Sara B. Fraser

Long Division

Black Rose Writing | Texas

The author grants the final approval for this literary material.

First printing

This is a work of fiction. Names, characters, businesses, places, events, and incidents are either the products of the author's imagination or used in a fictitious manner. Any resemblance to actual persons, living or dead, or actual events is purely coincidental.

ISBN: 978-1-68433-235-9
PUBLISHED BY BLACK ROSE WRITING
www.blackrosewriting.com

Printed in the United States of America
Suggested Retail Price (SRP) $18.95

Long Division is printed in Chaparral Pro
Author photo: Aidan Hamell
Cover art: Laura Fortune
Cover design: Conor O'Callaghan

For my mother, who did a far better
job than any of the mothers in this story.

"I do not, of course, mean that there are not battles, conspiracies, tumults, factions, and all those other phenomena which are supposed to make History interesting; nor would I deny that the strange mixture of the problems of life and the problems of Mathematics, continually inducing conjecture and giving the opportunity of immediate verification, imparts to our existence a zest which you in Spaceland can hardly comprehend."
–Edwin Abbott Abbott

Long Division

Walnut Acres

Gertrude has never seen the young man before. He's wearing an apron, so she assumes he is a cook; though it's hard to discern, here in the Walnut Acres Municipal Nursing Home of Lynn, who does what and where: RNs, LPNs, CNAs, an unfathomable hierarchy of nurses. And then there are the doctors, rarely seen, and the handymen, the food-service workers, new ones replacing ones who have disappeared; as a resident, you never know why or for how long any of them will be around. He is outside her room, flirting with Jessie, speaking loudly enough for anyone to hear them, not that many can.

"What time you get off today?" They are talking across the cart that Jessie pushes from room to room with cleaning products, linens, and a big black trash bag hanging from the side. He puts his hands on top of the cart, leans forward.

"One o'clock." She steps away from his nearing face but keeps one hand on the cart.

"Will you wait for me? I finish at four-thirty, but I can probably get off a little early." He looks like Sylvester Stallone, but not so pinched-looking in the face. And the arms are more sinewy than bulky. He has an accent. South American? Gertrude is surprised at how nice it is to be looking at him. She is a twig on a mattress, watching them over the National Geographic that she has let fall to her lap. The man catches her eye. And he winks. He winks! They hold each other's gaze for a moment—the man grinning with one eye wider open than the other, elflike, and Gertrude, stunned into temporary paralysis. Jessie turns to see what he is looking at. Gertrude lifts the magazine in front of her face and angles it into the lower field of her bifocals.

Jessie turns back to the man. "What am I going to do waiting around this shithole for three hours?" Her arms are crossed; she's guarded, but offering something.

"Go home and come back." The flirtation reminds Gertrude of high school. She drops the magazine below the level of one eye so she can keep watching them; but without depth perception they look flat, like TV characters.

"Maybe I'll come back or maybe I won't. I live pretty close. You'll just have to wait and see."

He calls after her, "Come back," as she pulls her cart down the hall. He walks in the other direction, rubbing his palms together and starting to hum, and Gertrude is left with nothing to look at but yolk-yellow walls and the left edge of an art-nouveau print that from this distance looks like smudges of earwax.

Funny feeling this, thinks Gertrude. A little ... gregarious, a little bold. She's ninety-four, and it's been a long time since she's looked at a man as somebody to be embarrassed in front of, somebody to feel especially appreciative of, for his man-ness. She remembers this feeling of being in a *moment*, of being alive and aware, instead of going through the motions. She wishes he would come back, and simultaneously hopes to never see him again. She pushes the soft pads of her fingertips together. Her hands are flaccid and pale and splattered with stains. She remembers her daughter's little hands as they made the shape of a church steeple. And her fingers would wiggle: open the doors, here are the people.

She is tired of fighting to stay in the present and welcomes the quiet trance of memory, so long as it keeps its flavor of contentedness. So long as the arrows of regret don't pierce it. She weaves her bony fingers into a steeple. Opens the doors, there are the people. They've all got osteoporosis now, she thinks, and arthritis that keeps them from wiggling. She chuckles, picks up her National Geographic and runs her eyes over the paragraphs, waiting for sleep to overtake her.

Later, after she's dozed, Jessie comes into her room carrying a plastic box.

Gertrude pushes herself up as much as she can. Jessie plucks a clipboard from the plastic slot near the door and makes some marks on it.

"I'm almost outta here for the day. Good news, huh?"

"Yes. Good news." Jessie stands next to Gertrude's bed and takes her pulse.

"How're you today?" she asks, but without real concern.

"I'm a little tired."

"Tell me about it. I'm on my feet ten hours now." She writes Gertrude's pulse on the chart, wipes down the sink in the corner of the room. Jessie is one of the nurses who do everything: clean the people, the rooms, check vitals, keep company. She's not one of the bigwigs who saunter in sometimes full of purpose to administer special medicines and expertise. Gertrude watches her, curious. They are living beings inhabiting the same room. Moreover, they are females inhabiting the same room. Gertrude is surprised at her awareness of the fact and feels guilty for all of the people she's taken for granted. Her fingers fiddle at the glossy corner of her magazine and Jessie twists a stick to angle the blinds.

"You'll be tired for your date tonight," Gertrude tries. This gets Jessie's attention.

"Date? Huh? My boyfriend is in Iraq."

"Oh. You didn't tell me." Gertrude is wary, but hopes Jessie will continue to speak to her, to offer her the semblance of an adult conversation.

"You know something, Missus Littlefield?" Jessie sits on the edge of the bed, which makes Gertrude tip to the side. "It's terrible; I want him to come home. But I'm kinda, like, I guess I don't really mind him being gone. Not *that* so much, I guess it's more that, well, I'm more ... myself, you know, when he's gone. I feel bad about it."

"Yes?" Gertrude is leaning on one arm very heavily. "Can you ... just ... help," and she tries to push herself straighter. Jessie puts her hands on each of Gertrude's upper arms and yanks her into a sitting position. Gertrude makes a tiny squealing noise because of Jessie's strong grip.

"Anyway, you know the way relationships are. Hard." Jessie moves about the room slowly, not doing anything in particular. "I guess I'm not surprised you never heard me talk about him. We were together two years before he shipped out. A long time...."

But Gertrude is suddenly exhausted and disinterested in Jessie's life, Jessie's soldier in Iraq. She remembers her own soldier, Clive, her vision blurring Jessie into a human-colored blob moving about the room. The day Clive left her on the station platform. The tears that pooled in the corners of his eyes and the way he wiped them away as he stepped onto the train with the other soldiers. The pain in her gut as the train pulled away. The thought that she was about to collapse had brought her sharply into her body, and she'd realized later that the physical pain had saved her somehow—she'd had to forget about him and focus on herself, finding a bench, folding over, the top of her head dropping onto her knees.

Jessie stops talking and sits on the end of the bed, startling Gertrude from her reverie. She is picking at the thin blanket, plucking lint or dust from it and rubbing her fingers together to drop the bits onto the floor.

"What about the cook?" Gertrude says.

"What do you mean?"

"The one you were talking with this morning."

"Oh, that guy? Naw. Helio. He knows I have a boyfriend."

"He's good-looking."

"Yeah, he's okay."

"Nice arms," Gertrude goes on, looking past Jessie's head to the open door where she'd seen them flirting with each other earlier in the day.

Jessie laughs. "Nice arms, yeah. He's got nice arms." She looks at Gertrude, whose attention is brought back to the younger woman's face. "Funny you'd notice that. That's what you got those glasses for, huh? Checkin' out the guys?"

Gertrude smiles with thin lips and puts her hand to the rim of her glasses. If she could still blush—if she hadn't outlived her blood's ability to rush to the skin of her cheeks—she'd blush now. "Well, you were there. Outside my door. I could hardly have helped watching." Her chin hardens defensively.

"You know what? You're a lot more with it than most of the old folks in here. Didn't think you'd've been able to hear what goes on in the hallway. Sure, I know you could see us, since you could see his arms. You should be watching TV instead of paying attention to what goes on in the hall."

"Well," Gertrude says, "I saw."

Jessie launches a stray wisp of hair with an exaggerated puff and goes into the hallway for a moment. When she comes back with a folded towel, she says, "We weren't doing anything."

"Oh, it doesn't matter," Gertrude says. "This has grown out of proportion." She waves her hand in front of her face, as if there were a fly there. "Forget it. Just making conversation."

Jessie puts the towel next to the sink and takes the dirty one. Gertrude picks up the remote and turns on the TV, but keeps it muted. Jessie looks at the clipboard. "Time for pills."

"Do you miss him?"

Jessie is busy arranging cleaning supplies in the plastic box. "Do I miss who?"

"The one in Iraq."

"Of course I miss him."

"Men can be so difficult." Gertrude has the staccato throat of someone with stage fright, and she looks away, her voice trailing. Jessie has the spray bottle of orange liquid in her hand, and she holds it carelessly pointed in Gertrude's direction.

"We were really happy together," she says. "Are happy." Her face seems to have changed in the last thirty seconds. Gertrude can see it in her eyebrows. They're straight across, dipping towards each other in the middle, whereas before they'd been softly curved, making her face look open. "I'm going home after I get you your pills. Do you want me to bring you to the community room before I go?"

"No," Gertrude says. "Well, yes, okay." Jessie nears the bed, clutches the blanket as if it were a weed that needed pulling. "No. I'm too tired, and you have to go. Never mind."

Jessie is exasperated. "Make up your mind."

"I'm too tired," Gertrude says again. Jessie slides the clipboard into its holder on her way out. "I'll be back with your pills."

Gertrude picks up her National Geographic. It is from December of last year, one of the last that she received before canceling her subscription. She has read it already. On the cover are galloping zebras. She finds the article about a lost Amazonian tribe fascinating and likes to look at the pictures of them: their compact beautiful bodies, earthy jewelry, and hennaed hair. She wonders if their lives are less complicated, and imagines that their social contracts hold more weight than those between people in modern society. Here husbands and wives separate, parents leave their children for others to raise, children move to other states, other countries. Strangers care for senior citizens. Her daughter disappeared years ago, and now Gertrude interacts more regularly with a nurse than with anyone in her own family.

It's not so bad. At least she doesn't have to worry about upsetting anyone if she's not feeling well.

She lets her eyes close and the magazine drop to her lap. Minutes later, Jessie picks it up and puts it on the table. Gertrude can feel her glasses being taken from her face. "Come on and take your pills before you fall asleep." She holds a paper cup while Gertrude fumbles in it with her fingers, sips the water that Jessie hands her. The bed thumps and whines flat as Jessie pulls the lever on its side.

Leigh

Mark is a good man. He is.

We're getting married, but I'm petrified. I don't know if I can go through with it, and I feel stupid because I know I should be happy.

He picks me up after work most days, and we ride the T together. Separate homes, for the time being, but close to each other. He lives on one side of Davis Square, and I live on the other. Later this month, I'll be moving in with him, and then in August, we'll get married.

And I do love him. He's good and stable and reliable. He could be better than that or worse. Or maybe he's both. He's my dream man, the perfect compliment, and he's also the dark heavy blanket that's going to smother me if I let him.

I'm at my desk, and my knees are tingly, and my back aches because I've been on my chair for hours without a break. But the work soothes me. When the numbers add up and make sense, it's so gratifying, and here, in my small office, my computer hums amicably, and my shelves are neat, and many of my books are wide enough to stand without bookends. Mark, Gramma, Andy, even my Dad and his wife—everyone but my mother—are small pictures tacked into the frame of my reminder board. They are like tiny clouds hovering over the more imperative information: extension numbers, dates to remember. Every year, every month is the same, and the bank does the work it needs to do, and I am part of its machinery, feeding numbers into my computer and calculating outcomes.

By the way, not to completely change the subject, but I have this letter. From Nevada. Folded into the shape of a hexagon and tucked into a small pocket in the lining of my purse. It says that my mother is dead. I didn't even know she was in Nevada.

I'd like to stay at work forever, but it is six o'clock and Mark is here.

We go for Indian. It's Friday and college kids are out in raucous droves, celebrating the end of the school year. Mark and I find a quiet table. He knows about the letter in my purse, but there isn't much more to say about it. There are a lot of practical details to iron out concerning the wedding and moving in together. He wants me to get rid of my kitchen table, my dishes, my sofa.

We will keep my bed for the guest room … until … *the kids come.*

I imagine them knocking at the door, the kids, carrying their belongings in a bundle tied to the end of a stick, like Snoopy always carried when he had to leave his doghouse. It's easier to think of them that way, arriving at the house fully clothed. Easier than confronting the reality: first off, we're in our mid-thirties, and I don't feel at all ready to have children. Secondly, and more disturbing: growing a human inside my body and then pushing the whole thing out of the little hole that is my vagina. I hate to even say the word *vagina* out loud, let alone think about expanding it around the head of an infant.

And then there's the prospect of getting married.

How many wives have said, "He's a good man," just like I have, and then, on some TV news program, amended it to, "He *seemed* like a good man"?

Because then he shot up his office, or got caught pretending to be a different husband to a different wife in three different states. Or skipped parole and the wife never knew about the drug dealing, the gambling addiction, the sexual-abuse allegations. And the wife had children with him? A child molester?

How can anyone recover from the treachery of having been deceived by the person they trusted most? Isn't it best not to set yourself up for that?

Actually … if Mark is capable of having a secret gambling or prostitute addiction, if he's liable to sneak off in the middle of the night for a tryst in the bushes of a highway rest stop, then maybe I have the same potential….

What if I find myself, after I'm married, feeling so trapped and bored and frustrated, that I become driven to disappear and create a false identity in another state, another country? And worse yet, what if I have children … when the urge to run hits me?

It's not an unreasonable fear. It's what my mother did.

* * *

I tell Mark that I've planned my yard sale for the weekend of the fourth.

"Why not have it the weekend before? You can move in sooner."

"No one will be around. It's a holiday." I'm moving into his place a month before the wedding, which feels unnecessary, but it's what he wants. It takes too much planning to move and have a wedding all at the same time. Even though our wedding will be very small.

I told him I wanted to move in a week or two *after* the wedding, to keep things relaxed. But he looked at me, his eyebrows low over his eyes, and said, in a deep, accusing voice, "Is that what you want?" I could see that I had made a mistake by even suggesting it. I hadn't just hurt his feelings, but had actually shaken his faith in me as a person capable of wifedom. Or maybe I'm reading too much into an expression, as usual.

"I'll bring some stuff over," he says. "I've got some things I could stand to part with. Golf clubs. Did you know I used to golf?"

"Did you?"

"I loved it."

"Well, why don't you do it anymore?" He shrugs, and I worry it's because he's with me. I should encourage him to golf, maybe even take it up myself. "Don't get rid of your clubs. Maybe you'll play again."

"You never get rid of anything, Leigh. If I want to golf, I'll borrow or rent clubs."

"But you have your own...."

"We won't have the room."

"It's a three-bedroom. Why wouldn't we have the room?"

"It's just golf clubs. I don't use them."

We eat in silence for a while. I open my mouth to say that I want to keep my LPs even though he wants me to get rid of them, but I decide to move off the subject of our belongings and how we're going to merge them—two thirtysomethings with two lifetimes of habits and possessions. These conversations annoy us both. I keep my mouth shut, recognizing that Mark has pulled into the lead because he's accepted that my cat, Buster, will be moving in too—and he's not happy about it.

I watch him chew. He is paying attention to his food. He's so childlike sometimes, the way he can focus completely on something like eating.

"The food's good," I say, and he nods.

* * *

When I was a kid, I developed this theory that it should be possible to breathe under water. All winter long I thought and thought about it. In. Out. In. Out. That's all breathing seemed to be, and if you could do it with air, then I didn't see any reason why you shouldn't be able to do it with water. I was confident. I thought I'd change the world. I thought I'd be able to live under water. But it was still only a theory, and being the sensible scientist that I was, I knew the theory would have to be tested.

We were at Bright's Pond. I stripped down to my pylon-orange one-piece with the figure-skater skirt, and went to the shore while my mother, Beverly, set herself up with a magazine; Daniel, my dad, laid down on a towel; and my brother, Andy, slept in his stroller under a tree. I took my time. I imagined how scared they'd be, and then how they'd rejoice when I resurfaced after a full hour under water; the police cars, ambulances, and divers would applaud and carry me to the Smithsonian in Washington, where I'd get a medal, and they'd offer me a job—setting a Guinness World Record for the youngest scientific researcher. And then, when I needed to get away from it all, I would have a home down at the bottom of the sea, in a cave, and I'd lie down on the ocean floor and look up through the swirling sunshine above, in silence. I'd have fish and frogs and turtles as kind pets, and they'd love me best because I was the one who'd figured out how to breathe under water.

Under I went, face first. In. Out. In. Out. The water sloshing around the inside of my mouth. And of course, I had to come up, coughing, sputtering for air. Daniel was mid-push-up and he sighed and shook his head before lowering himself onto the towel. He turned and said something to Beverly, who moved her magazine to the side and waved.

It's silly, but I used to be confident. I used to trust my instincts, and I thought I was smart, funny, and that I'd always have plenty of friends and lead a happy life. I know it didn't change on that day, but it's the first time I can remember feeling these things: Regret. Inadequacy. Companions that I've since learned to live with. How stupid I thought I was. How disappointed in myself. I vowed that I would make sure to get all the facts next time I had an idea, before believing in it. I mean, any intelligent being would have done some research. An intelligent being would have understood that human beings have lungs.

* * *

Back at my place, Mark grunts in disgust as he moves a pile of books and magazines from the couch to the coffee table and sits down.

"Beer or tea?" I ask him, ignoring the way he barely masks his hatred of my apartment.

"Beer."

I come back with two bottles and sit next to him. We've been seeing each other for a long time. I don't know why we can still feel so awkward together.

"Watch TV?" I suggest. He shrugs.

"Will you be able to find the remote?" he motions with his nose in the general direction of the middle of the room. My apartment is small. It's just my cat, my belongings, and me, but my belongings refuse to stay put and they end up all over every surface in the place, along with the cat's fur. It does feel out of control at times; I can't seem to keep it clean. There are mugs on the coffee table and on the windowsill. Some have grown mold; some have been there long enough for the coffee or tea remnants to have crystallized inside of them. Books and magazines are stacked on the floor, along with half-finished projects—checks written but bills unsent, an iron that needs to have the plug replaced (I've been meaning to get a book on how to do that), a pillow that needs to be stitched losing its stuffing next to the couch. I get tired just thinking about cleaning. Where would I start?

"Of course I know where the remote is." I pull it from between the cushions of the sofa and click it toward the television. We watch in silence. I wonder whether or not Mark wants me to change the channel. He sighs. His eyes are not on the TV. He is gazing toward the middle of the room. I regard him angrily.

"I know. I know," he says, acknowledging that I sense his annoyance. He stands and brushes his hands down his pants. "I'm sorry, Leeby. It just makes me feel so...."

"It's my place. I can live how I want." I take a swig of beer and keep my eyes on the meaningless little people on TV.

"Your office isn't like this. How come you can keep that clean? We could have gone to my place. We'll both be living there soon enough." I think about Mark's apartment, my soon-to-be-married-woman-home. The entire interior is painted stark white, and the only things allowed to hang on the walls have been pre-approved by various museums' print departments and gaze glassily from their sleek black frames. Books and magazines are put away promptly when they're finished being read.

When Mark's iron breaks, he throws it in the trash, the trash gets taken to the sidewalk, and he buys a new one.

The only reason we ever come to my place at all is because Mark still has a roommate.

"Charles is there," I point out. Charles is always awake and always in the living room, listening to classical music CDs or watching reality TV shows. He likes reality shows because they help him "keep in touch with the masses." I'm not kidding; he actually said that.

"He's okay. He's moving out soon. I don't know why you don't like him. He never did anything to you."

"It's not that I don't like him. You know that. It's just that I don't see why we should go over there, where we'll disturb Charles, when I have my own apartment."

"You have your own apartment because no one else can stand to live this way."

"Well, why on earth are you marrying me?"

"Don't start that," he says, as if what I'm saying isn't a logical line of questioning.

"Mark, I'm tired. I want to go to bed." He stands there, nodding at me.

"With me?"

I look at him. I don't want him here. I want to be alone. Where will I go at times like these when we're married?

"Well, you don't like it here."

"So you want me to go?"

"What do you want? Why can't you just say what you want? If you want to stay ... if you want to go." But he's right that I want him to go. I know I'm being manipulative and I feel vaguely guilty about it, which makes me angrier.

"Aw Leigh, that's not fair. Just tell me if you want me to stay or go." His voice is whiny.

"I just don't want to argue about whether or why I don't clean my apartment."

"You said you wouldn't make my place messy when you move in."

"Well, I haven't moved in yet, have I?"

"Come on, Leigh. I'm not being unreasonable."

"Neither am I."

"That's not fair," he says.

"What are you talking about? We're not talking about what's fair or not. You've decided to start a fight with me over the way I live."

"I never said anything, Leigh. Leigh. I know I can't live in the middle of junk. That's just normal. Anyone would be the same. It will make me unhappy if I have to live in such a mess."

"Mark." I try to choose my words with precision. "You know me. We've talked about this. I'm going to do my best, and you're going to be patient."

He cuts me off: "If I'm too patient, you'll revert to your ways. Someone's got to take control."

"I don't want you taking control," I yell, an electric current of anger rising up. "I'm not a child."

"Leigh," he puts his head in his hands, like he must carry it so it doesn't fall off. "I'm not being unreasonable. Why are you yelling?"

"I'm not yelling," I yell. I am heading for the pack of Camels I keep in the utensil drawer for emergencies.

"Leigh, don't smoke," he pleads. "Come on, you have a cold." I blow my nose and then strike a match. In a burst of angry clarity, I see that he's trying to make me be Normal and that he sees himself as some kind of savior who will help me to be a part of the ordinary world, the right world, if only I would allow him to.

"I can't stay if you do that. You know what it does to me." I exhale a cloud of blue smoke. He waves his hand in front of his face and backs out of the door.

"I'll call you tomorrow," he says. As the door closes, I get the mayonnaise lid that I use as an ashtray and deflate onto the couch.

It's a fight we have often.

We'll get over it; we always do. But at the moment I'm not sure I want to. I don't know who's right and who's wrong. I feel that I'm being drowned out, but I could be wrong. I may be paranoid and over-critical. Perhaps getting past that, learning to compromise, will make me a better, gentler person.

* * *

About the letter. It was addressed to Gramma, but I've been handling most of her mail, so I have it. She doesn't know. Mark says I shouldn't tell her. Tomorrow, I'll visit her, as I do every Saturday. I need to tell her, but I'm not sure how. *Oh, by the way, Beverly's dead. You got a letter.* How will it make her feel? I don't know how it makes *me* feel. And Gramma, she's ninety-four. The last thing she needs is to be told that her daughter has died.

But there's simple honesty. The letter was addressed to her. *Dear Mrs. Littlefield. Your daughter, Beverly Fortune, died last night. I'm very sorry.* Signed someone I'd never heard of: Simon Walsh.

Maybe Gramma knows Simon Walsh. But I doubt it.

It feels so distant and strange. My mother. My mother is dead. I say the words to try and drive the meaning deeper, but it doesn't want to go deeper; it sits out there on the periphery, outside the circumference of my existence, like something important I've forgotten to do.

January 1950

Clive tossed and turned and sweated. Gertrude could hear him whimpering, his voice growling up out of his throat.

She sat up, threw the covers off and slid into his bed. He was damp with sweat; it felt as though she were climbing right into his body, not just under the covers.

When she touched him, he woke with a start.

"You're completely soaked," she whispered and helped him strip off his T-shirt. "What is it? What were you dreaming about?"

He cleared his throat with a cough. "Damn thing gets in my head."

"What thing, darling? What is it?"

He turned away. She lay with her shoulder tucked into his armpit and waited. "You don't want to know," he said. But she did. She wanted to know what wives are kept from knowing.

"I don't need to be protected from it," she insisted. "Honestly. And anyway, it might do you good to talk. Maybe if you let it out, it won't haunt you." He was silent for a long time, breathing heavily. Then he started to talk.

"It's not really a dream. It's, well, it's something. This thing that happened, in Palau." He tried to turn away, but she held onto him and he didn't resist. "We smoked some Japanese soldiers ... out of their hiding place."

Gertrude waited.

"There was an underground cavern. One of them came out, with his hands on his head. He wasn't wearing a shirt. He was so small, with little black nipples and no chest hair. Just a kid. Probably not even twenty. Jim, you know, I told you about him, was there with me, and another guy, name of Patrick. Irish guy.

"He was surrendering. So we were happy. No one was going to be killed.

We'd bring him back to camp. Like a trophy. But then this other guy comes out of the hole ... and he's shooting, and it happened so fast ... and he shoots Patrick ... so we shot back." He was quiet then, and Gertrude could feel his whole body tense and relax, and then tense again, and she knew he was crying even though his face was turned from her and he was quiet. She stayed still, stilled her breathing to make herself invisible.

"Jim shot the guy who'd shot Patrick, but ... I ... I shot the other guy. He didn't have a gun." And he tensed again, turning his head away, shaking with it. "Jim and me, we didn't discuss it, ever.

"Jesus. I don't know if I did the right thing. I tell myself it was self-defense, but I don't know if it was a hundred percent." He began to calm as words came rushing out of him. Gertrude noticed that his speaking relieved the tension, the shaking, and he softened under her chin. "I don't know what I have inside me. The things I can do even if I know it's wrong, and my anger, it makes me do something. Maybe it's stupid to be thinking about it. Talking about it.

"Maybe the guy didn't even know that his buddy would try to take us down. Who knows? And I'll never know. Christ, I'll never know."

"Was Patrick ... your friend?"

"A good guy. I think he was from Indiana or someplace."

Gertrude stroked the side of his face. "The man killed your friend, Clive. Anyone would have done the same. You watched your friend get killed."

"It's all in that split second." Clive finally looked at her. "You think something your whole life. Think you're a certain kind of person, and then a moment comes and it takes you over and then all of a sudden you know that you're not really the person you thought you were. You do something you didn't ever think you'd do." He seemed to be pleading with her. Gertrude shifted and propped her head up, so she could see more of his face. She wondered if there were other things Clive had done, worse things, and she held herself as still as she could. He blinked and looked away; he would say no more.

"But we're all the same, in the center." She put her hand on the top of his head, drew it down the side of his face. He was not much taller than Gertrude, and their toes touched at the end of the mattress. She left her finger rest in the indentation at the tip of his chin. "We're all the same, Clive. The only difference is you got to see it. That's all. You're no different from anybody else."

He shook his head, squeezed her tight as if he could drive away whatever was inside him by merging himself with her. "I wish I never did see it, Gertie. If that's the truth, then I don't want to know about it."

"It's the truth," she said, sliding her hand down his stomach. "But so is this. So are we. And I love you, you know that?"

* * *

The next morning they sat together in the kitchen, eating homemade spice cookies and drinking black coffee.

Gertrude read some of the headlines from the back of the newspaper as Clive held it in front of his face, but she was giddy with the closeness that she hoped Clive felt too. "You don't want to talk about it anymore, do you? I mean I always want to be there to listen when you need me to."

Clive shook his head. "We already talked about it."

"Okay. But I think it's best to be able to talk. You know, it might help ... so you don't have nightmares."

"I talked."

"Okay." Gertrude dipped a cookie into her cup, nibbled at the edge. "You know something, I have a feeling."

"About what?"

"I could be pregnant." He lowered the paper to look at her, and she grinned over her cup.

"You wouldn't know that yet. It was less than a couple hours ago."

"I'm just saying I have a good feeling."

"Okay. Good. I wouldn't say anything until we know for sure."

She put her cup down and fingered a crumb on the table. "You wanna go out for dinner tonight?"

"Sure, we can go out for dinner." Clive gulped down coffee, turned the page.

"You wanna go to the Whaler?"

"Yeah."

Gertrude put her hands around her cup to keep them warm.

"I don't want to be late." Clive folded the paper and tossed it onto the chair next to him.

"But it's only seven."

"Yeah. I have a lot to do." He stood up, leaving his cup on the table.

Gertrude opened her mouth to complain, but she swallowed her words instead.

He dressed quickly, and she walked with him to the front door of their apartment. He kissed her on the forehead and rushed down the hall.

* * *

In her nightstand were the letters that Clive had written to her when he was away in the war, from islands in the Pacific that she'd never heard of. He'd written to her every week, and she'd saved every letter, and tucked them into the back of the drawer. She always read through them when he'd upset her. When he'd made her feel insecure. In his letters, she could feel his love. She was content with the Clive in the letters. More content, sometimes, than she was with the real thing—in those times when he could be so moody and distant.

My dearest Gertie,

I can't tell you how much I miss you. When I close my eyes at night, even if I'm sleeping outside in my clothes, surrounded by the smell of gunpowder and unwashed men, I can sometimes smell your smell. Gertie, I can smell your hair if I close my eyes and try real hard. Right now, as I write this letter, I'm imagining my hand on that hair, and I'm pressing my face into your neck and— Ha ha, Gertie, you should have seen it! I was trying to smell you, here in this infernal heat with guys suffering horrible bouts of dysentery, and my buddy Jim (you'll meet Jim when we're back in the States—you'll like him), he just saw me—I guess my eyes were closed and I was breathing in deep, imagining you—and he says, Hey, what're you writing? Describing a walk through a field of daisies? And then he called me a poet. So I'd better be careful how I act. Anyway, daisies don't even smell as good as you do.

Remember when we were courting, Gertie? Remember how long we'd stand on your porch for? I'm thinking of those nights right now. They were the best nights of my life.

Yours always, Clive

She sighed and leaned into the armchair, holding the letters on her lap. Of course he loved her. They were married for heaven's sake. But then, doubt crept in. She wondered about Jim. How close had Clive been to him? Maybe he was closer to Jim than he was to her? Maybe Jim knew the secrets that she'd never know. Clive was so hard to understand, so distant; sometimes he made her feel desperate, unsure of herself, and she wondered if he was easier with Jim, or for that matter, with his colleagues at Security Trust. Did other people get the best part of Clive?

But this was the real Clive—distant, unreachable, and for every opening up, like when he told her about shooting the man, there would be a closing, when he'd act as if he ... what? Resented having opened up to her? Regretted being vulnerable? Most of the time Clive was charming, easy to be around. When he was on top of things, nobody could resist him.

She wanted him to always be warm and charming, of course, but also she wanted to be the one who knew everything about him, who was his only confidante. If the price for his having opened up to her was that he'd shut down and become distant, then, she thought, maybe these moments of insecurity were a reasonable price to pay. She could wait it out until the return of the charming Clive, the one who could light up a room with warmth and humor, and who made her feel special and loved.

She tucked the letters back into the drawer and went to the kitchen. She slid her hands into her rubber kitchen gloves and set about washing the morning's dishes.

Gramma's door is closed when I arrive. I tap lightly. It opens a couple of inches and a woman's form fills the space. She's young and pretty; she looks like Jennifer Lopez, which makes me suspicious—and then immediately guilty. Honestly though, she should be bounding up the steps of a sorority in a cheerleader's outfit.

"We'll be done in a minute," she says and shuts the door again.

I sit on a stiff-backed couch in the hallway, surrounded by nursing-home sounds: the soft hum of voices, nurses' sticky clogs, beeping monitors.

I know that Gramma can't live much longer. She's ninety-four and her body is becoming less and less cooperative, though her mind is still edgy as glass. I can't believe she might die though. I can't imagine life without her.

It's quiet behind the door, and I have a fleeting moment of horror when I imagine that the nurse has smothered her. I've read of nursing-home killings, impostor nurses, poisonings, mercy murders ... you can never be sure. But I remind myself that a young pretty nurse like that wouldn't want to go ruining her future by murdering an old lady. So now her good looks are making me trust her more. I really am all over the place. Am I always like this or is it the letter in my purse? No. I'm always like this. But maybe the letter is heightening my natural neuroses.

Soon I hear voices, muffled, the nurse asking short questions and Gramma grunting. Satisfied that she is still alive, I get a bag of Fritos from the vending machine and sit back down.

The nurses go by, pushing carts and carrying cups with bendy straws perched on their rims. When I was a kid, I loved those straws, the noise they make when you push the accordion part in and out, and the way you can sip a drink even if you're shorter than the glass on the table. I wonder who invented them, and how much money that person has made just by thinking up the idea of a straw that can bend.

Daniel used to say that with just one good invention, you could be set for life. He'd sit at the kitchen table and pull out pens and paper and make Andy and me look around at everything we could see, and imagine how we could make things work more efficiently. Or we'd try to think up toys like the hula-hoop. Beverly would be making dinner around us.

"What are you doing, Daniel? You think one of these kids is going to make your millions for you?"

"You never know. Kids are smart, Bev. They can see things that grownups can't." And he'd wink at us. He'd start out excited and focused and then as we came up with one flop after another—Andy wanted to build a mechanized nose picker so the user wouldn't have to get his finger dirty, and I imagined a bum wiper—we could tell it was next to impossible for him to control his frustration. So we'd really try. We wanted to please him, and he was giving us the opportunity to ... if only we could come up with the next big thing. But then his patience would be gone and he'd give up as he realized that neither of his kids was a genius. He'd slam the papers and pens away in a drawer and stretch out on the recliner in front of the TV. Beverly would chuckle to herself and you could tell she meant *I told you so.*

"One simple thing, Bev. The simpler, the better. Kids are good at this stuff. It's a matter of paying attention."

"You're a dreamer, you know that?" He'd snap open a newspaper to hide behind. She'd flick it with a dishtowel. "Don't know when you'll wake up, grow up."

"They need to focus, that's all. They need direction. Leigh anyway. She could do it. I know she could." Proud as I was that he believed in my potential, and regretful that I hadn't lived up to it, I hated the implication that Andy wasn't as smart.

Daniel had the idea that kids have this natural creativity, but it seems, now that I think about it, pretty futile to expect anyone to come up with an invention on demand.

That must have been just before he moved out. I was about eleven and Andy would've been seven or eight. He was there, trying to get us to invent things, and then he was gone.

Somehow it was decided that Daniel would take us for half the day Saturdays and for lunch or dinner on Tuesdays, depending on whether or not we had school. He always took us to Dill's, because, he said, that's where they made the best tuna melts. But that was hardly the reason; our waitress was always Delilah. Andy and I figured out pretty quickly that Daniel and Delilah were girlfriend and boyfriend, even though nobody ever said as much. I guess Daniel's strategy was to expect us to absorb the information without ever saying anything. Maybe that made him feel as though he were including us in his life, and at the same time ensure that we wouldn't tell Beverly. And that's the way it worked too, for a while, though I can't imagine it was a conscious plan. It seems too sinister, too smart for Daniel. He would have acted the way he did out of inertia, and an inability to own his decisions.

When I brought up the fact that Daniel and Delilah were girlfriend and boyfriend, Andy would shrug and say, "I know that." I guess it didn't really bother me either, that our father was in a relationship. He hadn't been around the house much anyway because he worked a lot, so when he moved into the loft at the back of the Mercedes garage, we actually ended up seeing more of him. Lunch on Tuesdays was time dedicated specifically to us, and we would spend Saturday afternoons in the garage, listening to the metal clank of tools underneath peoples' cars. We could lie on his mattress—it smelled like motor oil and was covered with an Indian tapestry—and look over the edge of the loft at Daniel's legs sticking out from underneath a car, and at the two other guys who worked there, and listen to them yell to each other, their words muffled but their laughter distinct.

I don't remember the transition. I remember Daniel living in the house and then I remember him not living there. I guess my parents kept their negotiations private, working out their separation after Andy and I were in bed. So it was quiet and without fanfare. Even Beverly seemed fine with the arrangement. At first. Somewhere along the line, she found out that he was seeing someone. It didn't seem too bad at first, but when she figured out that he'd been seeing her since before they split up, that blew the lid off of her. Their separation had been mutual, or so she'd thought. She had thought it was just to give them space. She had thought it would make them appreciate each other more when they got back together. When she learned of Daniel's affair, she began to hate him with all the passion she had.

And then he told us that he was moving away.

It was a Tuesday, of course. I was watching TV in the living room. Daniel pulled up in somebody's Mercedes. He had a different car every couple of weeks, which was cool, but we had to be careful in them, to not get the seats dirty. He got out and fingered his hair as if it were still long, as if he were pushing a strand of it behind his ear. He had cut it about 6 weeks before he moved out of our house. ("*She* probably got him to cut his hair," Beverly had raged; she knew there was a *she*, but at that point, she still didn't know who *she* was.) As he came up the path to the door, the unbuttoned cuffs of his flannel shirt flapped about his wrists. He'd probably been working in his T-shirt and, rather than change, threw a clean shirt on over his work shirt. It was one of those amenable summer days when you could be comfortable wearing a lot or a little. I remember summers being more like that when I was a kid—now it seems that it's always either too hot or too cold, too wet or too dry. The weather's like an annoying toddler who won't stop pinching you.

I was on the sofa with my knees tucked up near my chin. Andy was in his room playing Barbie. Beverly wouldn't open it, and Andy's hearing was bad. (Nobody realized it at the time, not until years later, when he got tested and got his hearing aids. Our parents must have thought he was just being obtuse.) I went upstairs to get Andy, leaving Daniel standing at the door and Beverly huffing around the place, slamming doors, berating him. It was always like this, now that Daniel's affair had come to light. It depended on whether she was drunk or hungover. Drunk, she'd yell at him. Hungover, she'd give him nasty silence, derisive grunting, the murderous sucking and exhaling of her constant cigarette.

I sat in the front, and Andy got in back. There were newspapers on the floors so we wouldn't track in dirt. "Well, what do you think? Should we dine on pheasant under glass? Frogs legs? What're you in the mood for?" Daniel always said this, so it wasn't as funny as the first few times, but it was comforting, especially after being chased from the house by Beverly's rage. I watched the telephone poles fly past as we drove into town.

At Dill's, Daniel kept fingering the rim of his ear, leaning forward, putting his elbows on the table, sitting back into the red vinyl seat, back and forth. I missed his long hair. He used to let me practice reverse French braids on it while we watched TV in the evenings. From behind, he looked more like a bridesmaid than a Mercedes mechanic. I would lie on the couch behind him, inspecting the braid and the side of his face, with the soft sideburns and the tiny hoop he wore in his left earlobe. He looked different with short hair, and it added to the strangeness of him; I wasn't really sure who he was anymore.

"Do you miss your hair?" I asked.

"Sometimes."

"I liked it long," Andy said.

"Yeah." Daniel kept touching his ear. When he smiled, it was as if he were trying to stretch his mouth longer, but like a rubber band it kept snapping back into position. When Delilah floated over to the table, I ordered a side of French fries and Andy ordered a burger.

"Coming right up, sweetie. Leigh, honey, are you sure you only want a side of fries?"

No matter how nice Delilah acted, I couldn't like her. She called me *honey* and Andy *sweetie*, but she wore too much makeup, and her hair was too perfect for waiting on tables, and she seemed like she expected something from you. Like she was saying *sweetie* and *honey* because it was her job and she wanted to be paid for it. The result was that whenever she was around, I felt as if I had somehow landed in a parallel universe, where things felt one way while everyone was pretending they were some other way. It was exhausting, and I wanted to get away from her, but I sensed that if I rejected her, I'd have to give up on Daniel as well. If I had known that he was about to give up on me, I'd have beat him to it and charged out of there with Andy in the crook of my arm.

Daniel cleared his throat, said he had some *news*. Andy was eating his hamburger; he had ketchup on his chin.

"Andy, don't eat the whole thing," I said. "You know you're supposed to be on a diet." I looked at Daniel, hoping to make him feel guilty for buying Andy a burger when he knew perfectly well that he should have been having a salad.

Daniel smiled absentmindedly and tousled Andy's hair. "Just half. Then we'll have fruit salad, okay?" Andy dropped his forehead onto his arm and started moaning. I knew it was a joke, but Daniel got alarmed and started to get up from his seat.

Then Andy stopped the charade and smiled devilishly. "Okay. Just half, okay?"

Daniel sat back down, looking even tenser than before, and began fidgeting again: ear, forwards, back. Ear, forwards, back. Andy chewed and I sat on my hands and waited for the *news*.

Then Delilah was suddenly hovering. He looked at her, and when he looked back at us, I caught a glimpse of how his eyes had been: frank and open and relaxed. I wanted him to look at *me* like that, like a grownup that you don't pretend with. I wanted to shake him, him and his guilty, apologetic avoidance and rubber-band lips that were always saying something that sounded like it wasn't everything.

"We," he motioned toward Delilah, "are thinking of moving to Delaware."

"Both of you?"

Delilah smiled, her eyebrows furrowed in apology but her eyes defiant, victorious. I looked at each of them, Daniel and Delilah, back and forth, like a caricature of someone watching a tennis match. Daniel nodded.

"Are you getting married?" I asked.

"No."

But Delilah cleared her throat and put her fingertips on the tabletop. Her nails were painted orange, like her lipstick. Her hair was pinkish. Or maybe she was wearing a ribbon in it. She dyes her hair blond now, but I can't remember what color it actually was back then. Either way, she reminded me of some kind of sea anemone. "I don't know," Daniel amended. "Not right now, anyway." Satisfied, she moved off to the kitchen to pick up someone's order.

"Well of course not right now," I said. "We're in a restaurant right now."

Andy laughed through his nose, his fist to his face. Ketchup jumped a ride from his chin to his hand, and he wiped it on the edge of the table, leaving a shiny little blob. I glowered at him, annoyed—envious really—that he could be so oblivious to the tense situation we were in.

I didn't want dessert and Andy had fruit salad, which came out of a can and was saturated with sugar. (It was the seventies. Only extremist health-food nuts thought about what they were eating. As far as our parents were concerned, fruit was fruit, no matter how long ago it had been picked, how unnaturally red the cherries.)

"Where's Delaware?" Andy asked with his mouth full. He always talked with his mouth full. Grownups tend to overlook the simplest of solutions: between teachers and school counselors, nobody seemed to be able to do anything for Andy, whose condition was described as "slow." Yet his life would have improved enormously if someone had just taught him how to swallow before talking.

"It's south of here," Daniel told him, looking away from the ashen fruit churning in his son's mouth.

"Is it on Cape Cod?"

"No." He was taking out his wallet. "We're on Cape Cod. It's south of Cape Cod."

"I know that. I know we're on Cape Cod. I just didn't know how far away it was." Andy was becoming alarmed because Daniel was getting increasingly irritated.

"It's near Washington DC," I told him quietly. "Where the president lives."

"Wow!" Andy said. "You're going to live near the president."

"That's right. And you and Leigh can come and visit. You can come in the summer, and you can come at Christmas too."

"That's great," Andy said. He hated change, but for some reason, he didn't seem to mind Daniel's moving away. I guess he could sense, although he would never have said or even recognized it, that he was a disappointment to our father.

I stared at the ice melting in the bottom of my glass.

After we left, we walked along the sidewalk in front of the restaurant. I looked in the window and saw Delilah wiping the table where we'd been. She picked up the paper placemat from where Andy had been sitting with her thumb and forefinger, as if it were dirty underwear, and I could see her talking to someone in the kitchen and motioning with her free hand like there was a bad smell in the room. If Andy had been looking, he would have thought she was making a joke. He'd never have believed anyone could be so intentionally cruel. I could see that Daniel saw it too, but he didn't say anything. He didn't catch my eye; he didn't shrug his shoulders at me or shake his head. He just pretended it didn't happen and I knew he was going to move to Delaware anyway, even though it was obvious that Delilah only pretended to like kids so that Daniel would stay with her.

It took me years to admit, but I don't think Daniel himself liked kids all that much either. Even after they moved back to Cape Cod, Daniel left us with Gramma in Lynn. He could have taken us to live with him and Delilah in their big house in Truro, but he didn't offer. I never thought to question it at the time, but in retrospect, it seems strange, that a parent could so easily let someone else raise his children.

*　*　*

The nurse finally opens the door and motions me in. I sit in the armchair after kissing Gramma's cool dry forehead.

"How are you?" I ask her. I turn to the nurse because Gramma is looking out the window. "How's she doing?"

They both answer at the same time. "I'm fine," says Gramma.

"She's just great," says the nurse, too brightly. She's older than I originally thought, late twenties-early thirties, and she's not wearing any makeup, which is comforting.

I lean back in the chair, follow Gramma's gaze out the window. There is a single tree in the courtyard. A maple. Its leaves have recently unfurled themselves and they dangle greenly in the breeze. Gramma looks tired. The vinyl wheezes as I shift in my seat; Gramma's mouth twitches in recognition of the sound that announces my presence in the room, but she is on the verge of sleep; her mouth is already slackening. I pick up her National Geographic and flip quietly through the pages while she sleeps.

April 1953

It was lucky the Oak Ridge Motel finally appeared on the horizon: The car's headlights didn't work and night was falling. Clive turned in and cut the engine. When Gertrude reached under the cave beneath the dashboard to pull on her shoes, Clive leaned over and ran his hand up her stockinged calf. "It looks like a dump, Gertie. You sure you don't mind?"

"Of course I don't mind. I wouldn't even mind sleeping in the car." She finished twisting her heel into her shoe and squeezed his hand. "It's an adventure."

Clive took their cases from the trunk. The man behind the counter had greying hair combed back from a leathery face and was reading a newspaper. Clive set their cases down.

"We'd like a room."

Automatically, without looking at them, the man set a form on the counter. "Sign here." He turned to take a key from a row of hooks on the wall behind him.

"We're starved," Clive said. "Anywhere we could get a bite to eat?"

"Bout three miles," the man motioned toward the west, his hand a couple of inches from the countertop.

"Good food?" Clive asked, looking up from the form he was signing.

"Mmm hmm."

Gertrude waltzed the periphery of the room, looking at pictures, mostly reproductions of paintings of various types of dogs, and picking up the few postcards that were propped in a metal holder.

"Do you like dogs?" she asked the man.

The man shook his head. "Not especially."

"It's just there are a lot of pictures...."

"They were here when I bought the place," he cut her off.

"Well, goodnight," Clive said, picking up their cases. The man grunted and went back to his paper. Outside, on the way to their room, Clive huffed, "Don't know what's eating that guy."

Gertrude laughed. "He wasn't very friendly was he?"

"Couldn't hurt the man to look at a person when he's talking to him."

The key stuck in the lock, then the door stuck in the frame. Clive gave it a kick, and it finally pushed open. The mattresses on the two twin beds sagged like wet sponges, and the bedspreads were stained and threadbare. The bathroom was tacked onto the side of the room as an afterthought. The sink was next to one of the beds.

Gertrude opened her case and took out two skirts, held them next to each other against her thighs. "Which one? The blue one or the brown one?"

"I don't care, but the brown one is ugly," Clive said from behind a mask of lather. "God this place makes me claustrophobic. Look at the dirt on this." He unrolled a wad of toilet paper from the bathroom and wiped furiously at the mirror above the sink.

"You never told me," Gertrude said.

"Told you what?"

"That you didn't like my skirt."

Clive put his hands on the sides of the sink, his face half-shaved. "I didn't want to upset you."

"So you waited until now? You decided to upset me now?"

"You know the way you get."

"No, I don't know the way I get. How do I get? I wouldn't have been upset." She sat on the bed, the skirts over her knees. "Clive?" He continued to shave the rest of his face. "Clive, why didn't you ever tell me that you hated my brown skirt? I don't get upset about things like that. Just when you say it in such a mean way."

"I should never have said anything."

"It's not what you said, it's how you said it," Gertrude pleaded.

He laughed, meanly. "Sure, that's fine, whatever you say, Gertrude. You're the one who's always right."

"I never said I was...." she began, then threw her brown skirt into the garbage can, pulled herself into the blue one, and waited in the car.

She didn't want to fight. They'd been having too good a time.

They'd been trying for a baby for a few years and had decided to take this trip as a way to enjoy themselves again, to relax in each other's company. They both loved to drive, and a road trip with no known destination seemed like the sort of adventure that would perk them up, renew them.

She knew Clive's moods, the way he could seem content one minute and then callous the next, but she was determined not to let herself get pulled down with him. She resolved to pull him up instead. Clive got into the car and reversed out. He handed Gertrude a flashlight, saying, "We'll have to use this til we can get the headlights fixed," and Gertrude shined it into the night so he could see the road in front of them.

They drove in silence, slowly, following the dull beam of the light, until Gertrude swung the flashlight into the woods, crying, "Whoooo! This way, Clive! This way!" The road in front of them went pitch black. "Turn here! You missed the turn!"

"Stop it. You'll get us killed," he said with a grudging smile. He took his foot from the accelerator and the car hummed. Gertrude swung the light back. They bumped along the packed-dirt road. Again, she turned the flashlight to the side. This time Clive sped up. Gertrude whooped, then turned the light back onto the road. They were too close to the side and Clive swung the wheel, straightening them out. Gertrude fell against the door, laughing. "You're just crazy," Clive said. "I'm married to a crazy woman."

"You're the one who sped up," she laughed.

"Just trying to teach you a lesson."

"Oh come on, don't say that, darling, or I'll have to challenge you." And she turned the light off. They both yelled and careened into the dark.

"Okay," Clive said, slowing down. "You win. Turn it on!"

"I win. I win," she laughed, and flicked on the light.

There should have been enough time for it to get away. But the sudden light stunned it. Clive slammed on the brakes, but it was too late. The sound was thick, belying the smallness of the animal, a fawn. Gertrude's right arm had been out the window, and she winced with the pain of it hitting the rim of the door. The car ticked in the darkness.

"Give me the light," Clive said. It took her a moment to maneuver it from her right hand into her left and Clive snapped it away from her and crunched to the front of the car. "Aw gee," he said as he approached. He slid the flashlight into his pocket and dragged the animal to the side of the road. Gertrude sat, immobile, watching the line of light where it seeped up out of his pocket, waiting for him, clutching her arm near the shoulder.

She took the flashlight from him with her left hand, and leaned her teary face out the window until they arrived at the restaurant.

Clive was halfway across the parking lot before he realized that she hadn't gotten out of the car.

He walked back. "What's the matter?" he asked, leaning his head down to the passenger-side window.

"I'm coming," she said.

"You okay?"

"My arm hurts. I deserve it, though."

"Come on," he helped her up. "It's not your fault." She looked into his eyes. "Well, it is your fault. But everybody makes mistakes." He grinned.

"It's not funny." But she smiled, her face folded in misery, tears making rivers down her cheeks.

"Oh, come on, let's eat." He took her by the shoulders and gently glided her into a booth.

He cut her meat for her, and she ate slowly, maneuvering each forkful into her mouth with her left hand. They ate quietly, phrases such as *Would you like steak sauce?* and *Let's get another drink* passing softly between them. Clive drank vodka and Gertrude had a Manhattan. She ran her hand up and down the side of her glass, twirling it, bouncing the underwater ice gently.

"Its mother," she said finally. "Its mother must have been nearby."

Clive nodded. "I'm sure she was. I heard her, a rustle in the woods. I think it must have been her, but I didn't see her."

"It's the worst thing that could happen to her," Gertrude said. Clive nodded, shook two cigarettes out of the pack and lit them. He pushed a strand of hair back from her face.

"Stupid," she muttered. "I was only trying to cheer you up." She stared at the ice in her glass.

"These things happen." He snuck the tip of his nose through her hair and brushed her ear with it.

They stayed at that motel for three nights, avoiding the owner (laughing like high-school kids as they ducked behind a car when they saw him). In the mornings they walked—there was a lake about a mile away—and in the evenings they ate dinner at the same restaurant. Always back at the motel before dark, they spent the evenings in deck chairs in front of the door to their room, Gertrude with her arm, which was still sore, tied into a sling that Clive had made from the brown skirt he'd fished from the garbage can. They turned off the lights inside and looked up at the brightest stars that either of them had ever seen.

Many years later she told Beverly about the Oak Ridge Motel, and that her daughter had been conceived there. But she'd left out the part about the fawn. She didn't think it integral to the story. It had been a happy time. That's what was important, she thought, that they'd been happy.

Leigh

The nurse pokes her head in and asks if Gramma wants to go to the dining hall, or if she'd rather have soup in her room. Gramma makes a face, her lips disappearing into her mouth. "Neither, thank you."

I offer to get takeout. Gramma loves Chinese food. She leans over and starts pushing around pillboxes and pens and Lord knows what else she's got in the drawer of her nightstand, to get money to pay for lunch. I have two thoughts simultaneously as she's doing this: One, it strikes me how personal these little possessions seem. Junk that she keeps in a drawer by her pillow. Pens from her bank, a metal lipstick case, hairpins, all of it hers: Gertrude Littlefield's. Nobody else's. It's not something you think about when you tuck away the case from your previous pair of glasses, a button that popped off of your blouse, a keychain from the dry cleaners, yellow post-it notes with black lint dulling the sticky strip. You don't think of anyone looking at that repository and thinking that these things are yours, they are you, the person who sees them feeling like they've glimpsed a private part of you, like a birthmark peeking out of your waistband. And you never think that your knick-knacks may even make them feel despondent, excluded. These personal artifacts might suggest the solitary soul of their owner, her independence, her resistance to being fully understood by anyone.

And the second thought I have concerns how much my gramma wants to hold onto her dignity, her place as matriarch. She wants to pay for my lunch. But I can see that the search for money is exhausting her.

"Stop that, Gramma. I can pay for it." I pull my purse onto my shoulder. She sighs and relaxes into the pillow. She used to always insist on paying for things, and she'd persevere despite my protestations, but now the fight is leaving her body. I take my purse, with the letter from Simon Walsh inside it, and go around the corner to the Wok N' Roll.

Walnut Acres

Leigh leaves Gertrude's room and they're at it again: Jessie and Helio make their way into the frame of her open door. This time, it is Jessie who seems to be the propellant in their magnetic dance. She moves close, and he backs up. Finally, Helio stops, and Jessie pushes up against him.

Gertrude wonders if they're doing this on purpose. There are so many places they could go, but here they are, putting on a show, it seems, for her in particular. Or perhaps she's being egocentric, imagining she is of any interest to these people. Imagining they see her has anything more than a room number or a last name, as any different from the other people in here—wrinkled, used up, nearly dead. Then they kiss, and Gertrude swears she can see their tonsils, pink inside their mouths as they slip across each other. They move along, now out of Gertrude's view, but she can hear them. Jessie giggles and Helio says something and then, here they come again, back into view, first the back half of Jessie, brown ponytail and Helio's hand on her waist, emphasizing her figure, and then they are full in the frame of Gertrude's door and she finds herself suddenly more disgusted than fascinated.

"Stop that!" she yells. "Stop!"

Jessie pulls away from Helio and turns to face her. Helio takes a step back and puts his hand to his mouth, scolding his own lips, and Gertrude feels badly because he looks ashamed.

"Sorry about that," he says, then whispers something in Jessie's ear and pats the small of her back before exiting, stage left. Jessie leans against the wall with her arms crossed and stares at Gertrude. Then suddenly she starts laughing. Gertrude doesn't want to laugh. She wants to keep her composure, but with the inevitability of a physical response, Jessie's laughing infects her, and she starts to laugh too.

Then Jessie is gone, and Gertrude is left with humming lights, canned television voices, wheelchairs clicking, and people's middle-aged children, daughters mostly, full of purpose on blocky, sensible heels. The sound of nurses in neighboring rooms, cleaning residents one by one like bathroom stalls.

Gertrude looks out at the tree in the courtyard and can see the wind ruffle the leaves, but she cannot hear it or smell it so it isn't quite real.

Leigh

Gramma chews each bite of lemon chicken for an eternity. Residents who can't walk get a rolling table like the ones they use in hospitals so patients can eat meals in bed. Hers is above her knees and each forkful has to travel a foot and a half to get from the plastic box to her mouth.

"You want me to move that table closer?"

She puts her fork down and sighs. I swallow a bite of broccoli.

"I'm not sure I like that nurse."

"Which one?"

"Jessie. Any of them."

"She seems okay." I'm hungry, and I gobble my Buddha's Delight.

"Left her shift, while you were out getting our lunch."

"Did something happen?"

"I was hostile. I never used to be hostile. At least not to strangers."

"You can be as hostile to the nurses as you want, whatever you wish. Just don't get Alzheimer's. I'm so glad you never got Alzheimer's."

She looks at me for a long while and then hoists another forkful of chicken across the gulf between the box and her mouth. "You want me to push that table closer?" I ask for the third time.

"You're the one who sounds like you have Alzheimer's. I'm fine. I can eat like this."

"All right, all right," I laugh. "So what's with the nurse? Why the hostility?"

"I don't know. I know it sounds crazy. Maybe it's because she reminds me of Beverly."

"Beverly made her own choices, Gramma." She is quiet.

"Yes, of course. We all do."

I look down at my plate of vegetables in slippery sauce. The plastic fork is too debilitated to pierce the lightly cooked vegetables and I have to chase them around the perimeter of the Styrofoam tray. I give up for the moment, resting the fork against the rim.

I'm starting to have this strange electrical feeling that there is something supernatural going on, the way Gramma is mentioning Beverly. We don't usually ever talk about her. I wonder if she knows somehow that her daughter is dead. Maybe she is developing psychic abilities. I look away, suddenly afraid she'll be able to see through me to the letter from Simon Walsh.

"I'm sure the nurse is just doing her job," I say. She pushes the rolling tray further away from her, as if she cannot stand the smell of it. "Eat your lunch," I tell her. "You have to eat."

"I don't. I don't do enough to burn the calories, so I'm not hungry."

"You're feeling well, though?" She nods her head and then changes the subject.

"How are the wedding plans coming? Did you book something?"

"Mark's doing most of the planning." She nods. "You'll be able to come, won't you?"

"I don't know why you'd want an old fart like me there."

"Gramma, women don't refer to themselves as farts, no matter how old they are. It's just not done." She laughs, wiping the lower rims of her eyes with the top of her hand. I get the feeling she is laughing at more than my joke. "What?" I ask, laughing myself to see her so tickled.

"Oh, your grandfather. He used to say that exact thing. He used to tell me to never refer to myself as a fart in public."

"It's better than a lot of the things you could be called."

"Yes, like old cow," she says.

"Old witch would be pretty bad."

"Yes, it would. It would. So would old bitch."

"Never to your face!" I laugh.

"Still, we were actually young then, even though I didn't realize it. It was wonderful to be young."

I nod my head vaguely. "I don't know," I say. "Being young wasn't so great."

"Oh, sweetheart. You are still young," she says, emphasizing each separate word. "You. Are. Still. Young."

* * *

Beverly had been working for Dr. Silvieri for a couple of years, answering phones and scheduling appointments in his chiropractic office, but not long after Daniel moved away, she lost her job. She said it was because he wanted her to work more hours than she was able to. But it probably had more to do with the vodka-sodas and Daniel's moving to Delaware with Delilah, whose name, once Beverly learned of it, was only ever pronounced with a hiss or a spitting sound. I didn't like Dr. Silvieri at first. I had gotten free adjustments because my mother worked there, but he never gave Andy adjustments, and I used to hate the way his crusty-feeling hands massaged my lower back, nearly to my crack.

Beverly said that now that she was out of there, maybe she would be a paralegal and wear a smart mauve suit. Or she would open a muffin bakery and wear an apron, like the St. Pauli girl but with flour on her hands. She conjured these make-believe jobs in the evenings, while Andy and I ate pizza and she drank vodka-sodas. She would sit on the couch pointing a cigarette toward the ceiling and waving a sweating glass in her other hand. Her talk was dreamy, and it made me tense, because I knew none of it would ever happen. Andy loved it. We'd eat pizza, and no one would tell him not to have a third slice. Andy, with sauce on his chin, would tell Beverly about the castle he'd like to live in, where he'd have Barbie dolls of every hair color, with their conversion vans and convertibles and bedrooms and nightclubs. Beverly would laugh, wipe the sauce off his chin with a paper towel, take a big slug of vodka-soda, and tell him how she was going to build him a temple of Barbies on a big cloud in the sky, as soon as she got that wicked good job, and then we would all be happy and have everything we wanted.

I tried on hopefulness like a new skirt. But it never fit right—I just didn't look like me in it. I wanted to feel the way I pretended to feel, seeing Beverly buoyant and full of hope, but I could already envision the next morning. Beverly would forget that it was summer vacation. "What are you doing here?" she'd cry when she'd wake up to find Andy and me watching TV. "You have to go to school." She'd sob and rant, calling herself a bad mother and a terrible person. But soon she'd move on to the next thing—remembering that Daniel was gone and that she had lost her job—feeling sorry for herself and scanning the room, angling for a drink.

After Daniel and Delilah moved to Delaware, Beverly found out everything: who Delilah was, where she'd worked, and that Andy and I had been taken to Dill's Tuesday after Tuesday, for months. She found out after they left, so she never got the chance to go down to Dill's when Delilah worked there, to knock her onto the floor and pull her hair—which is what I'd like to have seen her do. She was furious for days, and I thought she'd want to stay far away from the memory, real or imagined, of Delilah and Daniel. But weirdly, she started taking us to Dill's a couple times a week.

We'd get sandwiches and sodas. Beverly would order coffee or beer and maybe a grilled cheese. I can still see her, her elbows on the table, nibbling at the edge of a sandwich and smoking, staring toward the kitchen, watching the waitresses as they came in and out of the swinging doors with trays of food.

She was getting a little nutty—morose and obsessive. She started asking us all these questions about Delilah—how she wore her hair, what kind of music she liked. "Tell, me something," she'd ask with rabid masochistic glee. "Does that Dee-li-laa whateverhernameis have a car?" I'd tell her I didn't know, and she'd get nasty, "Oh, sure you don't know. Your father only brought you to see her every week. At Dill's." And she'd lapse into a trance, and suddenly she'd be a private investigator: "You find out for me, what kind of car she drives. Ask your father when he calls." And when he did call, Beverly would be there, nudging me, reminding me to ask him. I'd ask him, and he'd tell me—with the bemused sort of distractedness that distance offered him.

Eventually, Beverly stopped taking us to Dill's. The food stamps we got were good for groceries, and, believe it or not, she could slip packs of cigarettes in with the food, but we couldn't use them in restaurants. She stopped asking us about Delilah too. I thought maybe things would go back to normal, but they didn't. They seemed to for a while, on the surface. Her drinking didn't slow down, but she became quieter for a while, and responsible, home when we came home from school and up in the mornings to make us breakfast. But in reality, things were weirder than ever. We didn't know it, but she'd taken a job as a waitress ... at Dill's.

This is how I found out about it: It was the day Andy broke his nose.

Some kids in the playground stole Andy's Barbie. They were smaller than him but, like wasps, could be overpowering when assembled into a swarm. The little shits. How could kids in second grade be so cruel? Take any one kid, and he'll be kind and usually shy. Put a bunch of them together, and they're a tribe of monsters. *Lord of the Flies*, it's depressing to admit, got it right.

Kids in our school used to play Push: in between the parallel bars, back to back, one team of kids would push another team of kids, like tug-of-war but backward. Andy was so big that he'd take on a group all by himself. And so kind-hearted and credulous that he wouldn't know he was being laughed at. He'd think that his classmates wanted to be friends. Andy, putting every ounce of strength into the game. Trying to be good. He was always trying to be good, and to be liked. He always *was* good, though he wasn't always liked. His face hardened into a rectangle, and the veins at the sides of his head pulsated, his eyes closed and like a true adept all was forgotten except the task at hand: Push.

His ass pushed up against the back of the kid who was against him. His hands scraped the ground, his feet rose up into the air and then finally, after sweating through the acrylic Globetrotters hat that Daniel had sent him from New York City, he fell, face first, onto the gravel, and eight or nine boys fell on top of him.

He lost his Barbie in the skirmish. She was one of the classics, with sunshine hair tied into a ponytail on the top of her head, and she was naked. At home, Andy liked to dress his Barbies in different outfits—but he always kept a naked one in his pocket as a sort of talisman. Daniel had bought him a worry stone, but he preferred his Barbie, with her smooth, slim waist and the space between her pert nipple-less breasts—the perfect nesting place for his thumb. I wonder if the whole thing might've been less catastrophic if she'd been wearing the halter-top disco gown or the sporty convertible-driving outfit. Maybe if she'd at least been decent, the boys wouldn't have turned into animals over her, like testosterone-mad cavemen.

The boys took her and, in a skittering dusty formation that the teachers and aides must have pretended not to notice, held her in the center of what looked like an undulating mole on the face of the playground, pulling her limb from limb, while Andy picked himself up, dusted off his Wranglers, and ran over to see what his friends were looking at. When he saw his Barbie, and tried to take her back, he ended up underneath the whole thing, the whole mass of boy-backs and boy-limbs, with their angular elbows, their converse sneakers, and their smell like molasses and dirt. And he broke his nose on the pavement.

I was sitting on the curb that separated the playground from the parking lot with a group of girls from my class, and we watched what was going on, but nobody did anything. I'm sure I couldn't have helped anyway, but the fact that I was just standing there, my fists clenched and my breathing tense, made me miserable; I imagined afterward all kinds of things that I could have done, should have done. All kinds of alternative outcomes that involved me in some way or another playing a heroic role. I could have hurled rocks at them. I could have pulled one of the aides out of her slumber and made her break it up sooner. Or gone over swinging my fists, yelling like Tarzan. Anything.

Finally, it got broken up and I saw him being led away by one of the aides, trailing splashes of blood. Finally, I went running to him, but the door closed behind them and I was left on the playground. I couldn't fathom going back into class after that, not knowing what was going on, how he was, so I pushed through the low-growing sumac trees and around the clump of dusty black-raspberry bushes at the edge of the playground and ran all the way home.

I had left my house key in my locker at school and the door was locked. Beverly wasn't home, and neither was her car. I had hoped to tell her that Andy was hurt and then to curl up on the couch with *I Dream of Jeannie*; it was on during school hours, so I hadn't seen it since the summertime. (I used to fantasize having my very own bottle in which to live, a soft place lined with pink couches and plenty of pillows.)

I figured the school must have called her and that she was in the nurse's office, or the hospital maybe, with Andy. So there I was, a runaway from school, locked outside of my own house, and nobody knew where I was. I began to feel less sorry for Andy and sorrier for myself. I started walking. At the end of my street, I took a left and headed for downtown.

That's when I saw Beverly's Mustang parked in front of Dill's. I looked inside: crumpled cigarette packs on the passenger seat, empty potato chip bags on the floor of the backseat. Nothing to indicate what it was doing here, downtown, and not at home, at the school, or at the hospital. I hated Dill's because I hated Delilah, so I didn't want to go inside, but I looked in the window, thinking that maybe Beverly was sitting at one of the booths having lunch. But it was worse. She wore an apron and was taking somebody's order.

*   *   *

Gramma and I finish our Chinese food—well, I finish mine and pack up the rest of hers, write her name on the bag and put it in the refrigerator down the hall. Gramma's eyelids are damp and pink, and they remind me of wild mushrooms. They want to drop down over her rheumy eyes. She's too tired; I can't bring myself to take out the letter. I unzip the pocket in my purse where it is tucked away. I touch its edges. But then my fingers retreat, leaving it there.

Andy shows up, earlier than usual.

"We just ate," I say to him. "There is some left over..."

"That's okay. I ate a Subway tuna on the way here." I try to hug him, but he puts his arms in a wide arc and aims his head far from my shoulder. "Don't get too close, I don't want to catch a cold." He smells like mayonnaise.

"It's not contagious anymore," I tell him. "It's nearly gone." I have only the tiniest roughness left in my voice.

"Still," he says, "I can't miss work." He sits in the chair next to where Gramma is propped up on the bed. "Hi Gramma."

"Andy. When are you going to cut that hair?" Her hand floats toward him. His heel pumps up and down, jiggling his knee.

"I don't like the barber," he says, leaning away from her hand.

"Well, find a new one," I tell him. "You don't have to always go to the same place." He looks at me with that combination of confusion and pity that I know means I can say all I want but I'll never understand the simple rules he needs to live by. Loyalty to a barber, even though he's old and surly and he pulls your hair and snips at your ears is one of those rules.

"So, you still getting married?" he asks me, and turns to Gramma: "Leigh's still getting married, huh? Ha! Leigh married." And he sings, "Goin to the chapel, and Leigh's gonna get married," and laughs, his fist to his forehead. He's got wrinkles and a few gray hairs, but when he laughs he looks to me like he's still in the third grade. He's been practicing the song for months now, and rarely makes it through to "goin to the chapel ... of love" without breaking into laughter.

"Uh huh," I say. "Yes, still getting married. And I have to go. Mark and I have some things to do." I pull my purse onto my shoulder, the folded letter inside of it, and kiss Gramma's soft cheek goodbye.

I kiss Andy quickly before he can pull away, saying "Oh, come on Leigh, I told you I don't want to get sick." I tousle his shaggy head and make my way to my car.

I drive several circles around the Powderhouse rotary, calculating its approximate diameter, imagining it as a sphere. I already know more or less what its area is, because I do this often. The road on which I'm driving becomes Saturn's ring. Going in circles calms me, and the other cars that pull in behind and in front of me are visitors, and since they are visitors, I am polite, and I drive slowly, and I let them in and then watch them veer off.

The letter in my purse is like something I have forgotten to do but can't remember what. It slips in and out of my consciousness like that, something I have to interact with in some form or another, but elusive and less solid than the paper on which it is written or the hexagonal form that I have folded it into, with hard edges and clear lines.

And Mark. Thinking of Mark gives me a similar feeling, of a thought recently forgotten, but whose essence remains, like a smell. I can talk about the wedding, who's going to come, what we're going to eat, what music will be played, but when I'm alone, it feels unreal, as if it were happening to someone other than me. Someone I'm watching on TV. Barbara Eden and Larry Hagman. In fact, Jeannie and her master did get married, in 1970. I saw the re-run. Jeannie full of joy, devoid of doubt. I can definitely relate more to Tony, who was a wreck up until the time of the ceremony. I only hope I recover the way he did.

Mark and I haven't spoken since our fight last night and I don't particularly want to, so, after a few more slow turns around the rotary, I go home, lock the door and unplug the phone. I put the letter from Simon Walsh on the windowsill and consider it while I sip a bottle of beer.

June 2004

Gertrude was in bed, in her apartment in Lynn, when there was a knock at the door. In her nightgown, she cracked it open, knowing it had to be either Leigh or Andy—it was too early for anyone else.

"Hi Gramma." Leigh kissed her grandmother's cheek, and as she walked in, motioned toward the dark-haired man behind her. "This is Mark."

He shook Gertrude's hand and said, "We brought muffins."

Gertrude excused herself and went into the bedroom to change while Leigh and Mark made coffee. Gertrude could hear them talking in low voices, two- and three-word phrases. Leigh hadn't told Gertrude about Mark, just hinted that she was seeing someone, so Gertrude was unprepared; wasn't even sure if the man in her kitchen was her granddaughter's boyfriend or not. How was she going to know what to ask, what to talk about? When she returned, they sat around the coffee table, Gertrude in an armchair and Mark and Leigh on the sofa.

Mark helped himself to a muffin and poured cream into his coffee. "I've heard a lot about you," he said, and Gertrude nodded and smiled and didn't know what to say because she hadn't heard anything about him.

Leigh jumped in: "So ... this is where I grew up."

"I thought you grew up on Cape Cod," Mark said.

Gertrude tried to figure out what they meant to each other. It was odd, she thought, that they were having this conversation here. If they were in a serious realtionship, wouldn't she have told him this early on?

"Yes, 'til I was twelve. But then I came here." Mark was silent, and Gertrude tried to assess how much he knew about Leigh's mother.

She changed the subject. "So, Mark. Where are you from?"

"Rhode Island. But I've been in Boston since college."

"He went to BU too," added Leigh.

"Uh huh," Gertrude nodded. "Is that where you met?"

"No, no," said Leigh.

"It's a big school," said Mark. He took Leigh's hand in his. Gertrude was alarmed to see that, even though she was at least satisfied to have the mystery of what they meant to each other solved. *Alarmed* is a strong word to use for a grandmother watching her granddaughter hold someone's hand, but Gertrude had never witnessed it. Leigh had never before brought a boyfriend home; if she'd had boyfriends, then she'd never talked about them. Gertrude had fleetingly wondered if her granddaughter was gay. In fact, she'd hoped she was, because the other option was that Leigh's childhood had been too traumatic, too damaging, and had left her incapable of having a relationship. She'd tucked her worries away, knowing there was nothing she could do.

"So then where did you meet?" Gertrude's voice was uncertain.

"Well, that's a bit of an issue. Actually," Leigh began.

"Yes?"

"Well, I guess you could say that we're just coming out of the closet, in a sense."

"We met at work," Mark said. "Out of the closet is completely the wrong term."

"The upshot is, I'm going to find another job."

Gertrude knew it was odd for Leigh too, introducing this Mark to her grandmother, holding his hand. Both women knew there was nothing wrong with the whole thing, but Leigh's hand, there in Mark's, seemed so exposed. Leigh: one half of a couple now. She took her hand out of his and reached for her cup.

"But why?" Gertrude asked.

Mark shifted, adjusted himself. Gertrude could tell he was used to holding meetings. "It's better that way. It's not necessarily company policy. I'm her boss, basically. You see?"

"I guess so." Gertrude was reminded of Clive and his lover. Clive had been Marianne's boss, too. Mark cracked his thumbs by making fists around them. Gertrude winced at the sound.

"So where will you get a job?" Gertrude asked.

"I'm sure I'll find something," Leigh said. "Anyway, I don't have to leave right away."

"I'm sure it's uncomfortable for the other girls." Gertrude sipped her coffee.

Leigh laughed. "Gramma, honestly, I'm an accountant. It's not a harem. There aren't *other girls*."

"Well, you know what I mean," she said, and looked to Mark for some kind of acknowledgment, but he was gazing toward the window.

"Have you lived here long?" Mark turned to Gertrude.

"Oh gosh, yes." Gertrude said. "Since I got married. We were going to move up to Gloucester or Marblehead, but we never did. We got separated instead." Mark nodded. Gertrude couldn't tell if his nodding meant that Leigh had already told him about Clive, or whether he was uncomfortable with her honesty. "Well, that's life," Gertrude went on.

"Yes. Yes," Mark and Leigh agreed with her, leaving a gap in the conversation.

"I suppose it wasn't Lynn, Lynn, the city of sin, back then," Mark said, leaning back, smiling, making things lighter.

"Oh, it certainly was," Gertrude laughed. "It's always been that."

"Some reputation, huh?"

"Oh, it's not really like that." Leigh put her cup on the table and rested her hands on her lap. "Well, it wasn't anyway. It was a great place to live."

Mark looked around. "I bet there's some great detail in this old place, if you were to uncover the floors and strip the paint."

The curtains had been pulled back with matching ties for so long that the sun had bleached them; they were darker in the folds where the light didn't reach. Gertrude watched Mark as he considered their surroundings and saw, through his eyes, that her apartment had become an old woman's home. Hers and Clive's ancient books were still on the shelves, though a row of paperbacks semi-concealed them. The sofa was sunken in the middle, and both of the armchairs were shredded by the cat she'd had for nearly twenty years. She wasn't so much embarrassed by it as she was agitated by Mark, the way he had drawn their attention to it.

"So, Mark, do you get back to Rhode Island much?"

"Yup," he said, cracking his thumbs. "I go every couple of weeks."

"Do you have any siblings?"

"A sister."

"That's nice. Are you close?"

"We're pretty close."

"His sister, Jane, is a lawyer," Leigh added. "But she's moving to Mexico." A look passed between them that Gertrude couldn't read.

"Oh," Gertrude said, "That's nice. Why is she moving to Mexico?"

Mark ran his hand over his gelled hair. "She met a guy there. I don't think she should go, that's why it bothers me."

"Bothers you?" Gertrude said. "But why should it bother you?" She put her coffee cup down on the table and sat back into the chair, relieved that the focus of the conversation had shifted to someone else's life—someone she'd never met.

"She met someone," Leigh began.

"No, I'll tell her. You'll make it sound like it's just me being paranoid." Mark turned back to Gertrude. "Leigh and I disagree on this. You see, Jane has a great job, at a law firm. A really good job. But she goes off to Mexico for vacation, and she meets this guy and now, all of a sudden, she's dropping everything and going to live with him in some mud hut on the beach or something."

"No, no, Gramma," Leigh laughed. "Don't listen to him. The man is in telecom. He has a job." She turned to Mark. "You know very well they're not going to live in a hut or a hammock or anything else. And besides, she's always played by the rules. It's about time she did something spontaneous." She turned back to Gertrude. "And anyway, Gramma, the law firm where she works? It's their dad's firm. She can have her job back any time she wants."

"Not really," Mark said. "She's almost a partner. She'd have to fall back down the ladder and work her way up."

"Anyway, Mark exaggerates, is all I'm saying."

"Well, I can see both of your points," Gertrude began.

"You know something, Missus Littlefield?" Mark interrupted her. "This granddaughter of yours is really something else. It's why I love her, but it drives me crazy."

"Oh, I see...." Gertrude said, unsure what he was talking about.

"She keeps me real," Mark clarified.

They all sipped coffee, Mark beaming, Leigh looking intently at the leg of

Gertrude's armchair. Gertrude could see how hard it was for Leigh to have a boyfriend, to bring him here, to be given attention. As far as Gertrude could tell, he seemed a little too satisfied, too sure of himself. But it appeared certain that he loved Leigh. He seemed like he'd be loyal, if it's possible to tell such a thing at a first meeting. And he was nice, without anger … maybe just a little too … content, a little … dull. But Gertrude was being judgmental, a fault she had spent most of her life trying to overcome. What did she really know about him? Generally, she found him nice enough. Still, she wished that Leigh seemed more comfortable. But Leigh might never feel comfortable. Maybe Mark was just what she needed, an extrovert to balance out her shyness.

Later, Gertrude and Leigh were in the kitchen, putting the dishes into the dishwasher.

"So, this is the new boyfriend?" Leigh nodded. "I wish you'd told me you were coming, I'd have been better prepared."

"Sorry, Gramma. It was last minute." Gertrude waited for her to elaborate, but she was straightening plates on the bottom rack of the dishwasher.

"I would have made cookies."

"I didn't want to put you out. This way, you didn't have to go to any trouble."

"You know I wouldn't mind." She put the juice into the fridge. "He seems nice, honey. He seems nice." Leigh was leaning against the counter, looking worried. Gertrude hugged her, and her arms around her were warm with the memory of Leigh as a child.

"He is nice, Gramma," Leigh said. "He's nice." They stood facing each other. Gertrude took a strand of Leigh's hair that had fallen in front of her face and rubbed it between her thumb and fingers. Leigh picked a lint ball from the shoulder of her grandmother's sweater. "Well, we better go," she said. "We're bringing Andy to the movies."

"Okay, honey," Gertrude said.

"He hasn't met Andy yet."

"Well. It's a busy day then."

"Yeah." Leigh absently straightened a jar on the counter so the word Flour faced out, then dusted the lid of the Sugar canister with her fingers.

Gertrude's eyes vaguely followed her granddaughter's movements. Suddenly Leigh brushed both her hands down the front of her pants. "Well. We better go." Gertrude followed her out of the kitchen.

At the door of the apartment, Gertrude hugged Leigh again and shook Mark's hand. A good firm shake, and she'd always been told that was a good sign. They turned away, and Gertrude watched them walk down the hall. At the top of the stairs, Mark reached over to Leigh's head and took the clip out of her hair; Gertrude couldn't hear what he said, but could see him shake his head, as if instructing Leigh to fluff out her hair. She had long hair, but she tended to always wear it back, off of her face. Leigh took the clip and turned to catch Gertrude's eye. Gertrude looked away quickly, pretending to examine a splinter in the door frame.

If they'd been strangers, Gertrude would have been satisfied to have witnessed such a moment of intimacy, but because it was Leigh, she felt embarrassed and unsettled. She hoped that Leigh was making the right choice. She heard their footsteps padding down the stairs as she closed the door.

Walnut Acres

Gertrude looks at the red buzzer, dulled by people's fingers, hers and previous residents', and reaches over to push it. A few minutes pass before Shannon, a mountain of a woman with shoulder-length brown hair, comes in.

"Yes, Missus Littlefield. What's the problem?" she huffs her way to Gertrude's bed.

"It's just ... I'd like to sit by the window."

"Okay, let's get you moved." Shannon puts a meaty arm behind Gertrude's back and supports her as she makes her way into the chair. Gertrude notices how different Shannon's touch is from Jessie's. Jessie is all angles and tension, where Shannon feels soft, like a pillow, but dull, and she smells like cigarettes.

"Okay?" Shannon asks, breathing heavily, putting her hands on her hips.

"Yes. Thank you."

"It's okay. I was going to come in later and help you get up anyway. You should be moving as much as you can. Keeps the body limber."

Gertrude looks at Shannon, her heaving chest, her round body.

"How old are you?" she asks.

"Thirty-nine. Be forty in a couple of months."

"So young," Gertrude says. "You should take better care of yourself, you know."

Shannon grunts. "Whatever," she says, and leaves.

The ground around the bottom of the tree in the courtyard is bare dirt, and there are tufts of whatever weeds can survive on the three or four minutes of sunlight that make it down there each day. The tree's leaves are a young and tender green, not having hardened into the full summer color they will wear until the fall. Gertrude is pleased to be noticing the leaves at this stage. Spring usually passes before she has even realized that it has begun, and she thinks that this will most likely be her last one. She tries memorizing the leaves, appreciating them, but becomes distracted by the windows on the other side of the courtyard. Most have their blinds pulled, but some of them are open and Gertrude could see into them—if she had her glasses on ... which she doesn't.

She looks at the glasses on the table on the other side of the bed and then at the red button, which is closer and more easily reached. She puts her hands on the arms of the chair and tries to push herself up, but sits down again, sighing. She counts to a hundred and reaches over and pushes the button. Waits. Counts up to eighty-five.

"You're busy, I'll do it," Jessie calls over her shoulder as she enters the room. She must have just arrived to work: She is wearing a short satiny jacket that leaves a bare ribbon of skin exposed above the waistline of her jeans and pointy shoes with heels as narrow as the middle of an egg timer. "What is it, Missus Littlefield?"

"I just want my glasses. I'm sorry for the trouble." She points to them on the table.

"Uh huh," Jessie says. "No trouble. But you know you should think of these things when there's already somebody in here. That button is supposed to be for emergencies. An aide stops by every half hour or so. You should wait for one to get you things like your glasses. Understand?"

Gertrude nods. She takes the glasses from Jessie and leans her face down to slide them on. When she looks up, Jessie is gone.

"And you should cover yourself up better," Gertrude says to the empty space where Jessie had been.

"What's that?" Jessie pokes her head in from just outside the door.

"Your parka," Gertrude manages. "It's too short." Jessie looks at her with eyes like black pebbles, and then, after holding her gaze for several seconds, turns away. Gertrude isn't sure if the sound she hears is Jessie. It sounds like a feline snarl, but it could be a rusty hinge somewhere. She breathes slowly, her hands holding tight to the arms of the chair.

Clara Honeywell's room is on the other side of the courtyard. Gertrude can tell it is Clara's room because her son is there, pacing back and forth by the window. Gertrude has seen Clara Honeywell's son a number of times in the community room, a nice looking man, always in corduroys and a turtleneck, with a dignified shock of grey hair above each ear. It is hit or miss whether or not Clara herself will recognize him, but Gertrude thinks he is a nice man. She remembers him on several occasions squatting next to his mother's chair, and Clara, staring into the distance—but for an emotional instant holding his head between her hands, a crystal ball in which she'd caught a glimpse of everything that had ever meant anything.

He looks like he might be crying, the way he's rubbing his face. Gertrude turns away, taking a deep breath. When she looks back, she can see the back of his head and Shannon, standing next to Clara's bed. Then Shannon goes to Clara's son and hugs him. Gertrude thinks she can hear the young man moan and even hear Shannon's whispered condolences, but of course she can't, because the windows are closed and the room is on the other side of the building. Then Jessie is in Clara's room; she is in her scrubs now and has her hair pulled back. She goes to the bed and crosses herself. She turns to Clara's son and holds his arms, his gaze. Shannon is still there too, leaning against the wall.

Gertrude adjusts her glasses with a trembling hand. She is leaning so far forward, toward the window, that slowly, like a big tree being cut down, she tumbles onto the floor; as she lands on her hip and her arm, her glasses go skating underneath the bed.

June 1954

Clive's footsteps came softly down the hall and then his keys tinkled outside the door. Gertrude, who'd been pacing their apartment like a caged cat, her head wound up on a worried neck, her ears straining to hear him come home, raced for the bedroom and lay down. Behind her eyelids were red splotches of treacherous anger.

So it wasn't a pair of policemen coming to inform her that Clive had been in an accident or had a heart attack. No. It was Clive himself, nonchalantly unlocking the door at four o'clock in the morning. Gertrude's fear and worry turned to rage ... and relief.

Already she began willing herself to believe the story he would tell her in the morning. What had it been the last time? There'd been an elaborate explanation: someone's house had burned down, and Clive had needed to stay at work until well after midnight to go over their insurance papers. There could be any number of reasons for him to be late. A client in some trouble that couldn't wait. Paperwork that had to be filed on a deadline. Food poisoning that kept him in his office, throwing up into a trashcan. But four a.m.?

She feigned sleep, but there were clenched knots throughout her body. She heard him undress. The metal thud as his belt buckle hit the doily-covered dresser top, rustling cloth, breathing. The tiny chorus of springs as he lay on his mattress, and then again as he turned over, sighing, and fell to sleep. Gertrude could hear his breathing slow, and could hear the way it moved up into his nasal passage, as it did when he slept. Somehow, as on those other nights, Gertrude fell asleep too.

In the morning, her eyes sprang open. She lay on her bed with the blankets pulled up to her chin and stared at the ceiling. Clive was still asleep.

She got up, went to the kitchen, spooned coffee from the can into the percolator, lit the stove. Her hands on her hips in her nightgown, a blue shift with satin ribbon around the neck that Clive had given her a few months earlier as a gift for their tenth wedding anniversary.

Fifteen minutes later, the coffee, taking most of the grounds with it, was gurgling from the spout onto the stovetop and she had collapsed onto the floor in the corner of their bedroom. In her hands was a letter she'd taken from his jacket pocket.

My Darling Clive, the letter crooned. It was written on stationery from the Kensington Arms Hotel. Gertrude and Clive had been to the bar several times. It was close to the docks, near the building where Clive worked, at Security Trust. She could picture it: The bar on the right, with dark wood paneling and a deep blue fabric on the chairs. The hotel front desk on the other side of frosted glass panels.

I've been thinking of you every day. When I see you and can't touch you, it's torture. Until the next time. Your Marianne.

The writing curly like a doll's lashes. She wondered, with a level of clarity that surprised her, whether they had gone to the bar for a drink first, or did they go straight to bed? Clive and Gertrude knew the bartender—not well, but he'd have known the woman wasn't Clive's wife. Gertrude wondered about that—pictured them in the bar, Clive, Marianne, the bartender— winking at him? Complicit? Or disgusted? How was she to know anymore what people were capable of, now that the one she'd never questioned had done this?

She curled like a C over the letter, as if it would spill if she tipped it, the painful coarseness of the woman's perfume. She let it enter her, and it was as though her pain were the entity with substance and she was nothing more than air or smell or smoke.

She knew Marianne. She'd spoken to her. She worked at Security Trust, as a receptionist.

On top of the dresser were a hairbrush, Clive's belt, and their wedding picture, oval in a square frame. Clive and Gertrude stuck inside it like a snow globe. Clive's hand on Gertrude's waist, and she looks as if she could fall forward in her uncomfortable dress; his chin is tipped to the sky.

Gertrude picked up his shirt and threw it over the frame, and then collapsed again, back onto the floor in front of the closet, with the letter perched between her hands; she pulled her knees in toward each other, against her arms, to stop the trembling.

Clive flopped onto his belly and cocked his head; one eye opened, looked at the clock. He was late for work.

"Gertie!" he called. He got out of bed and went down the hallway to the bathroom. "Gertie!" she heard him call again, over the rush of urine hitting water in the toilet. Against the closet door in their bedroom, Gertrude sat, biting her lip until she could taste blood. "Gertie, it's late!" He trudged pajama-bottomed into their room, plastic toothbrush handle and white froth coming from his mouth, and saw her. He put the toothbrush down carefully on top of the sleeve of his shirt where it was draped over their wedding picture and swallowed the foam in his mouth. He kneeled down, took the letter from her, threw it behind him onto the floor.

As if the letter had been holding her steady, she began to tremble after its removal.

"It's not what you think it is," he started to say. But he knew that there was no way out. "I'm sorry," he said. "I'm sorry. I'm sorry. I'm so sorry." They stayed that way for a long time, Gertrude motionless, staring past him at the letter on the floor, and Clive with his head on her knees.

He helped her up and led her by the elbow to the living room, went to the kitchen, turned off the stove, poured the burned coffee, brought two cups to where she sat on the arm of the sofa. She took the cup he offered and splashed it down his leg, soaking his pajama bottoms. "I deserve that," he grimaced, crunched over in pain. The fabric had been made transparent and she could see the skin was crimson. He lifted the material away from his leg and limped into the bathroom.

"How could you?" Gertrude said, over and over again, but her voice wouldn't work well enough for him to hear it over the sound of the cold running bath water that washed over his thigh. He returned quickly.

"This coffee is terrible," he said, returning with another cup. She looked at it, and at him. Clive's cup. This is Clive, she said to herself, but it was hard to believe.

"Let's go out." he said, "Let's talk. Let's get some coffee." and she nodded meekly.

On the way to the diner, she doubled over, putting her hands between her thighs, and heaved. She didn't vomit; nothing came up. When she looked into his face, she sobbed, "We were going to have a baby." Clive assumed she was talking about the fact that they'd been trying to get pregnant. When she realized that he'd misunderstood, she decided to keep the secret. She was pregnant. She hadn't seen her doctor yet for confirmation but she knew she'd finally conceived and her head ached with the bitter irony of it.

She slid into the booth first, while Clive hung up their coats. She wiped her eyes with the backs of her hands as he slid onto the vinyl across from her. Over by the door; their coats hung together on a rack, and she imagined Clive's coat tossed onto the back of an armchair at the Kensington Arms Hotel. And Marianne waiting in the bed.

"Gertie," he began, and her head spun in his direction, her eyes glaring. He stopped short, never having seen such anger in her. He spoke to her elbows instead of her face. "I know there's not a damn thing I can say. Or do. I know I've been stupid. Real stupid."

"Yes," she said, gazing at their coats.

"I just wish ... there was ... something," he tried to keep silence from developing between them, but was unable to think of the right words. "Gertie, I'm sorry."

Gertrude looked at him, and he looked at her, and it was as if their previous selves were fractured like a faulty film. They flickered in front of each other, their old selves interspersed with the selves that had been created by this treachery.

"You remember the Oak Ridge Motel?" He asked her.

"Of course I do." She was fingering the cuffs of her shirt. The waitress brought coffee.

"You were a damn fine woman, Gertie. You know what? No other woman would have stayed there without a fuss."

"Marianne likes nicer things," Gertrude said, through pursed lips and gritted teeth.

Either he didn't hear or he chose to ignore her. "You were, well, just the best a man could...."

"Stop it, Clive." They were silent for a long while. Gertrude went on, "Why do you want to bring up that trip? Have I changed since then? Have I changed in ... what ... two months?" She was draining of rage. "Have I changed? Is that what you're trying to say? That this is my fault?"

"No, Gertie. No you haven't. Not at all. Of course not."

"Then why, Clive? Why?" He shook his head. Clucked his tongue quietly against his top teeth. "Why?" she demanded.

"I don't know. I honestly don't know. You're the best thing's ever happened to me."

She sipped her coffee. Clive excused himself quietly and went to the restroom.

In her peripheral vision, she watched as he came back to the table; he was like a stranger. Worse than a stranger.

"What do you talk about with her?" she demanded after he sat down.

"What do you want to know that for?" He squinted, his bottom lids fluttery. His head was at an angle as though he were listening for distant sounds.

"Do you talk about me?"

"No. Of course not."

"I'm just wondering what it is you found ... what you found in her that you couldn't find in me."

"It's not like that."

"It has to be like that," she said, her voice trembling. "If I was enough, then I'd be enough."

"No," he said, "you don't understand."

"No, I don't. I don't understand. And I don't want to. I can't even try. I don't have enough left to...." She was about to tell him about the baby.... But she kept it to herself. The baby would be her weapon. She and the baby, together, would punish Clive, would hold him accountable. But when she doubted that for an instant, when she feared he'd abandon them both anyway, that he'd be unreachable, as he'd been so many times, even before this, the fear made her dizzy and nauseous and she had to get away.

"I want you out," she said. "By the time I get home this afternoon." And she left. Clive stared at the place where she'd been sitting and heard the whoosh of her coat and the slam of the metal door.

By the time she got home—after wandering the streets of Lynn for four hours, looking into shop windows, walking the beach, resting on benches—he was gone. He'd taken most of his clothes, his winter coats, his briefcase, his pipes, tobacco pouches, pipe cleaner, and the big brown ashtray with the pipe holder that sat on the low table between their two chairs.

Gertrude crawled onto his bed and wept.

Leigh

Simon Walsh's number isn't hard to find—his return address is on the letter, written in a shaky hand in the top right corner, along with the date. It is a formality that I have a hard time associating with someone my mother had known: a return address, a date. My experience of my mother was that she never knew the date, never mind bothering to put it on a letter.

A young voice that couldn't possibly go with the handwriting on the letter answers, but when I ask for Simon, he says, "Yup that's me." The phone has suctioned itself onto my ear. "Yes, hello," I manage. He is silent, waiting for me to say more. I stumble along, *umm-ing* and *uh-ing*, before I finally get another word out. "I'm Leigh," I say.

"Well, hi there. Leigh. I'm so glad you called. I thought I might hear from one of you."

"Fortune," I say my last name anyway, because it had been poised to come out of my mouth and had nowhere else to go.

"Yes, I know. I know," he says. "Your mother told me all about you."

"She did?" I'm blown away. I had no idea. How could I have known that she ever thought anything about us at all?

"Of course she did. You're her daughter." As if it were totally normal for a mother to abandon her children and then talk about them anyway. As if there were a connection between Beverly and me that had continued past my twelfth year. The phone makes a soft pop as I pull it away from my ear.

"How's Andy?" he asks.

"Andy's fine." I can't find any more words.

He clears his throat and then is silent. The silence goes on for longer than I am used to.

I'm trying to figure out how to ask who he is, how my mother knew him, and I finally blurt, "So who the hell are you?"

Then I mumble, trying to formulate something gentler to say, to ease what I've just let out of my mouth, something that will better disguise my ignorance, and, after a short pause, Simon Walsh begins to laugh.

"Your mother and I were good friends," he says.

So now I have to figure a way to ask exactly what that means.

"So you were...." I trail off and this time he jumps in to help me.

"We were friends. Nothing romantic." He laughs at something private and then continues. "We met at AA. I'm surprised your grandmother didn't tell you. Beverly's mother. I thought you were close."

"We are," I say defensively. "We are close," I repeat, trying to buy some time to figure this out. So Gramma knows Simon Walsh? She never told me. I'm like the kid in the class who's being called on to answer a question about a book she never read. I thought I was the smart one, the one with the letter, the one who was keeping a secret, and it turns out that Gramma's been hiding my mother from me ... for how long, I have no idea.

"I'm close to my Grandmother too," Simon Walsh says, tangentially.

"Oh," I say, "that's nice." He must be young enough to have a living grandmother. I picture Simon Walsh and his grandmother as a Norman Rockwell painting, a heavy-chested matron offering a tray of cookies to a little boy in short pants and suspenders. But then, I can't imagine how that picture could in any way be related to my mother.

"I don't know if you know this, but I actually didn't know where my mother was." I am suddenly full of words and disregard for what this man might think of me. "Did you know that?" I ask, not waiting for a reply. "She disappeared from my life when I was barely a teenager, and now that she's dead, she has the gall to show up again? What am I supposed to do with this information? I don't even know my mother. Didn't even know my mother...."

I trail off; I feel like I might cry, so I focus intently on the shape of the telephone base and do a quick calculation to figure out its area. Its curved edges complicate things. I'm tempted to speculate how much area the phone base loses in those curved edges, but I need specifics, so I pull a ruler from my purse on the floor and hold it up, look for a pen, paper.

"Well, it's none of my business," Simon Walsh says. "Beverly didn't ask me to contact you. She just said, when she was bad and we knew she wouldn't last long, to contact her mother. To let her mother know. And so that's what

I did."

What am I supposed to do with this information?

"She didn't care about us at all." My voice sounds robotic. I look for a pen.

"I can't tell you if she did or she didn't," he says and I sit up, because I had expected him to console me, to tell me that she did care for me.

"It has nothing to do with you," I say. "I didn't mean to bring you into it."

"Damn," he says. "I don't mind being brought into this. She was a friend. If there's anything I can do."

"I'm sorry," I say quickly, because the fact that Beverly had a good friend and it wasn't me is more than I can take now after all of this and I hang up the phone and collapse onto the floor where I cry for a good long time, my body thankful to rest against the hard wide plane. The smell of Buster's fur is comforting in the thin rug under my face.

*　*　*

Downtown Wellfleet. Beverly's car outside of Dill's; Beverly working inside. It might've been Delilah's old maroon apron tied around her waist.

I dropped into a squat, so that Beverly wouldn't look up and see me. But then, realizing how ridiculous I must have seemed, crouching underneath the restaurant's window display (red plastic lobsters, sand, starfish), I got up and walked in the direction of the library. I passed the checkout desk, but the stacks of books seemed so tall that I thought if I leaned against one of them, which is what I wanted to do because I was dizzy, it would come crashing down. It was too quiet in there; behind my ears was a dull howling.

I couldn't go back to school. You can't run off and play hooky at recess and then expect to go waltzing to your desk in the middle of class. I have always wished I could be more impulsive. My whole life I have listened to people tell me about incidents in which they acted on an instinct that they couldn't control: yelling at a stranger, telling off a rude boss. I wish I had marched into Dill's and confronted Beverly, just as I should have tried to rescue Andy from the kids who took his Barbie. But it was too late, as usual. If I went back and confronted Beverly, what would I say? Why didn't you tell me you had a job? Why are you obsessing about Daniel's girlfriend? What are you, a psycho? Are you planning on finding them in Delaware and driving your car through their bedroom in the middle of the night?

And then there was Andy, bleeding in the nurse's office with no one to help him. I would have to do it for Andy. I had forgotten about him, even though he was the reason I was in this predicament in the first place. The first thing I was going to do when I got back to our house would be to throw his stupid Barbie collection in the trash. Didn't he know he was asking for trouble? And Beverly, worse than just allowing it to continue, had even encouraged it, had said it was okay for a boy to play with girls' toys. I left the library, walked back to Dill's, and, after taking a deep breath, pulled open the door. I expected her to be right there in front of me, but she wasn't. I decided she must be in the kitchen and I sat down at a table to wait. Another waitress came over, her arms behind her back as she tied on an apron. I didn't recognize her, but she knew who I was.

"Hi there." She held a small pad and poked the butt of her pen into her cheek. "Your mom just left."

"I'd like a ginger ale, please." She nodded and turned away.

"It's on the house," she said when she came back with the glass.

I figured Beverly must have heard about the accident by now. Either the school knew she was working here and had called her, or her shift had ended and she'd find out when she got home. They'd be calling her there for sure. I wanted to ask the waitress if the school had called, but she was busy with some other tables and I didn't feel much like talking anyway. I was about to go home when a hand pushed a dollar along the table in front of me. It was Dr. Silvieri, the chiropractor. He had shaved his mustache so now his upper lip curled, bald, into the top of his mouth.

"That's okay, it's paid for," I told him, and tried to squeeze by to leave. He stood there, grinning at me as if he were playing a game that I was enjoying too. But I wasn't enjoying it.

"Ha ha," I said.

"How's your mother?" he asked. "She still out of work?"

"No."

"Well, the girl I got to replace her didn't work out, so tell her if she wants her job back, I'd be willing to give her another chance."

"She's working here," the waitress said, picking up my empty glass. "You're talking about Beverly, right?" We both nodded. "Yeah, she's working here," she said to Dr. Silvieri, then looked at me. "Isn't she?" I wasn't sure if the look on her face, her eyes intent, was concern for me or scorn for my mother, or a little of both. Or maybe she didn't know anything about my mother, Delilah, my father, or Dr. Silvieri. But I doubted that. Wellfleet was a pretty small town.

"Sure," I said and then pushed right toward Dr. Silvieri, which made him have to move aside. I ran out, leaving the two of them standing next to the booth where I'd been.

Andy was on the couch, watching TV. His eyes were bloodshot, the skin around them puffy and dark; he had a bandage over his nose, white tape across his cheeks, almost to his ears. Beverly was on the recliner, the phone in one hand and a vodka-soda in the other. She looked up when I shut the door.

"Oh thank God," she said to whoever was on the other end. "She just walked in the door." She made a sort of grimace at me, like she was mad but relieved too. She left her glass on the coffee table and crouched down in front of my face. "I could kill you. Where have you been? Do you know the school called? What is going on?" She took off my windbreaker and hugged my head at the same time. Andy was almost asleep; he looked up and said, "Like my shiner?" and then turned back to the TV.

"I saw Dr. Silvieri."

"You left school because you had a subluxation?" She laughed. "I was worried sick. I had to pick Andy up at school, and then they tell me that you've disappeared as well. I thought, my God, it's my lucky day, one kid injured and the other gone, kidnapped or whatever, all in a day!"

"I was at Dill's."

"What were you doing there?" she asked, moving about the house, retrieving her glass and heading for the kitchen. She acted as though there was nothing strange about my having been at Dill's, but there was a slight catch in her voice.

"I had a ginger ale."

"Uh huh." She splashed more vodka into her glass.

"Dr. Silvieri says he'll give you another chance if you want your job back."

"Does he? The bastard. Did you tell him I wouldn't work for him again if he paid me a hundred dollars an hour?"

"No."

"I don't need him."

"But you need a job," I ventured. Her movements slowed down as she remembered the lie she had to protect.

"That's true."

* * *

Two days later, I brought Andy to Dill's. We peered in the window, but we didn't see her.

"She was there, I swear it," I told him. We were on the sidewalk, Andy with the rapidly deteriorating white bandage over his nose, a delicate lace of blood on the rim.

"Even if she was, so what?" He was annoyed with me for bringing him there. He wanted to go home and watch TV. I wanted to pull him along with me, to know everything I knew and to feel as betrayed as I felt. I didn't want to feel alone; I needed a partner.

"We'll have to go during school hours," I said.

"No way." He shook his head, and his hands started to tremble. If I didn't calm him down, he'd begin wagging them all around himself, in a mad dance. He couldn't be trusted to be secretive or subtle, and he got very nervous at the suggestion that he disrupt the routine that he was used to.

"Okay, okay. Never mind."

"Why don't you just ask her?"

I looked at him. We both knew I couldn't ask her, but neither of us knew exactly why not. She used to tell us everything, so when she started hiding things, I guess it seemed that her secrets must be very dark and unreachable. If she didn't tell us things, then we didn't ask. Andy looked away.

I had no one who would understand the significance of this development. No one who was up to the investigative task of figuring out my mother and her intentions.

So I let it go.

After that, I'd bring it up sometimes: "Do you think she's still working there?" And Andy would answer that he didn't know and it was clear that he didn't want to know. It didn't last long. She went back to Dr. Silvieri's office soon after my encounter with him at Dill's. Who took whom back was never very clear. I assume that it was difficult for Dr. Silvieri to keep a receptionist for very long. Beverly didn't have many options. She was hungover so much of the time that I'm sure she must have gotten fired from Dill's. I wished she'd realize how stupid she was being—slathering herself in the memory of the woman who'd stolen her husband—and had quit. But I'm sure that's not the case.

* * *

I still can't feel bad for her. I still feel like the victim, all these years later. And now I find out that she went and made friends with Simon Walsh, instead of coming back to Lynn and being with her family. It feels like a punishment, like at twelve years old I should have known how to be a better friend to her. If only I'd been as good a friend as she found in Simon Walsh, then she wouldn't have had to leave. "That's ridiculous," I tell myself out loud, and get up off the floor. Finally, I go to the bathroom and wash my face.

Over the sound of running water, the phone rings. My first thought is that it is Simon Walsh, calling me back, but when I look at the caller ID, I see that it is Mark. I shut off the volume and go to bed.

Walnut Acres

Whenever someone dies, there is extra bustle in the hallway: the important-sounding hush of rubber-soled shoes, the medics, the rolling gurney. Clara Honeywell's room is on the other side of the hallway from the nurse's station though, so Gertrude supposes that's why no one is coming in to check on her, or even passing by on this side of the building—all the action must be over there.

She can see her glasses underneath the bed. She can see the side of the emergency call button, far above her. She calls out, but—most likely because of Clara Honeywell's passing—the nurses are occupied. She lays her head on her palm and waits. The chill from the floor moves further into her body. She can feel it like a weather front, creeping closer and closer to her bones, her right leg, her hip, her ribs, her shoulder, her arm. She imagines her bones, thinned with age, dry, liable to crack. She counts into the seven hundreds and then hears a voice, finally.

"Oh shit, what happened to you?" It is Helio, the man who was flirting with Jessie. The man who winked at her. He kneels, puts his face down practically onto the floor in line with hers. "You okay? Should I get someone?"

"No. I'm just cold. Nothing broke. Could you by any chance help me up?" He squats and maneuvers her into a sitting position so that she is leaning into his chest. He feels warm against her back. Then he puts one arm behind her and the other under her knees and picks her up into the air. She wants to relax against his chest, but resists, strains her head in the direction of the bed. "Thank you." She's more relieved than embarrassed. "You're kind."

"You don't want to go for a walk or anything? Pretend you're my bride and we're on a honeymoon?" He smiles into her face and his teeth are white, his eyes kind.

"No, I guess you'd better put me down."

After he lays her onto the bed, he sits down on the chair. "You sure everything's working?" She moves her hands, opening and closing them, and then wiggles her toes.

"It appears that I am fine," she says. "Thank you so much...."

"Helio."

"Helio," she repeats. "Yes, I remember. Jessie told me your name. It's different."

"Cape Verdean." He puts his hands on the arms of the chair but doesn't get up.

"Jessie is ... very angular," Gertrude says, conspiratorially, with squinted eyes.

"Angular?" He leans toward her.

"You know, all angles. She needs to put on some weight."

"You mean Jessie who works here?"

"Yes, that one."

"I don't know, she's pretty fine as she is." Helio makes a gesture with his hands as though he is scooping water from a stream, or cupping a part of Jessie.

"I'm cold." She motions toward the blanket at the bottom of the bed. As he arranges it over her, she says, "I would say that Jessie is a woman who doesn't have many friends."

"I don't know about that...."

"But then I never trusted anyone with too many friends." Gertrude is looking past him, toward the door. "Women especially. Men can have a lot of friends, but if a woman has too many friends, then there's something wrong."

Helio is quiet, watching her.

"Helio," she says suddenly. "Would you mind, my glasses, they're under the bed."

"Sure. Okay." She can feel his warm presence underneath her as he retrieves them. He hands them to her, and she holds them on her lap with the hinges open. He seems about to leave, but sits back down again. "So, what were you doing anyway, lying on the floor like that?"

She slides her glasses onto her face. "I fell."

"I kinda assumed you fell. I didn't think you were down there doing Capoeira."

"Capoeira?"

"It's a Brazilian martial art."

"Like karate?"

"Naw, nothing like karate. You do it to music. It's beautiful. You'd like it."

"I don't imagine I'll get the chance."

He stands. "I'll come and visit again, if you want."

"Oh, I'm all right. Don't worry."

"I'm not worried. You know, I'll just check in."

She isn't sure what to make of Helio. She wants him to leave her alone, because she doesn't know him, but she also wants him to stay. "How long have you lived in Lynn?" she asks.

"Ten years. You?"

"Seventy-four."

"Wow."

"It's changed a lot."

"For the worse?"

"I don't know about that. If Lynn has changed for the worse, then the whole world has. Which may be the case."

"It's diverse." Helio props his foot on the edge of the chair and ties his shoe.

"Well, it's always been quite diverse, just with different people."

"I'd love to have seen the world back then. You know that?"

"It was simpler." He nods, but doesn't respond. "Clara Honeywell died," she says, breaking the silence.

"Oh yeah ... just now. News travels."

"I hardly knew her." Gertrude looks at the window, but she can't see into Clara Honeywell's room from her bed. "Has Jessie gone home?" she asks suddenly.

"Man, what is it you got about Jessie?"

"Nothing. I saw her in there, in Clara Honeywell's room."

"How'd you see that? Out the window?" He leans over and squints. "Oh, is that how you fell? That's how you fell isn't it? Man, you got a real curious side don't you?" He laughs. "Oh, now come on, I won't tell anyone."

"Do you really think I care whether you tell anyone anything? I'm ninety-four years old."

"I was only kidding anyway." He claps his hands together in front of him, as though asking forgiveness. "If I was in here, I'd be watching out the window too. This place is as boring as ... and you know what? Besides that? It's depressing! Shit, you gotta find something to do."

She beams at him. "You do. You've got to do something with your time."

"Anyway, I gotta get back to work. Don't be falling on the floor anymore, alright?"

He turns to her from the doorway and clicks his tongue against his teeth.

And just like that, Helio becomes Clive. It is as though in Gertrude's brain there is only room for a certain number of people, and the spaces have all been used up. Everyone is someone else, someone from the past. That sound he makes with his tongue against his teeth, he's just like Clive. There is a physical resemblance as well. Helio, like Clive, is compact, and with short dark hair. Then Shannon puffs past the door, sighing, and suddenly she is Beverly, only heavier, sulking, not taking control of her own life.

Gertrude gazes at the few people who pass. Clara Honeywell's relatives, she guesses. A woman lifts her hand to her hair in a particular way and she is Marianne, Clive's lover, dark-haired and treacherous, but Marianne's face has morphed in Gertrude's memory into the face of Liza Minnelli, fat and over-painted. She counts and categorizes the people as they pass. Each person's passing leaves something as tangible as smell, and it lingers around Gertrude, touching off memories that play like movie clips.

* * *

Gertrude wakes in the middle of the night. She feels a cold breeze inside her body, and she's certain that it's Clara Honeywell. That's how you know a soul has passed by. You feel the breeze beneath the skin instead of upon it. At the nurses' station, somebody types; the clicking sound moves around her thoughts like water through reeds. She pushes the emergency call button. Waits.

Jane, one of the night nurses, stands in the doorway; she is a heavyset woman with hair like a puppy that naps across her shoulders.

"I'm just ... a ... little..." Gertrude begins. Jane waits, a hip against the doorframe. "Scared, I guess." Jane looks down at her fingernails, cleans dirt from under one of them.

"What do you have to be scared of? You afraid of ghosts or something?"

"Yes. I am."

"There aren't any ghosts around, Missus Littlefield. I told 'em all to stay away. So don't worry."

"I'm thirsty," Gertrude says.

"Well, that I can help you with." She turns away, toward the kitchen area down the hall. Soon she comes back with a plastic cup and puts it on the table.

"Anything else?"

"No. You've been very helpful."

"That's what I like to hear." Jane squeezes Gertrude's bony forearm. Gertrude lifts the cup to her mouth and sips. Water. She pushes the button again and waits. She can hear Jane sigh and flop a magazine onto the desk at the nurse's station before clomping back to her room.

"Now what?"

"Juice. I'd like juice. This water tastes like chlorine."

"What are you worried about, your health?"

Gertrude takes as big a breath of air as she can manage, and says, "Why don't you like me?"

"I do like you," Jane says benignly.

"You do not. You're nasty to me."

"Missus Littlefield, I really think you should get some sleep. You're being belligerent."

As she goes out the door, Gertrude yells after her, her voice tremulous. "Don't forget my juice," and then whispers, "Bitch." She closes her eyes and tries to sleep, sure that she isn't going to get any juice.

Leigh

Andy and I are at Friendly's.

"Do you remember when Beverly worked at Dill's?" It is ten o'clock on Sunday morning, but he doesn't eat ice cream all week because of his perpetual diet, so it's the first thing we do together. He laughs. I'm not sure what he finds funny.

"That's gross. Close your mouth."

He swallows the chewed-up cone and yellow ice cream, with his fist in front of his face, like he is holding a microphone to the space between his eyebrows.

"Yeah. Why'd she do that?"

"That's what I was going to ask you."

"Who knows? Are you going to have ice cream, Leigh? You're not going to just have coffee are you?"

"It's too early for ice cream."

"Never too early or too late or anything else," he pops the last inch-an-a-half of cone into his mouth, "for ice cream."

"It was weird though, wasn't it?" I ask. He nods. "She used to go through things so quickly, didn't she?" Andy nods again. I continue, "She would get totally obsessed with something, and then she'd just forget about it, like it never existed."

"Like us," Andy adds. He isn't laughing now, and his face has changed. It is like a thief who pulls a stocking over his head, the way suddenly everything angles down toward the ground and his features become dull and nebulous.

"Yes, but why on earth would she want to work where Delilah worked? I mean, why did she want to think about it all the time? To be surrounded by memories that were painful?"

"Maybe she wanted to match up with Delilah." Andy's foot is tapping, and his eyes look small and red behind his glasses.

"You mean she wanted to try and be like her? She wanted to figure out what she didn't have that Delilah did?"

"Yeah."

"No, I don't think so. At least not in a conscious way. I bet she never even thought about what she was doing or why."

"Whatever. I'm going to get a cookie, okay?" He is moving toward the edge of the booth to get up.

"I know you know better than that. Your whole life you've had to watch your weight. You don't need me to tell you this."

He laughs and gets the cookie anyway. He makes his own money, and he's an adult after all. He works at the CVS in Everett Square, processing photos. He's been there for ten years, and he loves it.

When we leave Friendly's, the air is warm, and there is the green smell of summer, buoyant despite the car exhaust and the dripping hum of air conditioners that stick out of people's windows. In the passenger seat of my car, Andy hits his fist against his knee and turns up the radio.

"So how's Mark?" He yells over the pounding of Kiss 108. I nod at him and mouth the word "fine."

We are heading from Andy's neighborhood, in Everett, to Gramma's nursing home in Lynn.

"Andy, I have to tell you something," I shout over the music. He's looking out the window and doesn't hear me. "It's about Beverly," I say to the steering wheel, too quietly. "She's dead, but that's not the worst of it." I look at the side of Andy's head, the plastic hearing aid attached to the back of his left ear. "The worst is that Gramma knew where she was. And she didn't tell us."

"I love this song," Andy says, and turns up the radio even louder.

* * *

Stan Silvieri took Beverly back on as his receptionist, and Andy and I would go there after school to wait for her until she finished work. There was a Dunkin Donuts in the strip mall where his office was, and we'd check in with Beverly and then go for donuts and orange juice, sit at one of the orange tables and get powdered sugar and juice stains on our homework.

That only lasted a couple of months. He fired her again, right in front of us.

It was ten-to-five and we walked back across the concrete to meet her as she finished work. They were fighting; Beverly slammed the filing cabinet drawer shut, knocking a cold cup of coffee off the top when she did.

"You're fired," he yelled at her, un-originally.

"Shove your job," she said, pulling Andy's hand and motioning for me to follow. We piled into the car, and Beverly jammed the keys in and screeched out of the parking lot. "Frig him," she said into the rearview mirror.

"What happened?" Andy asked.

"He's a bastard. It's no wonder nobody wants to work for him." We were quiet; I stared straight ahead, willing the car to not hit anything or anyone as it sped toward home. "He thinks he's some kind of a God, like I should feel grateful to serve him."

"Like a god, Beverly?" Andy asked. He loved Greek mythology, and had a series of books about their gods.

"Like a god. He wants me to do all of this personal stuff for him, on top of what I'm there for. I'll never meet a man who's not an asshole. Christ."

I looked back at Andy, to see if he'd feel insulted, since he was male, but he didn't seem to.

* * *

A few days later, and Beverly had been on a tear, drinking vodka-sodas all day long. Andy and I usually walked home from school together, now that we didn't meet her at the chiropractic office, but I had been working on a science project after school, and so was walking home by myself. Dr. Silvieri pulled his car over to the side of the road and leaned across the front seat, pushing out the passenger-side door.

"Hi Leigh. You want a ride?" It was only the second time I'd ever seen him when I was by myself, and again he was trying to be too friendly.

"No thanks." I pulled at the straps of my knapsack, hoisting the weight of it further up my back. When I was around other kids from school, I usually let it hang, long, from one shoulder, but I was on my way home. I started walking faster, but Dr. Silvieri drove along beside me.

"You sure?"

"Yeah. Thanks anyway."

"Well then, shut the door for me, will you?" I stopped walking and kicked the door closed. He drove away. That was the first time. I don't know what he was doing driving around when he should have been in his office, cracking people's backs. But there he was again two days later. I was with Andy this time, and he slowed down and waved at us, motioned with his forefinger to the seat of his car.

"He wants to know if we want a ride," I told Andy.

"Beverly might not like that." Andy wiped his nose with the back of his hand.

"No, but it's kind of cold today," I said.

"It's up to you."

He was driving along, waiting, heading in the same direction.

"Oh, what the hell." I opened the passenger side door. Andy got in the back and Dr. Silvieri pulled away from the curb.

"How was school?" he asked.

"Fine," we both said. Andy started telling him about the *B* he'd gotten on a math test, and Dr. Silvieri nodded and looked at him in the rearview mirror as he talked, but he looked at me too, beside him in the passenger seat, and grinned. He didn't seem nearly as creepy as I used to think he was. He didn't mention the fact that we'd seen each other that time in Dill's, or ask anything about Daniel or Daniel's girlfriend, or about Beverly working at Dill's. I was thankful for that, and I smiled back at him.

"Say hi to your mom," he said as we got out of the car.

"Thanks for the ride, Dr. Silvieri," Andy said.

"Call me Stan. We've known each other for a long time." He was looking mostly at me.

A few days later, I was alone again, and he showed up in his car. I got in. He had bought me a present: a thick headband. Nobody had said anything about the hair that was missing from above my ears. I'd started pulling the hair out of my head around that time. I'd go into the bathroom and pull out hairs one by one, and flush them down the toilet, or I'd lie in bed and drop them down onto the floor between the bed and the wall. I thought I had hidden it from everyone by letting the hair from the top of my head fall over the bald patches. And I used to try to keep my head still, because if I held it just so and there wasn't any wind, I thought no one would be able to see the baldness.

"Thanks." I looked at him suspiciously, to see if he was going to say anything more. He didn't.

"I thought you'd like the color."

"I guess it'll bring out my eyes," I said. It was green, and I liked to imagine that my hazel eyes were more green than they were yellow or brown.

He looked at me, like a man looking at a woman. It was weird. It scared me but excited me at the same time. I think it was my first glimpse of myself as ... well, as a woman, I guess. Not a little girl. Even though that's what I was. I slid the headband over my head and pulled the rearview mirror toward me. It worked well, covering the bald spots completely.

"You want to go to the beach or something?"

"Why?" I asked, avoiding any kind of commitment, but making sure that the conversation would continue. It was attention and I craved attention.

"Why? I don't know. It's nice there. It's a nice day."

"Why did you fire my mother?"

"It was mutual," he said, as if he'd been expecting the question.

"What happened?"

"We weren't getting along."

"Getting along? Why do you have to get along? You weren't married. She was just working there."

"Your mother is ... well ... she's not very ... reliable."

"Tell me about it." I rolled my eyes. But while it was great that someone could understand my plight, I felt as if I were being disloyal to her at the same time.

"You're very different from her, you know, Leigh?"

"I don't know."

He had grey hairs in his eyebrows and at the sides of his head. He had a little paunch that rested in the hammock of the terrycloth tracksuit top he used to wear with nothing underneath it. The zipper was sometimes pulled all the way up and sometimes would be left open to the middle of his chest and you could see the brown hair that grew there in patches. I missed Daniel. I knew that Stan would never be my father, but I enjoyed the attention he was paying me, making me feel special.

He drove to the beach and parked on the side of the road. He got out first, and I sat in the car, watching him walk toward the ocean. He lifted his arms toward the sky, shook his head to let the wind fluff out his hair. He had shaggy hair like Barry Gibb. I opened the door, and the wind blew against my back as I turned to push it shut. There was no one there. It was October, too cold for swimming. The college kids had left town, and the tourists had gone home, and everyone else was warm in their homes, doing their homework, their housework, being responsible. At my home, Andy was probably up in his room, with his Barbies; Beverly was probably asleep on the couch, half-naked with the ratty blanket that served as a slipcover pulled over her, the television on, nothing cooking for dinner.

I ran up behind Dr. Silvieri and pushed him.

"Whoa, there, little missy." He turned and leaned toward me like a sumo wrestler. "That's asking for trouble." I put my arms out at my sides and squinted, daring him, but when he started toward me, I screamed and ran. He caught me from behind and swept me up in his arms, carried me over to the dunes, laid me down and held my hands above my head. Then his head was hovering over me, and his lips touched mine, and I squirmed and turned my head. He got off and sat down next to me.

"Guess I lost my balance," he said.

"It's fine."

"You ever kissed a boy, little missy?" He ran a finger down the side of my face.

"That's none of your business."

"You're a beautiful girl, you know." Him telling me that was like an injection of helium into my body, making me float. I let myself believe him.

We were silent for a long while, Stan staring out at the ocean and me lying on my back, watching the clouds' hasty flight.

"You wanna go home?" he asked finally.

"It's a little cold." I pulled my coat around me and sat up.

"Let's go." He jumped to his feet and started walking away. I ran after and followed him to the car. On the drive home, he asked about my science project. He listened as I told him about it—a model of the respiratory system made of tubes and balloons. Beverly didn't even know I was doing a science project.

"Thanks, Stan," I said as I got out in front of my house.

"You bet, little missy."

Beverly had been watching from the window, one hand pushing back the curtain, the other holding a vodka-soda with a cigarette stuck out at an angle to the glass.

"What the hell are you doing with that prick?" Her voice was acid.

"He was just giving me a ride home."

"You said you wanted to walk. I offered to pick you up."

"The last time you said you'd come, you fell asleep," I reminded her.

"Well, that was just once." Remorse made her try to hug me, and I pulled away and ran up to my room. I could hear the clink of bottle on glass as she poured herself a refill in the kitchen and then the couch springs as she sat down.

I think Beverly had been beautiful. That's the way it seems from the pictures I've seen of her. She used to have light brown hair that gently framed her face and pretty lips that didn't seem strained, fluttery, and anxious the way they became later. She had started bleaching her hair metallic blonde just after Andy was born, and she would color it sporadically, and in varying degrees of thoroughness, so that it always seemed to be half-done.

I used to figure that she had two brains, one that controlled her mouth, and another that controlled her eyes, because there was this dissonance between them. Her mouth could be smiling, but her eyes looking angry, or her eyes could look drowsy but her mouth tense. In the photos I found of her at Gramma's, she didn't look like that. She was smooth and beautiful, though always solemn.

By the time I was school-aged, she'd grown a plump second chin. It never went away after she lost all the weight she'd gained when she was pregnant with Andy, even when the rest of her body was skinny and jagged. It seemed like her face continued right down to her breastbone. But she could still look beautiful sometimes, if she'd turn in a certain direction or lift her head up and laugh. She was usually sloppy with her makeup, but on the days when she got that right—without too much blue into her eyebrows and without getting the pink lipstick smudged on her teeth, when she'd get the foundation to actually hide the bulbs that were forming below her eyes, then she could still be beautiful.

It was hard enough to find a job in the winter on Cape Cod, but for Beverly, it was even more difficult. I'm sure Dr. Silvieri had every right to fire her. She was difficult, and her drinking was becoming constant. She wasn't always ripping drunk, as she was most weekends, but there was usually a little alcohol running through her; if not, she'd get shaky and morose. But Dr. Silvieri never talked badly about her to me.

I spent another afternoon with Stan Silvieri, later in the winter. We went to his condominium. The idea of owning a condo was futuristic in itself, but he also made it look space-age the way he decorated. I wasn't aware of the term "bachelor pad," but every time I have heard it since, it makes me think of Stan Silvieri's condominium. He had a sleek orange sofa and a coffee table made of brushed aluminum. He had hundreds of LPs neatly lined up on a shelf against the wall. When I saw them, I ran over and started pulling them out, but he scolded me.

"Ah ah ah, little missy," he said, taking the flat faces of mismatched Simon and Garfunkel out of my hands. "They're alphabetized. You have to be careful."

That was something I'd never encountered. Nothing at my house was off limits. We never went into Beverly's room, not because it was forbidden, but because there was nothing in there that we wanted. Everything else in the house was equally ours. Nobody ever said, "Don't touch."

I flipped through them, trying to read the titles off the skinny ends.

"Your mom gotten a job yet?" he asked.

My fingers kept walking the record spines. "Nope."

"Should I give her another chance?" My fingers stopped. I shrugged.

"Up to you."

"I've got another girl, you know."

"A girl?"

"In the office. I have a receptionist."

"Oh you have Gordon Lightfoot," I said, leaving my fingers there to hold the place. "Can we listen?"

"Sure."

I pulled the album out and handed it to him. He took it gingerly and slid the album out of its jacket, laid it on the turntable. We didn't have a record player at our house, even though I had a couple of Beatles records that I'd picked up at the flea market. I had them propped on my desk like photos of friends—Revolver and Sergeant Pepper's Lonely Hearts Club Band. I sang along to Carefree Highway.

"You have a nice voice," he told me. I flopped onto the couch.

"Not very soft," I reported. He looked at me. "The couch. Must be better for your spine." I laughed, but he didn't.

"Where was your brother today?" He had driven past me on my way home; it was becoming a habit. Usually he'd just drop Andy and me at our house.

"Stayed home sick."

"Too bad."

"Beverly says he's a walking oxymoron," I laughed, kicking my shoes onto the floor. "He's the strongest kid in the school; he's even stronger than the older kids, like the kids in my grade, but he's always getting sick. Like his muscles took all the strength out of his immunity."

"His immune system. Why do you call your mother Beverly?"

"That's her name."

"I know. But kids usually call their mothers *mom* or something."

"Yeah. I don't know. I guess I just heard other people calling her that and so I did too." He took one of my feet and started rubbing it while we talked. *Let me slip away, slip away on you*, I sang.

"Did you know that 25 percent of your body's bones are," he began.

"In my feet," I finished for him. "Yeah, I know."

"Very smart, little missy," he said, pulling each of my toes, one by one, his other hand resting on my shin.

"You got anything to eat?"

"No. Not much," he said, staring at my foot as he rubbed it.

"I should get home," I said, pulling my foot from his hands. I was wearing the headband he'd given me, and I pulled it into place from where it had slipped back on my head.

"You're a beautiful girl, Leigh," he began. I leaned forward and pulled my sneakers on. "But what has happened to your hair? Your lovely hair?"

"Nothing." He reached his hand toward my ear, to touch my head and I batted his hand away.

He recovered his composure quickly, but I could see his temper flare for a moment after I'd hit him. His hand flew back into striking position and his face went grey. But he smiled and dropped his hand to his lap. I didn't want to get to know that temper. An expert at sliding beneath the tectonics of people's emotions (having survived Beverly's and Daniel's ups and downs) I eased a bland smile onto my face and got us into the car. He dropped me home and I didn't see him again for a while.

* * *

Andy and I step off the elevator in front of the nurse's station: a desk in front and a room in the back; both areas littered with magazines, clipboards, stacks of folders. Down the hall there is a huddle of four or five people. A woman on a vinyl sofa next to a vending machine is crying, her red face affixed to a blossom of Kleenex while the remaining people talk to each other in mumbles and whispers. I nod at whoever might notice us and hope that my face conveys condolence. Gramma's door is open and she's watching TV.

Andy pulls the chair around so he can watch with her and I lean on the windowsill.

"Get a chair, Leigh," Gramma says and I nod, go into the hallway where there are extra chairs, and bring one in. I slide in next to Gramma's head. "Clara Honeywell died," she tells me.

"Was she a friend of yours?" She shakes her head.

"She had," her voice drops into a stage whisper, "dementia."

"Poor woman. It must have been hard for her family." Gramma nods, her chin jutted and her eyes wide. Then suddenly her features right themselves and she returns her attention to the television. Andy is watching as well, and is giggling at something funny.

"Andy," she says suddenly, startling him. "Tell me about your week."

"Nothing," he says, not turning away from the TV. "Same old, same old."

"What is that? Same old, same old. You'll be an old man one day, and you'll wish you had lived a more interesting life." She's speaking too quietly for Andy to hear her and I wonder if it's for my benefit she's saying this.

"Andy," I call over the tinny television. "How's Kevin?" Kevin is Andy's best friend. They live together in a sort of halfway house.

"Good," he says over his shoulder. "He got a girlfriend. Sorry, Leigh." He laughs at me.

"It's okay. You're the one who's been trying to fix me up with him."

"You had a chance too," he says. "He liked you." I smile at Gramma, who hasn't in any case been following our conversation. Her eyes have closed and her mouth is slack. I catch Andy's eye and motion toward our sleeping grandmother. He shrugs, settles deeply into the chair, engrossed in the television. Suddenly I feel bored being here. I come every weekend, am responsible, a good granddaughter. A good girl. I move close to his ear so he will be able to hear without me yelling.

"Andy, can you take the bus home today?"

"Sure. Why? Where are you going?"

"I don't feel very well," I lie, and put my hand on my abdomen. "Woman stuff."

"Aww, Leigh, don't tell me that." I kiss him on the cheek and he leans away from me.

"I love you," I tell him.

"I know," he says, as if I've just told him to wash the dishes for the seventh time. "I know. See you."

November 1954

The guest room was crowded with a twin bed, a crib, and a changing table. Gertrude's sister Estelle was on the bed with her chin on a pillow, her calves rocking back and forth like windshield wipers, reading a magazine, and Gertrude was washing their dishes from breakfast when there was a knock at the door.

"Stel, could you get that?" Gertrude called from the kitchen, her hands in the basin. Another knock. "Estelle! The door!" Estelle put her magazine down with a sigh and pushed herself up, but as she emerged into the hallway, Gertrude was already bustling past, snapping off her dish gloves. "Never mind, I've got it."

She swung the door open, and there was Marianne, her black hair shiny and styled, her lips painted pink, clutching a purse in front of her like a shield. The two women stood facing each other. Marianne's mouth opened but no sound came out.

"I'll give you two seconds to explain why I shouldn't slam this door closed right now," Gertrude said, the bulk of her pregnant belly filling the frame.

"Wait, Gertrude, listen," Marianne began. "I just want to say. Well, listen. I told Clive that he should go back to you."

"Good of you."

"I guess I'm here because I thought you should know that it's over ... between me and him."

"Well I'm sorry to hear that." Gertrude pulled the door close to her belly, put her fist, still clutching yellow dish gloves, on the wall and leaned against it.

Marianne went on. "Gertrude, if I'd known about the baby, I swear, I would never...." and she ran out of words.

"If you had that much control, then how could you have gone through

Sara Fraser   87

with it anyway?" Gertrude asked. "The baby has nothing to do with it. Never mind, I can't imagine you have an answer."

"He says you won't take him back. You should take him back, you know. He's a good man."

"I'd say I know him better than you do." Gertrude slammed the door shut. The two women stood on either side of it, equally stunned and momentarily unable to move. Finally, Gertrude heard Marianne walk away. Estelle was behind her.

"Wow. She had some nerve coming up here," Estelle said.

"Imagine her offering him back to me just because I'm pregnant. As if I'm someone to be pitied. As if he were something to be traded. The nerve of her. As if I'm only worth such consideration because I'm carrying a child." Gertrude paced to the end of the room and back again, her hands in fists at her sides.

"Okay, calm down. Just relax." Estelle took her by the arm, led her to the sofa and sat her down. Gertrude pushed herself back up and went into the bathroom, held her head in both of her hands as she peed. She sat for a long time.

"Hey, you okay?" Estelle knocked on the door.

"Fine. Just fine," she said finally. After she emerged, her face blotchy and red, Estelle followed her into the kitchen.

"She had a lot of guts to do that," Gertrude said. Estelle put the kettle on the stove.

"She's trashy, though. You know that, but they're not seeing each other anymore. Clive wants you back, Gert. Don't you think, for the baby?"

"He'll do it again, Estelle. He'll do it again. He did it once, how can I take him back? I can't."

"But to be a parent by yourself...."

"It's not an option." Gertrude said. "I can't take him back."

"I'm not going to be here forever, you know." Estelle put two cups on the table.

"I never asked you to." Gertrude wiggled her fingers into the dish gloves.

"Gertrude," Estelle pleaded. "You gotta listen to reason...."

Gertrude laughed. "Reason? You're going to lecture me about reason?

Good God, if you're the face of reason, then things have really gotten bad."

"Oh, come on. Listen to me."

"Okay, fine. I'm listening. But it doesn't mean I'm going to change my mind."

"So how are you going to do this by yourself? The baby needs a father. And not just that, but you need the help, the support."

Gertrude splashed suds around the basin. "Is that it? Are you done? Because I've been listening."

"And?" Estelle put her hand between her sister's shoulder blades.

"And what? I listened. That's all I said I would do."

"Honestly Gertrude, you're more stubborn than anyone I know." Gertrude put the last dish into the drainer and snapped off the gloves. Estelle poured hot water over tea bags. "I can't help you, you know. I'm not going to stay in Lynn forever. Lou and I are moving to Cape Cod. Soon."

"So you've decided for sure?" Gertrude sat down opposite her sister. Estelle held her hands together as if she were trying to crack a nut inside them.

"Yes. We're going as soon as the weather gets warm."

"Gonna go off the two of you and be artists, huh?"

"Something like that."

They sat in silence. Gertrude wound her hands around the hot cup that Estelle pushed in front of her. "I'll miss you," she said finally.

"That may be true, but if I stayed here, you know we'd end up pulling each other's hair out." Estelle laughed.

Gertrude giggled too, but it soon turned to tears. "Why'd he have to do it, Stel? Why'd he have to go and do it? We were happy."

Estelle put her hand on Gertrude's and waited for her to calm down. "You could forgive him, you know." Gertrude shook her head. "You could." Gertrude shook her head again. "Well, then it's your choice. It's your choice."

"I can't," Gertrude said. "I can't. I just can't. I'll always see that woman's face. I'll always wonder."

"Don't ever forget that it's you that made the decision, then. You had the choice."

"It's not so easy. Forgive or not forgive. It's not like that. It's not so simple."

"Okay. Have it your way," Estelle said. "Have it your way."

"Is it *my* way? It feels like the only way."

"Gertrude, can I tell you something?" Estelle put her cup down.

"Oh, I don't know. Do I want to hear it?"

"Probably not, honey, but I'm going to say it anyway."

"Well, if you're going to say it...."

"You're being selfish, Gert." Estelle said. "I hope I don't sound mean, but you have to think of the baby. The baby should come first."

"What do you know about it?" Gertrude demanded. "You don't know. You haven't had children, or been cheated on. Lou is still with you. So don't tell me I'm wrong." She got up and put her cup into the sink. "You might do the dishes once in a while to help out, you know."

"Forget it." Estelle stood up. "You don't want me here. You don't want Clive here. You want to do this all on your own, go ahead." Gertrude stood facing the cabinets as Estelle went into the guest room and closed the door. In her own room, Clive's bed was made; it still had the same sheets that were on it the day she found the letter from Marianne. All of his clothes were gone, and their wedding picture was in the bottom drawer of the dresser. She sat on her bed, immobile as she heard Estelle call out, "I'm going out. Goodbye!" And she heard the front door close. In the silence, Gertrude remembered how Clive had looked when he slept, his lips relaxed, the sheet tucked under his armpit and his arm, with its soft dark hair up to the elbows. She used to love to look at his hands when he touched her. They made her feel soft and small, and taken care of.

She put her hands on her pregnant belly. How tiny the baby was to fit inside there. She suddenly felt sad for Clive—that he hadn't been able to put his hands on the skin of her belly, to feel the child moving around. The baby kicked her hard in the bladder, and she got up to go to the bathroom. Without another person to marvel at the mystery of one tiny human living inside another, without another person to see it as something beautiful, she felt like a human factory, a warehouse for baby storage and she felt immediately guilty and horrid for thinking of her own child as a product, a tenant, and shameful that she wanted it out. But she wanted her body back to herself.

She resented the strange creature that would soon emerge from her in a torrent of pain. Not all the time, but sometimes, that's the way she felt. And now, not even Estelle would be here to help. But Estelle would be back, at least for a little while, until she moved away.

Gertrude went into the kitchen to wash the teacups. Estelle had left hers on the table; Gertrude picked it up, but it slipped from her hand and smashed into pieces.

Leigh

I still haven't called Mark, and I know I need to. I am on my way home, where I plan to listen to his messages and call him back, apologize for having ignored his calls—but instead I veer off 1A and head toward 93.

On some shallow level of my brain, I think I'm going to visit my father, but instead I end up in the Sand Bar, a weathered blue shack at the bottom of a dune in Truro, which is where the deeper, truer, but more dangerous part of my brain has directed me. I'm not sure why.

And I'm feeling a little ridiculous, because I am the oldest person here. The place is filled with late-afternoon-sun-dappled half-stripped wetsuit-wearing surfer boys. Late teens, early twenties, and a few young girls with perfect tans and bikini tops like bottle caps strung from one nipple to the other and around the neck, leaning over the pool table and giggling. I wouldn't be surprised if a bevy of camera-wielding assistant directors and tittering makeup artists came sliding over a sand dune, revealing this as the set of a soft drink commercial.

I order whiskey.

The Sand Bar wasn't a bar when I was a kid. It was a storage facility for boats. That was when people used to fish from rowboats and carry buckets home with fresh cod, stripers, and flounder. Now it seems that a whole generation has disappeared and been replaced by a young population of thrill-seekers with plenty of free time. You don't see much of the lower classes around the beaches, not in the summertime at least. When they're not working low-wage jobs, they're more likely at one of the ponds, spring-fed and blue but not as popular with tourists (and obviously surfers and their admirers).

At the pool table, an argument has erupted and a couple of girls are trying to talk sense into an angry surfer. He finally shakes his blonde hair away from his face and takes a sip of beer as a conciliatory gesture. I smile at him, and he observes me blankly, as if I were a barnacle stuck on his surfboard. Does that happen, I wonder idly? You'd have to be in the water a hell of a long time for a barnacle to get stuck to your surfboard. I guess if there *were* a barnacle on a surfboard then definitely this guy would look at it like he's looking at me, slightly curious but dumbfounded and unsure about what it is he's seeing. I look away, toward the bartender, and order another drink.

* * *

Beverly went out on a Saturday night, and on Sunday morning, I woke up to find Dr. Silvieri at our kitchen table, drinking a cup of coffee. I had encountered different men in our kitchen, but I couldn't believe that he, of all people, was there.

"Good morning, Leigh." I stared at him. "I haven't seen you in a while."

"No."

"There's coffee in the pot." He motioned toward the coffee maker.

"I'm too young. I don't drink coffee." As usual, no one had made orange juice. I took a can from the freezer, plopped the frozen juice into a carafe, and measured in three cans of tap water. I stood with my back to him, stirring the lump of orange juice with a wooden spoon.

"Where's Beverly?" I asked.

"Sleeping. She's still not working," he offered.

"I know. She's not going back to you."

"No." I was still trying to dissolve the frozen juice with a wooden spoon, but I could hear him sip his coffee and put down the mug. "I have another girl."

"So you've said."

"Where's your brother?"

"Still sleeping," I said. "It's Sunday."

"But you're up."

"I always get up."

"Yes, you do. That's not surprising." He smiled at me with one eye closed, as if he'd meant to wink but had gotten stuck.

"What's that supposed to mean?"

"Nothing, little missy. Nothing. Just that you're a good girl." I got my favorite Tom and Jerry glass and poured juice into it. I stood at the sink; I didn't have my headband on, and I didn't want to get close enough for him to be able to see my bald spots.

"I should get going." He stood up and put his mug into the sink while I twirled away from him toward the living room. His coat was on the back of a kitchen chair. He slung it over his shoulder as he opened the front door.

After he was gone, I finished my juice at the kitchen table and was suddenly exhausted, so I went back to bed.

When I got up again, Beverly was in the kitchen, drinking coffee and working on a word-find.

"I didn't know you went out last night," I said as I sat at the table.

"Uh huh. You wanna help me with this? I'm looking for 'compound.'"

"Don't you want to know how I know?"

"What's that? Oh, here it is, C-O-M-P…"

"How I know you were out last night."

"You know I go out sometimes," she said as she finished circling the word. "Just for a little while, to be with grownups, you know."

"I saw Dr. Silvieri this morning."

She put her pen down and propped her forehead on her hand. Her other hand shook a bit where it rested alongside the word-find.

"Oh God. Oh God. Oh I forgot. Oh God."

"You *forgot*?"

She was laughing, her teeth to the air now. "God, that's right! Of all the people! Oh well. I think I had fun, though. That's what counts right?"

Her mouth was laughing, and her eyes looked drowsy, the bottom lids sinking into her cheeks. I didn't feel like eating breakfast anymore, but she was standing up and shaking the Bisquick box to see how much was left.

"I'll make pancakes." Her hands shook as she poured the mix from the box and her lips looked swollen as she sucked on her cigarette. She kept laughing, saying, "God. Of all people." And "Oh well. No harm. Ha-ha." I sat with Andy in the living room and watched cartoons until we had the pancakes, burnt on one side, underdone on the other, and the middle tasting like aluminum. Beverly went back up to her room while we were eating. She had her own black-and-white TV up there and she turned it on; it played all day long while Andy and I entertained ourselves.

* * *

That surfer boy has a mysterious look about him, and a couple of the young girls are attracted to him because of it—they lean into him and laugh when he says something funny. But for some reason, he's drawn to me. I can see one of the girls pout and another one snigger as he pulls up a stool and sits next to me at the bar.

"Can I have a smoke?" he asks, and shakes one from the pack of Camels in front of me. I nod, but he hadn't waited for my response anyway. He puts a match between his second and third fingers and strikes it against the matchbook. I tell him I'm from New Hampshire and that I'm a middle school teacher and that I'm on Cape Cod for a wedding and that my name is Sylvia. He doesn't say much, which is a good thing. Instead of talking, he looks into my eyes, sending jolts of electricity right down into my gut. Against reason. The whiskey compounds things.

The leap isn't so far really. From not cheating to cheating feels like the tiniest little step, practically unavoidable. Because I was already two people, even before I climbed up into the dunes with Jared, the twenty-two-year-old surfer. There has always been the *me* who is getting married, who goes out to dinner with her fiancé after work most Friday nights. And then there is the other *me*, and always has been. The one Mark can't or doesn't want to know. I don't usually interact with her very much myself. I don't know her very well. This me, disembodied, but whole, and entirely in this moment, is enjoying the dune grass that is scratching at my ribs. Because it's so physical. All of it.

It's not that Jared is great at this. He's pure muscle and sinew and tan, sand, beach, salt, sun. He's inexperienced, that I can tell. Even I can tell this, I who am probably as inexperienced as he is. Apart from one time in high school, when I laid down for Alex Martin and let him pound away, and that other time, I have only really had sex with Mark. I'm not sure where I was throughout my early twenties, mentally. How did I avoid the dance that everyone was doing—in college, during my early working years? When everyone was single and hooking up with each other? Where was I that I didn't manage to enjoy … this? That's a question I'll have to look at … later. Not now. Right now, Jared's mouth is producing too much saliva and all of the danger he'd embodied when he was in the bar, flirting and so courageous, is dissipated as he puffs through lips swollen by too much beer and too little practice. I never stop to consider why I'm doing this, not until it's over and

I'm sticky with sand that won't come off, and he's nice now, he is. He doesn't go tramping off over the dune or anything like that. He's actually kind of funny, the way he grins at me and swats at the sand on my thigh to try and help dislodge it. After we've pulled ourselves together, and we slide down the dune to the beach, Jared goes back to the Sand Bar, and I walk as fast as the sinking sand will let me to the gravel parking lot and my car.

I thought it was a small step, but at the moment, I feel very different. The sand that is still inside my pants scratches at me accusingly. Inside my car there are takeout coffee cups on the floor of the passenger seat, newspapers from last month, receipts, tiny twisted apple cores and orange peels. (If I've inherited anything concrete from Beverly, it's my resistance to cleaning out the car.) I put the key into the ignition and peel out of the parking lot. I'm laughing, which makes me think that I must really be crazy. There's nothing funny about this, I tell myself. But I laugh until tears begin and the laugh turns, as this kind of laughter always does. I pull onto the side of the road near Bright's Pond and find a spot at the periphery of the small beach there, under the canopy of trees at the edge of the woods and I put my head onto my arms, without any ability to fathom what else I might ever be able to do with my life apart from sit here under these trees and cry. The future, even what should be the near future of getting back into my car, let alone going to work on Monday, is unimaginable.

* * *

Beverly called a family meeting. It was a weekend morning and she turned off the TV before sitting next to me on the couch. Andy was on the floor with his head on a pillow.

"Andy, sit up. Leigh. Kids. I have some news." We looked at each other, then back at her. "It's good news," she went on. "There's going to be a baby."

We weren't getting it.

"I'm going to have a baby. I'm pregnant. A brother or a sister for you two."

"Half-brother or sister," I reminded her. (It couldn't have been Daniel's. He was still in Delaware. We hadn't seen him since he stopped by at Christmas. What a day that was: Briefly, Santa left a few nice presents under the tree and a fresh new bottle of vodka for Beverly, who started celebrating early and was halfway soused by the time Daniel arrived. She wouldn't let us go with him, to Delilah's parents' house, and he said okay, gave in, left presents, and got back in his car. Andy and I watched him pull away from the curb, Delilah's bright blonde coif in the passenger seat. That was that. He didn't even call later on. As if we were in on it too. As if we deserved to be punished too.)

"Babies are so … small." Andy was getting nervous, unsure I guess of what he'd be asked to do.

"They're small, but they're cute," Beverly said, running her hand down the side of Andy's face.

I knew very well how babies were made. "Who's the father then?" I asked. She looked at me and smiled, a mad crazy smile, a smile of pleasure. How could she have smiled like that? "Stan," she said, and it took a minute for me to make the connection. Dr. Silvieri.

"Dr. Silvieri's gonna be our father?"

"Of course not," I told Andy. "Daniel's our father."

"You know what I mean." Andy was sitting up now. Every so often, you could see a part of Andy that normally you wouldn't know was there. As the male of the family, even though he was the youngest, he sometimes would suddenly seem mature, as if he felt responsible for taking care of his mother and his sister. I found in those moments, when I could see his courage, that I loved him more than ever. He didn't even have to say anything. His attention was full on our mother, as she gazed into the middle distance, one hand on her abdomen. He got up and poured her a glass of orange juice.

"Thank you honey," she said as he sat beside her on the couch. I went to my room and got under the covers in my clothes. To think. But I couldn't think. Nothing made any sense. Stan would never go along with this. I thought he was in love with me, that his having slept with Beverly was a tragic mistake, and that it was actually me that he wanted. Love, in the end, couldn't matter that much. It was so random and irrelevant and didn't seem to ever lead to anything good anyway. He definitely didn't love Beverly—that much was certain. What were they thinking? God she was pitiful, getting herself pregnant like that. I was only eleven and even I knew it wouldn't work out.

Boy was I smart. Smart and cynical. The tools for life.

But you know what? I was absolutely right. It wasn't going to work out. Not in the least.

Later that night, Beverly had gone to bed and Andy and I were in my room. He was on the floor building a racetrack out of blocks, and I was reading on the bed. "Do you think it'll be a girl or a boy?" he asked. I snorted.

"Well?"

"I don't know, Andy. I don't know what it's going to be."

"Why are you mad? Don't you want a brother or sister?"

"Of course I do. It's going to be fun to have a baby." I shifted onto my back and propped my legs against the wall. My fingertips made their way to my head, narrowed in on a follicle, and pulled. Andy was the only person I would pull my hair out in front of. I don't think it was so much that he didn't notice, as that he just didn't think it was such a big deal.

"Leigh?" he stopped what he was doing. "What if I drop it?"

"If you're afraid you'll drop it then don't pick it up," I reasoned, and released a hair between the bed and the wall.

"He tried to kiss me," I said suddenly, sitting up on the bed. Andy's face went ashen. "Dr. Silvieri," I clarified.

"Do ... do you want me to ... do ... something?" Andy pushed his hands underneath his haunches; his eyes were fixed just over my head.

"Naw, forget it," I said, lying back down again. "It was no biggie." I picked up my book and held it suspended over my face, but I wasn't reading. I was listening to Andy's breath, and then to the sound of the blocks, as he returned to his racetrack.

* * *

The water is cold like a slap, which is just what I need. I wade in in my underwear and bra and rub at my thighs and between my legs, moving parallel to the shore in a bid to escape what is washing off of me. I go under and swim toward the middle of the pond until my arms begin to feel numb and I turn back. It is when I emerge from the water that I realize I hadn't smelled or heard anything before my swim. Now I see that there are hundreds of chirping birds in the trees, going about their business and the air smells of pine and mint. I stand behind a tree and shiver until I am dry enough to slip my clothes back on. Out in the sunshine, on the sand, I can see the spot where, as a child, I had tried to breath under water. I wonder if I'd stayed under, which one of my parents would have been there to save me.

Walnut Acres

When Gertrude wakes up there is bustle in the hallway. She doesn't remember having fallen asleep, but she must have slept for a couple of hours. She is curious to see who will be on duty, so she presses the red button.

"What can I do for you?" Jessie asks, padding into the room.

"I want to go to the community room."

"You must be feeling frisky, huh?"

"I don't know about frisky. I just want to get out."

"Well, you'll have to wait. I told you already that the emergency call button is for emergencies. Remember? It's almost time to get up anyway."

"Yes, yes."

"Good. I'll be back in a bit." She saunters back to the hallway. Gertrude dozes, waiting for something to happen. For someone to do something, tell her something. Anything. She craves movement.

Eventually, she hears Jessie's voice. She leans over to the side, trying to see her. "Hey, you. You cooking today? Or are you the handyman?" Her voice is flirtatious, flouncy.

"Come here." A man's voice answers her. Helio. Then there is silence, quiet giggling. Gertrude leans over further, adjusts the glasses on her face. The couple slides into view. Helio's hand drops down to pinch Jessie's behind like it is breaking off a piece of French bread. The two of them are kissing. Again.

"This is why I have to wait?" Gertrude says more loudly than she'd intended. Jessie twists away from Helio's grasp and sees her, practically lying on her side in order to get a better view, her glasses trained on them. Jessie smiles, waves, then turns back to Helio. Gertrude harrumphs herself up as straight as she can and looks around for a magazine or something else to look at.

"I gotta get going," Jessie says finally, after kisses and whispering.

"That's alright. Me too," says Helio. "I have to fix some toilets."

"Yuck. Gross."

"No grosser than some of the stuff you have to do, I'm sure." The two of them laugh. Gertrude resents their laughter; it sounds metallic. Jessie passes Gertrude's door. Helio leans his head into the room.

"Have a nice day ma'am."

"Nice day," she mumbles. "Have a nice day. Sure."

Finally, Jessie comes back and helps Gertrude into a wheelchair.

"I saw you in Clara Honeywell's room," Gertrude says to her, after she's been arranged in the chair.

"What?"

"I saw you in her room."

"I'm sorry, Missus Littlefield, but I don't have any idea what you're talking about."

"You were in there, weren't you?"

"Missus Honeywell passed away, and yes, I was there. You're pretty nosey, huh? I don't even know how you could've seen her room; it's on the other side of the building. Maybe you were projecting your spirit or something?" Jessie goes on, more to herself than to Gertrude. "What do you call it ... I saw a show on it. On that cable station that has shows about supernatural stuff."

"I saw you and Helio too."

"Astral projection; that was it. Yes." Jessie gets behind the chair and pushes.

"I don't think anyone could have helped watching," Gertrude says. "The way you two were carrying on."

Jessie laughs. "Well, you have a TV. You don't have to be all nosey watching people, do you?" They turn into the carpeted community room. The walls are off-white, and there are reproductions of various paintings on the walls, landscapes and animals. In the corner is a piano, and more central is a television. Several residents sit in front of the TV in various states of awareness. Gertrude recognizes Joshua Cleggan.

"Over there by Joshua." She points him out.

As Jessie wheels her over, she leans down to Gertrude's ear and whispers, "Mr. Cleggan's pretty cute, huh?" Gertrude waves her away. Jessie parks

Gertrude alongside him.

"Haven't seen you in a while," he says, turning in her direction.

"I guess I haven't felt like getting out of bed."

"I've days like that *meself.*"

Gertrude is quiet until she sees that Jessie has moved away.

"How are your kids?" she asks.

"They're a bunch of Yanks."

"Yanks?" Gertrude laughs. She loves listening to his Irish accent. "Nothing wrong with that."

He shakes his head. "Shoulda raised 'em in Kerry."

"We all have regrets I suppose."

Joshua stares at his hands for a while. "You should come for dinner on Sunday, Gertrude. Katherine would love to meet you."

"Katherine?"

"Aye."

"She's dead, Joshua. Your wife is dead. Just like my husband. Remember?"

"Huh? Right," he says vaguely.

"This is what we're reduced to," Gertrude observes.

"What's that?" Joshua asks.

"I said, I was just thinking how it's a sad thing that we're here sitting around a television set."

"You know you're right," he says. "Why aren't we chatting? About current events, or the weather even?"

"Indeed why not?"

"What is the weather today?" he asks, and Gertrude laughs.

"I don't know," she says. "I don't know. I haven't been out. Next subject?" He gazes at her. "What is it?" she asks.

"I bet you were a fine-looking woman in your day. Katherine was beautiful too. You'd have liked her. She never did make it back to Kerry."

"I know, Joshua. I'm sorry about that."

"Aye, maybe next year, when I get the promotion." He turns back to the TV.

"Sure. When you get the promotion."

Her hands hold onto each other, and she can feel the bones under the soft, loose skin. Her hands feel like they could be someone else's. Gertrude looks at them. The hands of an old woman. Hers for a lifetime, and still they seem so strange.

She knew she would grow to be very old; her whole life she knew it. Somehow, even though there are no guarantees, she knew she would outlive most people of her generation. And it used to give her a feeling of power—her health, her strength, her longevity. Somehow she knew she'd *win*. And now here she is, staring at this pair of hands that seem as though they should have nothing to do with her. She craves some evidence of continuity, a reminder that she is the same person she's always been, just older. But that continuity is a restless empty hall if you have to feel it alone, she thinks. Without Clive, without her sister Estelle, without Beverly, who really knows her? Who can remind her of the person she was? Who can reaffirm that she is that same person? Nobody can look at this old woman and see the young wife, the young mother, the young sister.

Gertrude flexes her feet and then points her toes. She wants movement. She puts her hands on the arms of the wheelchair and pushes. Her thin buttocks scoot to the edge of the seat. Bedsores curse at her as they are dragged over the vinyl. She puts her right foot on the floor and then her left.

As she falls, she hears Joshua call out for someone to come help.

Soon Jessie rushes over.

"I just wanted to walk," Gertrude explains.

Jessie, with more strength than Gertrude would have imagined she possessed, lifts the old woman into a sitting position and, with her hands under her armpits, hoists her back into the chair. Gertrude is surprised at how little it hurts. She's starting to feel super-human, the way nothing has broken inside her.

"What is it with you, Missus Littlefield?" She sits on one of the side tables, a little out of breath. "Helio told me he had to pick you up off the floor just yesterday." Gertrude holds onto the arms of the wheelchair and looks at Jessie. "Well?" Jessie demands.

"I'm sick of it. I want to get up and walk. I want to walk on the beach. I want to do capo ... terra."

"What?" Jessie crosses her arms in front of her. "You mean that Brazilian thing that Helio does? Capoeira?"

"Yes, that." Gertrude taps her fingers agitatedly. Jessie laughs. She turns to Joshua Cleggan. "Can you believe this woman, Mr. Cleggan? Wants to go for a walk on the beach. Wants to do *capoeira*."

"The beach is nice," he says.

Gertrude nods. "See? The beach is nice. Thanks for agreeing with me, Joshua."

"Katherine loved the beach," Joshua says. "You should be more careful." Gertrude nods. "Yes, I should. Why? On the beach? What are you talking about?" But Joshua isn't listening anymore. She shakes her head in disgust at the way he forgets himself in the middle of conversations.

"Let's bring you back to your room, Missus Littlefield." Jessie is walking around Gertrude, to the wheelchair handles.

"No! No!" Gertrude gets agitated, trying to turn toward her, "I do not want to go back there. I want to talk to Joshua."

"Okay. Sure." She raises her hands like she's being held up. "But any more accidents and we're going to have to restrain you in bed, you understand?"

"Yes, I understand."

After Jessie has gone, Gertrude looks around. All the other residents look so tired, so completely spent and uninterested. Gertrude supposes that she looks the same.

But she feels interested.

On the other side of the room, a woman Gertrude doesn't recognize is talking with her daughter. The two women look so much alike that it is as if they are the same person, one having traveled backward or forward in time to meet up with the other. Both women wear their hair long, a rarity these days. Gertrude herself followed suit when senior-citizen fashion dictated short hair, usually permed to resemble snail shells tight to the head like a helmet. She cut it soon after Clive died. Her life in two segments: long hair and short. Optimism and disappointment.

The older woman's hair is tied into a bun, and the younger woman's is long down her back. They have the same smooth, rectangular noses and small chins.

Gertrude puts her hand on Joshua Cleggan's arm. "Joshua, look at those women over there." He turns to see what direction she is pointing in with her chin.

"I don't know them."

"No, but look how similar they are. They are so much alike. And so elegant."

"One's the daughter, visiting, I suppose, or maybe just dropping her mother off."

"They are so alike," Gertrude says again.

"Do you and your daughter look alike?" Joshua asks her.

"Oh that's my granddaughter, Leigh, you're talking about."

"No, that's not what I said. Her mother is your daughter, is she not?"

"People don't ask me about her very much, Joshua."

"I'm only asking if she looks like you."

Gertrude is silent for a long time, gazing at the mother and daughter across the room. "I assume she's dead," she finally says, startling Joshua.

"What? Who's dead?" he asks, and coughs into his hand.

"Oh never mind, never mind."

Gertrude turns her attention to the television and begins to feel sleepy.

When she wakes up, she is being wheeled down the hallway. Her head has been hanging over to the side and her neck is sore. As she starts to right herself, the saliva that had pooled in the corner of her mouth starts down her chin, and she has to wipe at it with the back of her hand. Helio's head appears next to her ear.

"Have a nice sleep?" he asks.

"Yes, thank you." They turn into her room. She dabs at the corners of her mouth to make sure the drool is gone. "I don't sleep very well at night anymore; I guess I dozed off." She smiles at him apologetically as he parks her and goes around to sit on the armchair.

"I hear you were trying to do capoeira again." She smiles, her mouth closed. She's never ashamed of the goldfish color of her teeth when any of the nurses are nearby, or Leigh or Andy. But she feels a little giddy with Helio.

"I guess I really want to learn."

"You'd like it, I'm telling you. You seem to have a knack for getting onto the floor, that's for sure." He is wearing blue-checked industrial pants and a white T-shirt. They sit facing each other, Helio looking at Gertrude and Gertrude gazing past him.

"Joshua was asking me about my daughter," she says, remembering.

"Nice old man, Mr. Cleggan."

"I wish I'd known him when we were younger. He's forgetful now. And forgetfulness doesn't make for a good conversationalist."

"Oh, it's not so important, is it?"

"Of course it is. It's important to remember what you're talking about if you're talking, wouldn't you say?"

Gertrude notices the brightness of Helio's teeth and concludes that he's never been a smoker.

"What exactly is your job?" she asks. "I've seen you wearing an apron, and I've seen you sweeping the floors."

"I do odd jobs, whatever they need me to do."

"I'm sure my daughter's dead." Gertrude tightens her lips.

"You're sure?"

"The last time I saw her, she was very sick. The thing I feel most ... guilty ... about is that I let her stay away." Gertrude looks at Helio and thinks it should feel odder than it does, telling him such personal things. She must sound like a crazy old bat, but the words are coming out of her anyway. These are things she can't tell Leigh. Leigh would never forgive her. Helio is quiet. "Well, you see, she left her children with me. I'm sure you've seen my grandchildren. Well, maybe not, you haven't worked here very long."

"I remember seeing a young woman in here with you."

"Pretty...." Gertrude says.

"Yeah, I guess so."

"My daughter dropped her children with me when they were young. Eight and eleven, or twelve. At any rate, they never saw her again."

"Was it drugs?"

Gertrude sighs, relieved that he can be so forthright, but thrown off by the explicitness of his question.

"She was a heavy drinker." Gertrude takes her glasses off and holds them open on her lap. Helio becomes blurry, chocolate hair, almond skin. She can hear him breathe. "I'm sorry, I have absolutely no idea why I'm telling you all of this."

"Maybe you just want to get it off your chest," he says. "There's nothing wrong with that."

"I'm usually the one to listen," Gertrude says.

Helio laughs. "I know that. You're listening and looking even when you're not supposed to be."

"I guess I'm nosey."

"Damn right you're nosey."

"Okay, I'm nosey. I know you and Jessie are dating."

"How about we get you back onto the bed, so if you fall asleep again you don't get a sore neck."

"That's okay. You don't have to tell me anything."

"Jessie's a nice girl. But, I dunno. I want a family, a solid family. Understand?" Gertrude isn't sure if he means he knows about Jessie's boyfriend, or if he means Jessie isn't the type of girl to settle down. But she senses that he wants her to understand without him having to explain.

"Of course I understand that."

"Yeah, I thought you would." He smiles, and she's pleased that he is happy with her, but she feels a little guilty for pretending to understand. She is doing exactly what she used to do with Clive, before they were separated. Back when she wanted nothing more than to be with him. She said what would make him happy, and would pay very little attention to what she actually thought or felt. But this conversation she is having, this is something special. They are telling each other things. Real things and she wants it to continue.

"Okay, come on, I'm going to help you up." He takes her hand and guides her arm until she is standing. As she shuffles to the bed, he puts his hand on her lower back. When she is sitting on the edge, he helps her swing her legs up, and he arranges the pillows around her, so she is comfortable. "Maybe you used to come to the Market Basket to do your shopping. I was a bag boy when I was a kid, first job."

She shakes her head. "I always go to ... went to ... Callahan's Market."

"I'll let you get some rest. I gotta run anyway. I gotta get back to work."

Gertrude thinks she'll stay awake for hours, thinking about the conversation with Helio, thinking about Beverly, worrying that Leigh will find out what she's known for a long time, wondering how to tell her, if she should tell her. Of course she should tell her. She should have told her a long time ago. Beverly didn't want to be found. That's why Gertrude kept her secret.

But none of it keeps her awake for very long. It exhausts her, and she falls heavily to sleep.

* * *

Later, Jessie pulls the door closed behind her. She carries a plastic tub and a sponge. When Gertrude first came to this place, she was sure that the sponges the nurses used to wash her were dirty. Now she looks away, refusing to think about it. Jessie pulls the nightdress up over Gertrude's head and washes her roughly with warm, soapy water. Gertrude remembers undressing Beverly the same way when she was a small child. Before the girl became difficult, stubborn and spoiled.

"Arms up in the air," Gertrude would tell her, and she'd lift her chubby arms, her hands like starfish; Gertrude would run a fingernail along her belly and Beverly would chuckle and gurgle and pull Gertrude to her, her arms around her neck.

Gertrude looks down at her breasts where they hang against her and laughs to herself.

"What's so funny?" Jessie asks.

"Oh. Just. I used to think there was something beautiful in growing old," Gertrude says.

Jessie puts a towel over Gertrude's back. "There, keep that on, so you don't get cold. No more nonsense, now, okay. There's nothing wrong with growing old. It's better than the alternative, right?" This is something that the residents and the nurses say to each other at Walnut Acres: that growing old is better than the alternative. It's such a common saying that Gertrude wonders if it had been proposed by the management, as a sort of marketing tool. Gertrude idly wonders what life is like in other nursing homes. Never having paid much attention to them, she has to use her imagination. She supposes that even in the more elite ones, the residents are the same. Age does equalize things in a very satisfying way, she thinks. Rich or poor, they all have to have some younger person wash them with a sponge, cut their nails, get them dressed.

"I'm not so sure," Gertrude pulls the towel around her shoulders. "It's easy to say when you're young." She watches Jessie take a clean nightgown from the shelf. "I'd like to travel in time. If we could travel in time, then we'd all be equal. Nobody would be older than anybody else."

"Okay, whatever."

"It's the kind of thing my granddaughter likes to talk about, other dimensions. Such things."

"I hate science fiction."

"She's a mathematician."

"Good for her."

"Well, she's an accountant." Jessie puts a clean nightgown over Gertrude's head and changes her underwear. "I'm sorry you have to do this for me."

"Don't be. It's my job." When Gertrude is clean and changed, Jessie takes a hairbrush and works at her hair. "You want me to paint your nails for you?"

"What on earth for? Are we going somewhere?"

"No, but I'll do it anyway. I have some extra time, so I might as well."

"Well, thank you. I don't like nail polish, though. It looks cheap."

Gertrude remembers a fight she and Beverly had over nail polish. Beverly was entering puberty, and was always looking in the mirror, fixing her hair, painting her nails. Begging for clothes, makeup. They were in Grant's pharmacy and Beverly stole a bottle of nail polish. Gertrude saw her slip it into the pocket of her coat.

Gertrude made her confess to the cashier and put it back, and Beverly didn't speak to her for the rest of the day, after yelling, "Well if you'd let me buy it, then I wouldn't have to steal it!" and Gertrude yelling back that nail polish was for hussies. When they got home, Beverly slammed the door of her room and didn't come out at dinnertime. Gertrude called Clive, who played Switzerland by not taking anyone's side, and she avenged his diplomacy, his non-allegiance, by being out of the house with Beverly when he came by for dinner on Friday.

Clive always accepted her vindictive, petty behavior with patience and calm, and showed up the next week without a word.

"Suit yourself," Jessie says. The hairbrush sticks and she pulls it through.

"Ouch. Please be more gentle." Gertrude holds tight to the blanket on her lap.

"Sorry about that. Your hair is awfully dry. It sure does get knotted."

Gertrude grunts. "I should bring in some detangler. My niece has some. My sister couldn't ever get a brush through that girl's hair. Until she found this detangler. You'd like it, smells like bubble gum."

"It sounds horrible."

"I'll bring some in, maybe next week." Gertrude remains silent while Jessie brushes.

"That's nicer," Gertrude says, enjoying the rhythm, the feeling of her hair moving, being touched. Jessie hums.

December 1960

Clive went to Fiore's Deli once a week to buy meat pies. Two would keep him for the week, along with a few cans of soup and a loaf of bread. He had a white box tied with red string in one hand and was on his way out when Gertrude pushed past him on the sidewalk. She had been Christmas shopping and the cold air made her cheeks bright.

"Gertrude," he said, his voice tight with surprise.

"Clive, what are you doing here?" Lynn was a city, but it was small, and it was stranger that they *hadn't* run into each other than it was that they were running into each other now.

"Meat pies." He held up the box.

"I'm on my way to Callahan's," she said quickly, as if she were afraid that he'd think she'd been following him.

"Yes. Yes. Well. You must be in a rush."

"I'll see you Friday evening?" Since Beverly had been born, they'd managed their relationship as a business partnership. Clive would eat with them on Friday nights and take Beverly for the afternoon on Saturdays. He'd show up at 6:00 every Friday and they'd eat together, as a family. They did it for Beverly, to keep things as normal as possible for her. They were civil, and Gertrude was proud of herself and proud of Clive that they'd managed things that way. They weren't quite friends, but they were well-mannered co-parents. In the beginning, when Beverly was a baby, Clive had tried to persuade Gertrude to take him back, but she wouldn't. And so they'd settled on this, a detached marriage, and had avoided either loving or hating each other in front of their daughter.

"Gertie," Clive said, his hand floating toward her arm, touching softly with fingertips.

"You haven't called me that in a long time."

"Sorry."

"It's okay. I like it." Gertrude looked at the sidewalk while Clive gazed at her face. Finally, he suggested they get lunch.

"I have to pick Beverly up," she began.

"Not until 2:30. It's only noon."

She didn't know whether it was courageous to accept his offer, or whether the courageous thing would have been to say no and to leave quickly. But she felt bold as she looked into his eyes and nodded. They walked together, Clive with his box of meat pies in front of him. His coat smelled like wool and pipe smoke. Her elbow touched his and she enjoyed walking beside him.

At the diner, he pushed the box in first and then slid into the booth across from her. The air around them was close and fragrant with the smell of French fries and sizzling meat. As soon as they'd settled in, conversation came easily, and they recognized in each other the person they had fallen in love with; they were both simultaneously surprised and unfazed by the reappearance of this easy rapport. Clive told her anecdotes from work, stories of his brother who'd moved out west. Gertrude told him about Estelle's break-up with her husband, Lou. When the waitress came to take their order, Clive asked Gertrude what she wanted and then reported it to the waitress, saying, "My wife would like the haddock. I hope it's fresh. She deserves the best." And the waitress smiled, her pen to her lips, looking back and forth between them. Perhaps imagining her own married future, hoping that she and her husband would one day be as content as this couple seemed.

It didn't come completely out of the blue: Gertrude's guard had gradually dropped over the years as Clive had been living alone, had been a gentleman when he came to the apartment for dinner, unassuming, responsible, and a truly loving father to Beverly.

"It's been nice having this time," Gertrude said, as the waitress cleared their plates and brought two cups of coffee. "You know, to talk."

"Gertie, I miss you," Clive said simply.

"I see you every Friday and Saturday."

"You know it's not the same."

"I know it's not the same. I miss you too." They ordered dessert. Clive had ice cream, and Gertrude had grape-nut pudding. "The last time we sat together like this was the day we split," she reminded him.

"Worst day of my life," he said.

Gertrude smiled, appreciative of the admission, but not convinced of his sincerity. She felt stronger without him, and she wanted to find a way to tell him that: that she loved him, would always love him, but that she had become stronger alone. "The day was bad," she began. "But you know, I think it was for the best ... in a way." He twisted his cup and looked at her with admiration.

"You know, I think maybe you're right." It wasn't the answer she'd expected and it took her down a notch, but she ignored it.

"I never did ask you. Clive. Did you and Marianne...."

"We didn't last long. She came to see you. You remember."

"Yes, of course. I was pregnant."

"She told me she was going to see you."

"She did?"

"I tried to stick it out with her at first. I thought I should, since, well, since you wouldn't have me back. Oh, she wanted me to. She had it in her head that I was going to leave you for her. But I didn't, Gertie. And I wouldn't have."

"Okay, so you've said," said Gertrude, frustrated but needing to hear it all.

"I told her I wouldn't marry her. And then we heard about you and the baby. And, Marianne's not a bad girl. She felt terrible. She went to see you because she knew it wasn't over. Between you and me. Baby or no baby it couldn't have been over. Not completely."

"Clive, you don't have to tell me..."

"It's still not over yet, Gertie, not for me." He reached across the table and took her hand.

"Oh God, Clive, I have to go," Gertrude said suddenly, pulling her hand away and looking at her watch. "I have to pick up Beverly."

"I'll go with you," he said, reaching for his wallet.

"Don't you think it would be ... strange ... for Beverly ... to see us?" She pushed her plate into the middle of the table and stood up.

"I'm her father. Don't you think she'd be happy to see me?"

"But you must have to go back to work?" she turned toward the door, where their coats were hanging. He remained at the table. "What's the matter?" she came back to him, pulling the sleeves of her coat up over her arms.

"Nothing. Nothing. I do have to get back to work," he said, and walked with her to the door. On the sidewalk, she faced him.

"It was a nice lunch, Clive. Thank you." He kissed her on the cheek. She tried to find his gaze with hers, but he touched her on the shoulder and turned to go. "Clive!" she yelled after him. He turned around. "Your meat pies! You forgot your meat pies."

That Friday, Clive came for dinner, as usual. Beverly answered the door. "Hi Daddy," she crooned, and threw her arms around his neck. "Come see the picture I made for you." She pulled him by the hand into her bedroom, to the desk. On it was a picture she'd drawn in school: her apartment building, her mother, her father. *For Daddy*, it said across the top. *I love you*. Gertrude, in an apron, stood at the door of the room with her arms crossed over her chest.

"It's the nicest thing anyone's ever given me," Clive said. "Thank you." He turned to Gertrude. "Doesn't your mother look gorgeous today, Bev?"

"Uh huh," Beverly said, pulling her father's attention back to the desk. "Look at this one. This is one I drew at home, not at school." Clive nodded and oohed and ahhed and winked at Gertrude, who stood back, watching them.

"You showed me that one last week," Clive reminded his daughter, when she'd run out of new pictures to show him.

"Dinner's ready anyway," Gertrude added. "We're having chicken."

"It's nice to have a home-cooked meal," Clive said, as they made their way to the kitchen.

"Fiore's meat pies are home cooked," Gertrude reminded him.

"It's not the same."

Beverly and Clive scraped their chairs from the table while Gertrude hummed a tune and pulled a golden-skinned chicken from the oven. Clive unbuttoned the cuffs of his shirt and rolled his sleeves up to the elbow.

Beverly cleared her throat dramatically before saying, "Daddy? Why don't you live with us?"

She had only just begun to realize, through friends at school, that it was abnormal for her father not to live with her and her mother. She'd never thought to wonder where he was during the week, so her parents were caught off guard by the sudden question. The smell of dinner settled in silence as Clive and Gertrude each retreated to their own camps to consider.

Clive tried first. He started to say that it was simpler for them to have different apartments and that he understood it was strange and different from most of her friends, but then Gertrude cut him off.

"It's not a thing you should be asking us," she said, and put the chicken on the table. "Beverly, would you like the leg?"

"Would you like me to live here?" Clive asked his daughter gently, winking at her while his hand reached towards his wife.

"Clive, stop it," Gertrude said. "White meat or dark?"

"I don't want chicken," Beverly said, pushing the plate away.

"Chicken's what we're having," Gertrude said, "so that's what you'll eat."

"Now, Gertie," Clive began.

"Don't you do that, Clive," she turned to him. "Don't undermine me. She has to eat what she's given. She thinks she can act like that. I was never allowed to act like that when I was a girl."

"Daddy," Beverly begged him.

"You have to eat what's for dinner, Bev," Clive said.

"I don't want it," she said again.

"Well then go to your room, and don't come out until tomorrow," Gertrude yelled, pointing toward the hallway with a potholder. Beverly stood up from the table, ran to her room, and slammed the door.

It was a miserable silence that was left behind. Gertrude slammed a bowl of peas onto the table and went into the bathroom. "Well I suppose you have it even worse," Clive whispered to the roasted chicken steaming peacefully in front of him. He filled his plate and started to eat. When Gertrude came back from the bathroom and sat across from him, he put his knife and fork down.

"What is it?" she asked. He shook his head, and took a drink of water. "She's got to learn how to behave," Gertrude declared. "She can't act like that. She has to eat what's on the table."

"What do you want me to say? I have no say in this; it's your project. I'm the weekend visitor, Gertrude, so what do you want from me? You're gonna do what you're gonna do, no matter what I say."

"You're the one who slept with somebody else!" Gertrude yelled. "This wasn't my idea."

"No *that* wasn't," he said methodically. "But *this* is. All of it. It's all your idea. You made all the decisions, and you know it." Clive's voice was starting to rise, and Gertrude began to feel a melting sensation in her stomach, with the knowledge that what had been nice was crumbling. She was beginning to regret her anger. But she couldn't stop herself.

"You said yourself it was for the best," she said. "You said it. It was what you wanted." And with that, all the disappointment she'd felt when he'd given up so easily a few days earlier came back to her.

"You said it first."

"You didn't have to agree with me," she sobbed, putting her head on the table.

"Stop it," Clive said. "This isn't what we should be talking about. What's it got to do with Beverly? Isn't she what's important?"

Gertrude cried even harder, as she felt Clive's affection for her dissipating. She regretted. It felt like she was digging at herself, and digging harder, wishing to go back in time to when he looked at her in the doorway of their daughter's room and said she was beautiful.

"Gertrude, stop it." But she couldn't. He turned to steel. "It's all about you, is it?"

"What do you mean? I'm feeling awful," she wiped her face with a napkin. "That's how you're going to make me feel better? Telling me my pain is selfish?" She rose from the table. "It's how I feel, Clive. I have feelings; you could acknowledge that. Instead of telling me I'm wrong. All the time, I'm wrong. I'm wrong. How can it be wrong? These are feelings. How can you say a feeling is wrong? It's not right or wrong; it just is."

Clive stood and paced back and forth across the kitchen. "Forget it. I give up. You want to blame me, blame me. You can't see what you're doing, fine. Don't see it." And he grabbed his coat and stormed out. Gertrude collapsed onto the sofa, curled up, and sobbed.

Beverly approached her mother, watching from a safe distance. She's just a little girl, Gertrude thought, innocent in all of this. She sat up, wiped at her face with the corner of her apron. "Beverly. Sweetheart. Come here." But Beverly stood her ground, arms crossed. She looked old. Stubborn and wise. Nobody was going to comfort Gertrude, it was clear, so she got up and began clearing the dishes from the table while Beverly went back to her room.

Whenever Daniel calls me—not so often, maybe once a month—he suggests that I come for a visit. I always make excuses. I'm glad I didn't call and tell him I was coming today. This way I can go to his house, and if he's not there, I can say that I tried. I can leave a note, for him and Delilah. That should get me off the hook for a while. Because I don't particularly want to see him.

Or I could avoid it altogether. He doesn't know that I'm here.

However, I need a distraction, so I decide to go. I don't want to think about the strange me underneath the even stranger Jared the Surfer. Like animals. I mean, What were we doing and how did we get there? Of course I've been attracted to men other than Mark, but I've never followed an attraction all the way to its thorough and physical conclusion.

I push the doorbell quickly, tentatively, but the sound it makes goes on for a full five seconds: a jingling, happy tune. Delilah is there on cue, as the doorbell winds down.

"Hi, Leigh! We weren't expecting you! Were we?" She looks as though she'd been expecting somebody: her hair is coiffed into a beehive and I marvel at it, how she keeps it like that. I never visited them in Delaware, never slept at their house in Truro, and so I've never been able to observe Delilah first thing in the morning. She is wearing a pair of pink capris, narrow at the ankle and a blouse with pictures of dolphins, one across each breast. She's still in good shape; I have to give her that.

"I was at the beach," I explain as she nods at me for a while before opening the door and letting me in. I think she's being rude, but then I realize that she must be startled. She makes a small squeak of discomfort when I sit on the couch with my wet hair and damp clothes, but she catches herself, clears her throat and pretends to be comfortable and easygoing. I lay my wet head onto the back of the sofa and watch her squirm.

"Daniel will be back any minute," she says finally. "Excuse me just a moment." And she practically runs from the room, as if we're two magnets and we've turned our north poles toward each other. I get up and nose around the living room. Delilah is an avid collector of duck things. Wooden ducks, duck bowls, duck carafes and platters, duck pictures, cute ducks and modern ducks and classic ducks and antique ducks.

I remember the time I gave her a pair of duck earrings.

I'd decided to spend Christmas with them one year when I was in college. Delilah's sister was there with her son, a tornado of a child whom you could see it took all of Delilah's wits to withstand, and Delilah's parents, an old couple who it seemed to me never addressed each other directly. From what I remember, Daniel spent most of the day talking to Delilah's father about golf and cars, and refilling people's glasses. Delilah spent the day trying not to appear to care about the juice spewing from the sippy cup attached to her nephew's hand—even as she ran around mopping it up with a rag, smiling and laughing mechanically with her sister—a nice enough woman, but not really interested in much other than her son; and I spent a lot of time gazing at the Christmas tree and getting drunk. "Thanks Leigh," she'd said, and put the earrings on the mantelpiece. I smiled at her and got another drink. I'm good at drinking—much better than Beverly, depending on how you define it as a skill—so nobody noticed.

It wasn't my best Christmas ever, but I'm sure it also wasn't the worst. Delilah did like the earrings at least; I've seen her wear them, which I consider a small triumph.

I can hear her in another room. She is on the phone, but I can't make out what she's saying. There's a picture of her nephew on the mantelpiece, in a duck frame. He must be in high school or maybe college, and I suppose he's calmed down by now. He looks serene in the picture, and handsome. There's a slight resemblance to Jared the surfer, I realize, and a flush of shame lights my cheeks.

"I'm just on my way to an appointment." Delilah saunters back into the room. "Do you mind, Leigh? Your father's on his way. Help yourself to whatever you'd like in the kitchen, okay?"

I smile to myself as I note how she specified *in the kitchen*. As though I might help myself to one of her ducks or something. I follow her to the door and wave at her as she pulls away in her squat, red Audi. I wonder what her appointment is for—her hair and her nails are already perfect. Maybe she's having her fortune told, or her feet massaged, or craniosacral therapy. I don't really know, because I don't know her well, but I imagine since she doesn't work and doesn't seem to have any interests other than duck-collecting, that she must spend a lot of time with manicurists, estheticians, and massage therapists.

As I close the door against the sound of Delilah's receding motor, I have a revelation. About my tryst in the sand dune. What it's done, this sex in the sand with a stranger, is it's made me more myself. I feel like I've taken something back. I know I sound like a fruitcake, but I feel like I've just taken back my self. From Mark.

And then I can't believe how bitchy that is. I mean, what do I mean by that and how would I ever explain it to him? Is it because I just found out that my mother is dead? No. That's me trying to excuse myself for having done something that I know is ... not just wrong ... actually, no, it's not wrong, per se. But it *is* fucked up. Because it hasn't gotten me anywhere I shouldn't be able to go on my own, without risk or deception. If I feel that Mark is sucking my individuality away from me, then there are certainly better ways of dealing with it....

"Well, hello. What a great surprise." It is my father, leaning awkwardly over me as I stand from the sofa to give him a small hug.

"I was in the area." I give him the same story I gave Delilah: went for a swim, decided to stop by, all that.

"Well, will you stay for dinner?" he asks. I'm hungry but the thought of sitting at the table with Delilah....

"Oh, I don't think I have time. Mark will be waiting."

We sit opposite each other, me on the sofa and Daniel on an armchair. The upholstery has nothing to do with Daniel. It's all about Delilah and her ducks; they're modern-art kind of ducks, dashed out in mustard and puce on a pinkish background.

"So how's Mark?" Daniel asks and I tell him *fine* and compliment the new bushes in the front yard.

He brings me to the garage to show me his latest metalwork. He took it up as a hobby after his parents died, and it turns out that he's a pretty good artist. Now he gets commissions for things like trophies and railings.

I don't intend on breaking down.

In fact, if asked whom I'd least like to break down in front of, I'd say Daniel. But when he brings me to the garage to show me the trellis he is making for Delilah's roses in their backyard—it's made of black iron, the heavy metal whittled down to delicate filigree in places and left chunky and earthy in other places—something about the sweetness and the simplicity of his labor, about the time and effort that he has put in....

"Beverly's dead," I say.

I thought it would come out as matter-of-fact, but this happens to be the moment it finally hits me and I crumple into Daniel's arms. It feels strange, and it feels good, being held by my father. I'm thankful for the moment, but I'm also angry that I had to go so many years without this. But he's never been very good at it and he's still not very good at it, and he backs away, saying that we should go into the house where it's more comfortable.

I can't quite pull myself together, and now I'm feeling ridiculous for crying.

"Gosh, I don't know what to say," Daniel says a few times, and, "It's really too bad."

I go to the bathroom and valiantly try to stop the tears and calm the weakness in my stomach. I make a show of looking at the clock on my way back to the living room and say, "I really have to go. I'm so sorry." I back out of the door, noticing that Daniel has brought a couple of glasses of something and a plate of cookies to the coffee table.

"I'm sorry, I have to get back," I tell him, and I think he's relieved, or maybe it's regret. I'm not sure. Maybe he'll go back into the house and feel inadequate, or maybe he'll relive the way he left Andy and me alone with Beverly, and then alone with Gramma. Or maybe he'll just be glad that it's over, this raw emotional encounter with his daughter. I really don't know. And I don't care. All I want now is to be back in my car.

* * *

Beverly lost the baby, which didn't surprise me.

We walked home from school one afternoon and Gramma was in the house. The place had been cleaned, and there was a bowl of Chex mix on the table. At that time, we weren't sure about Gramma. We hadn't spent much time with her. We walked forward slowly, and she approached us with as much caution. She hugged Andy first and then she moved toward me. She put her hand on my forehead, as though she were about to push back the headband that wasn't really covering the baldness anymore. I flinched, and she hugged me before bringing us to the table and pouring out glasses of juice.

"Where's Beverly?" I asked, reluctant to eat or drink until I knew what was going on.

"She's fine. She's in the hospital." Gramma crossed her arms and leaned her elbows on the table. "She's not going to have a baby after all."

Andy and I drank our juice. The look that passed between us over the rims of our juice glasses was some bland combination of relief and acknowledgment that neither of us was very surprised. Gramma went back to the sink, where she was soaking the coffee pot and the blackened teakettle in vinegar.

Beverly had been pretty far along, actually; she'd been showing, with a bulge the size of a honeydew. She was in the hospital for a week, though it seemed longer than that. I didn't care much about the baby, but it scared me that Beverly wasn't at home. Gramma took us to see her once during the week. We rode there in a taxi, which was thrilling.

The three of us slid into the wide back seat and the driver pulled away from the curb. The driver's picture gazed out from his taxi license on the back of the seat, and it looked like a wanted poster the way he stared straight at the camera. I imagined him kidnapping us to sell us as slaves on the black market. Now that would be an adventure. I was sure he'd be too charmed by me though, the way Stan Silvieri was, and that he'd change his mind about selling us on the black market and instead would take us on a vacation to Disneyworld.

There was a strand of beads hanging from the rearview mirror and he had some little toys glued to the dashboard—penguins and horses and wind-up frogs. I leaned my chin on the back of the front seat and watched the tiny plastic menagerie as we made our way to the hospital.

Beverly was sitting up in bed. She didn't look very sick, but Gramma had told me that she'd lost a lot of blood.

"How are my dear, sweet loves?" she said and pulled Andy and me toward her with a paper-braceleted, pale arm. "Thanks for bringing them over, Ma. I've missed these two."

There was a white hum about the place that made me uncomfortable, and I started to wish that we'd just stayed at home.

"So, tell me what you've been up to," she suggested. Andy and I shrugged. Gramma sat against the wall, next to the door. "Has Ma … your gramma … been treating you right?" We looked to Gramma, who smiled at us.

"You see for yourself that they're fine," she said. Beverly shook her head at her mother, with a malicious smile on her face.

"Be nice to them, Ma. Don't be an old mean bat, the way you were with me." Gramma cleared her throat and sat up straighter, her purse held tightly in her lap while Beverly started to laugh. Nobody laughed with her, but she didn't seem to notice. "Aw gee, I'm just kiddin'," she said, putting one hand on my shoulder and the other on Andy's. "Well, kinda kidding."

She leaned into the pillows, her hair greasy and two-toned and stuck to her temples. For some reason, I thought of the taxi driver, and of the little plastic toys on his dashboard. It seemed strange when adults kept toys. I didn't trust it. It was as though they were neglecting their role as adult. Like my mother.

"I'm sorry, kids, about the baby," she said, as if to herself. "Well, I know we all wanted a baby around the house." She looked at me. "Right?"

I shrugged. "I don't really mind." Andy shrugged too and started twisting the fingers of one hand into the palm of the other, like a human pepper grinder.

"Andy wanted a baby brother or sister, right Andy?" Beverly squeezed his shoulder from behind. He looked at Gramma, who smiled apologetically.

"Sure, it would've been fine," he said.

There was a strange smell as we sat around Beverly's room. Something full and gross, like someone's intestines, but also wet cardboard, lemon, and ammonia. There was a woman on the other side of a white curtain, but we could only see her foot—yellow against the sheets—and hear her cough. She often coughed, deep and throaty, and every time she coughed, we all looked in the direction of the white curtain, and the foot shuddered with the sound.

She groaned sometimes too, and I wondered if I should go over and make sure she was okay, but nobody else seemed to pay her any mind, so I tried to ignore it.

Beverly was her usual self: unpredictable. Happy and chatting one minute and morose the next; she was somehow enhanced and toned down at the same time. Like she was a TV program and someone had brightened the colors, but made the picture fuzzier. I guess it was because she couldn't drink in the hospital. And the baby had been a girl, she told us. Like me. She had wanted to name it Sky.

Gramma sat against the wall, and soon we forgot she was there, as Beverly and Andy and I played Go Fish with a deck of cards we'd brought from home. Beverly would never let us win. She was a competitive and sharp person, but she rarely did anything more challenging than word-finds or Go Fish. Andy won, and we put the cards away.

"I brought you your book," I told her and pulled the novel she'd been reading from a paper shopping bag: *Flowers in the Attic*, by V.C. Andrews.

"Thank God, Thank Leigh," she said, and took the book with one hand and squeezed my shoulder with the other. "What else you got in there?" she said, looking at the bag as I held it on my lap.

"Let me give it to her," Andy said, and took the bag from me.

"I brought it," I argued, grabbing the bag back.

"Leeeeeeigh," he howled, and held onto the side of it.

Beverly shushed us and slapped her own thighs, trying to make a spanking noise, though the sheet over her legs dulled any sound her weakened arms could have mustered. The bag ripped, and the books fell out onto the floor. We'd gotten her the next two in V.C. Andrews's series, from the drugstore/bookshop downtown. I grabbed one off the floor and Andy got the other, and we handed them to her.

"Thank you kids," she said, smiling so much her eyes crinkled up. "You have no idea how boring it is in here." As if on cue the woman in the other bed coughed, raking something up from her lungs. Beverly went on in a stage whisper, "Listening to that," she said, pointing her thumb in the woman's direction. We giggled. Gramma went into the hallway.

"What am I gonna do now, huh? Time to make a plan." Andy and I fell silent as we watched her. She sat up and pushed the hair from her face and then deflated again. "Oh, I'm too tired to make a plan. Too much. It's too much sometimes. I don't know how anyone is supposed to get along here." Her head almost disappeared into the pillow, and she closed her eyes. Her eye kept twitching, like it was trying to get a fly off of it, but there was no fly there. Then she started to snore.

* * *

Driving home, I am stuck in traffic on Route 6. In front of me is a pickup truck and a driver that looks, from behind, like Jerry Garcia with a baseball cap. He has a greying mop of hair that I imagine must itch his neck. He is smoking, and I can tell he's a local. He's pissed off and keeps revving up and stopping, revving and stopping. He is probably working, even though it's Sunday, and shouldn't have to be held up by this tourist traffic. It was stupid of me, too. It was stupid to drive to Cape Cod on a Sunday. Now, getting home, I'm paying the price. I light a cigarette and tap the lighter against the steering wheel, look out at the touristy shops and restaurants as they creep backward while I make my way, bit by bit, harrying the clutch.

Walnut Acres

Gertrude half-wakes to the sound of murmuring. Higher and lower tones, like deep water at the bottom of a river talking with the shriller flow at the top.

When she was growing up the people at the end of the street had horses, and she used to feed them long grass and dandelions that she'd pick from the sides of the road. It is there that her dream is taking place. The murmuring sharpens into voices; she is watching herself as a girl. She watches her younger self push handfuls of grass through the planks of the fence, holding flat her hand, and it is the horses who are talking, making the murmuring noises. Young Gertrude yells at them, "What are you saying to me?" The horses keep murmuring and the young girl threatens to stop feeding them if they don't speak more clearly. The horses' paddock is packed dirt, with throw rugs of green grass nibbled down to nothing. The horses continue to murmur.

Gertrude steps toward the girl. She takes her by the arm, turns her around, and starts to explain what the horses are saying, but realizes when she starts speaking that she doesn't know what they are saying either. She believes she knows, but when it comes time to translate their strange gibbering, she can't remember. The young girl's face is so expectant, needing answers, but as Gertrude fumbles, unable to remember what she'd sensed the horses were saying, the girl's face hardens into an expression of anger and disappointment.

"Now it's worse than it was before," the young girl says. "Now I'll never understand." And she turns away.

The horses are silent as Gertrude watches her younger self walk around to the other side of the paddock.

And then they start up again, this time louder and Gertrude's ears decipher more clearly, but the girl is gone. The horses are gone. The voices are coming from inside her room. Before she opens her eyes, she comes to understand that it is Jessie and Helio, and they're arguing.

"No trust. Not when...." This is Helio.

"What would you have done?" That from Jessie.

"Should have said...."

"I'm sorry. I said I was ... sorry."

Gertrude opens her eyes, and they are there, and the door is closed for privacy. They are using her room as they would a broom closet, and she is just a broom.

She watches them without moving for a while, trying to connect their voices with the stream and the horses, but she can't anymore. Helio and Jessie gesture and argue in stage whispers. Their arms flex and move about, but are subdued as well in that their elbows don't leave their sides. Gertrude imagines that if their voices were to rise, then their arms would gesticulate in bigger, rounder movements, taking up more space.

"She's awake," Jessie says, glancing at Gertrude. "We should go somewhere else."

"Naw," says Helio. "We're done." He turns toward Gertrude and says, "Hello, Missus Littlefield. Have a nice nap?" Gertrude nods her head. "Good," he says, and he leaves the door open on his way out.

Jessie throws her hands up in the air and says "Men!" before marching out into the hallway.

"Men indeed," Gertrude agrees, but Jessie is gone.

Later, Gertrude receives her first visit from a dead person.

It is Clara Honeywell.

"Is this a dream? What are you doing here?"

"No honey, it's not a dream," the woman says, and sits on the edge of the bed. "Haven't you been visited before?"

"Visited?" Gertrude pats her nightstand blindly, looking for her glasses. "No, I don't think so."

"Well. I was visited for a long time before I passed on," Clara Honeywell says. "It's wonderful to be done with all of it. You know, you shouldn't be afraid."

"I must admit that I'm a little scared now."

"I feel much better since I passed."

"You're sure this isn't a dream?"

"Yes."

"Tell me then, tell me what's to happen."

"I'm afraid I can't do that."

"I understand," Gertrude says, and in that moment she does understand. Clara Honeywell, whose hair has been recently colored and styled, with tea-colored curls, smiles at Gertrude, closing her eyes as she does so. Gertrude picks up her glasses from the nightstand, and turns back to find her visitor gone.

She slides the glasses onto her face and stares at the wall beyond her open door. Jessie hustles past, a stack of folded linens in her arms, but doesn't look in.

The ferry ride was smooth. Gertrude sat inside and Beverly sat on the top deck, looking for whales.

"There's one," Beverly whispered to herself, looking toward the horizon where the spray of a breaching whale was just visible. "Look at that!" she exclaimed, and scanned the deck for someone to share the sight with. There was only a snuggling couple tucked into the corner next to a lifeboat. Beverly looked back at the horizon, but the whale was gone. Gertrude was gazing out the window from the lower deck, but was on the wrong side of the ferry to have seen the whale. She was deep in thought anyway, and not really seeing anything she was looking at. She was wondering how things between her and Beverly had gotten so bad. Sometimes it felt like their personalities were simply incompatible. Other times, it felt as though her daughter were too much like her.

The plan had been for Beverly to spend the summer with her Aunt Estelle on Cape Cod. Gertrude was to bring her there a couple of weeks after she graduated from high school. But after three days of summer vacation, Gertrude suggested they go sooner.

"After all," she'd said to Beverly, "the summer jobs might be gone by the time we get there."

Beverly had looked up from the magazine she was reading at the kitchen table and said, "Yeah. Right. Okay."

"Well, when should we go?" Gertrude asked, straightening appliances on the counter.

"Ma, why don't you admit that you want to get rid of me?"

"That's not true," Gertrude lied. That was just the problem with Beverly: She said too much. And the worst was when she was right. It maddened Gertrude no end that Beverly could sense her mother's discomfort. But her discomfort always arose in the first place because her daughter said things like that. Gertrude felt that her whole life was under a microscope and that she was being judged constantly.

In moments of insight, Gertrude remembered how judgmental she had been of her daughter. Beverly wasn't as studious as other kids in the class. She was frivolous, caring only about nice dresses and parties. Even as she grew into a teenager and began to take more of an interest in the world; as she became concerned with civil rights, women's rights, the environment; Gertrude couldn't help but suspect that her daughter cared about these things because it was in fashion to do so. So now that the tables were turned, and Beverly judged her mother harshly—she was too cold, too calculated, too controlled—Gertrude realized that the only thing she'd really managed to teach her daughter was how to be judgmental.

"It's alright to admit that we're not getting along," Beverly had said to her, and gone to her room to pack.

"Don't say that. How can you say that?" Gertrude had followed her daughter down the hall and watched her lay dresses and skirts on the bed.

"Oh please, Mom. I'm just saying what's true. Let's just get me the hell out of here, okay?" Gertrude had gone back to the kitchen without a word.

* * *

Estelle met them at the ferry and brought them to her place, a two-bedroom attached house with weathered shingles and threadbare rugs on the painted wood floors. Beverly and Gertrude followed her into her studio. Dried blobs of plaster, gravelly sand and chipped seashells littered the floor. On a table was one of her sculptures, half-finished.

"It's a cloud formation, and the shells symbolize the sea," she explained to Beverly. "You see, it's about water. And water is life."

Gertrude sighed loudly, sarcastically. Beverly glared at her mother and moved her suitcase to the corner.

"No one expects *you* to get it," Estelle chided her sister.

"I'll just wait in the kitchen until you're settled," Gertrude said, moving out of the room.

"So," Estelle said to her niece, "you think you'll really stay for the whole summer? You won't be homesick?"

"I don't want to go back to Lynn ever again," Beverly said, without even lowering her voice. Gertrude had stopped in the hallway and was listening to them from outside the door.

"Listen," Estelle leaned against the wall while Beverly moved about the room, looking into tubs of her aunt's sculpture-making materials. "I know you're angry at your mom." Beverly nodded. "And your dad too." Beverly shrugged. "But you do need to go home and do that course in the fall. Where are you going to study again?"

"Katharine Gibbs School. Ugh."

"Ugh, nothing. It'll be a good thing. You have to support yourself. Look at me. Since Lou left, it's lucky I've got my art. Through that, I've been able to support myself. It's important for women, you know."

"So people buy these things?" Beverly asked, looking at the cloud formation. She added quickly, "They're beautiful. It's just, well, I've never bought art before. I don't know much about it."

"People do. I sell them down at the landing, you know, the ferry, and the tourists love them. My sculptures are really about place. About this place. Cape Cod." Estelle paused and breathed in deeply through her nose. "About the sand and the beach and the ocean. Tourists love that, because they're not from here, so it's like they're taking some of the place back home with them. I like to imagine one of my pieces living in a townhouse in Manhattan."

Estelle was fixing a scarf around her salt and pepper hair.

"That looks nice." Beverly stood looking in the mirror next to her aunt. She had long straight brown hair, and she wore it down; her face was wide with prominent cheekbones and blue eyes.

"You should put your hair up sometimes," Estelle told her, and walked behind her to pull her hair into a bun. "You have such a pretty face."

Gertrude listened to her daughter and her sister, talking more easily and affectionately than Gertrude herself had spoken to either of them in such a long time. She went to the kitchen, stepping lightly on creaky floorboards, and put the kettle on the stove.

Later in the afternoon, Estelle drove Gertrude back to the ferry. Beverly stayed at the house, to unpack.

"Don't worry," Estelle said as she hugged her sister at the dock. "I'll take good care of her. It's going to be fun!"

* * *

By the end of the first week, Beverly had gotten a job in an ice cream shop in Provincetown. She and Estelle would drive out there together in Estelle's matchbox Cortina, sliding out the flat road through the sand dunes and scrubby pines to the tip of Cape Cod.

Estelle sold her sculptures on the pier and Beverly would lean out the takeaway window of the ice cream shop and see her aunt, with various other artists. She'd point at whoever she was talking to, a cigarette between her fingers, and wag her head as if she were saying something really important, even though she may as easily have been talking about the weather or somebody's dog's new collar as politics or the war in Vietnam.

Beverly would lean back inside and rest with her hands on top of the aluminum freezer doors and wait for the next batch of tourists to pour off the ferry.

On her second day of work, a young man leaned on the ledge and stuck his head in the window. He had long eyelashes, chestnut eyes, and wispy sideburns.

"Mint chocolate chip."

"Cup or cone? Small or large?"

"Cone," he said, "Large." He was wearing a tie-dyed T-shirt and orange striped pajama bottoms.

"I like your shirt," Beverly said as she handed him the cone.

"I'm trying to waken the senses," he said. "Did it work?"

"Umm. I don't know," Beverly leaned her head to one side and studied him. He sat onto the hood of somebody's parked car and licked his ice cream cone.

"So where'd you come from anyway?" he asked her.

"Lynn," she said.

"Lynn? Lynn. Well, Miss Lynn, welcome to Provincetown."

"You from around here?" she asked, wiping the top of the freezer with a rag.

"I am. My name's Daniel. My parents call me Danny, but I hate that."

"I'm staying in Truro with my aunt," she said, and leaned out the window to point out Estelle.

"Cool. That's cool." Daniel licked drips from the periphery of his ice cream cone. "So, you have a name? Miss Lynn?"

Beverly laughed, "Well, I do, and believe it or not I'm named after a town ... but not Lynn."

Daniel took a long look at her and said, "New York?" Beverly laughed again and crossed her arms. The rag made a wet spot on her shirt.

"I said town, dummy, not city."

"Okay, okay. Let's see...." he bit his ice cream. "Nope. I give up. What's your name?"

"You didn't try very hard, did you?"

"No, but you'll tell me, I know you will."

"Now how do you know that?" she asked.

"Because I'm irresistible. You cannot resist me, no matter how hard you try."

"Oh really? Well. I guess I'm going to have to try then."

"Tell me," Daniel said in a hypnotist's voice. "Tell me your name. You must tell me your name."

Beverly laughed so hard she had to put her head on her arms on top of the freezer, not because what he said was so funny, but because Daniel was cute. And she was free of Lynn, free of her childhood. She was somebody new, in a new town where nobody knew her, and here was a guy, a funny and cute guy, paying attention to her. How much easier life seemed already, on Cape Cod with Estelle. Without her mother making her feel small and mediocre, her father's sporadic appearances, their stiff Friday night dinners where nobody talked about anything.

Beverly and Daniel arranged to go out after her shift. When he picked her up, she finally told him her name. "I knew you could not resist my charms," he drawled. They went to the beach, wandered along the shore in the darkness.

The next night, it was more of the same, but with marijuana, and the night after, they went to the beach again and made love on LSD.

* * *

Gertrude heard the story of her daughter's having fallen in love from both Beverly and Estelle.

"Mom, he's gorgeous," Beverly told her over the phone. "I think we'll get married. Can you believe it?"

And Estelle got on the line. "Don't worry, Gert. He's a nice kid. I've never seen Beverly so happy. She really loves it down here."

Had Estelle meant to emphasize how happy Beverly was? Had she meant it as a jab? Was she showing off?

She remembered when Beverly was born. Estelle was with her, soon after the birth. The nurse came in with the swaddled baby, and brought her to Gertrude, but she was overcome with fear. "No, I'm dizzy," she'd said. "I'm afraid I'll drop her. Just give me a minute."

But Estelle had moved in and taken the baby from the nurse's arms. "Look at that. She's beautiful. She's perfect, Gert. Look her fingers, they're so tiny."

Gertrude had watched her sister and it was as though she's held a million babies before. The nurse and Estelle, cooing and smiling while Gertrude looked on from the bed. Clive came in quietly and stood against the wall. Gertrude looked from the two women to Clive. She mouthed the word *hello*, and he came to her side.

"She's so natural," she said to him, looking at Estelle.

"You'll get used to it, Gertie. Don't worry."

"Here," Estelle brought the baby to the bed. "Here's your little girl. Congratulations, Clive." She turned to Gertrude. "Are you ready for her?" Gertrude nodded. When Estelle put the baby into her arms, Gertrude started to shake. The baby started to cry, and Estelle picked her up again.

"You probably just need some sleep," Estelle said to her sister.

"You hold her, Clive," Gertrude said. Clive took the baby from Estelle and Gertrude watched as tears flowed down his face. She twisted her fingers together on her lap.

"She's beautiful," he'd said to Gertrude. "Just like you."

They named the baby together. Beverly. One of their favorite towns. They used to spend summer days there early in their marriage, at the beach, eating fried clams and French fries from a box. "Beautiful Beverly," Clive had said, and Gertrude had started to let herself feel the joy of it.

After the summer ended, Beverly came home and started classes at the Katharine Gibbs School in Boston. Mother and daughter caught the train together from Central Square in the mornings, and they got along better than they had in years, maybe better than ever, and Gertrude ceded that Estelle had done a good job with her daughter. For the first month, Beverly walked to school from North Station, and Gertrude continued on to Harvard Square, where she worked in the University's museum as a receptionist. They chatted about Estelle, about Daniel, about the weather, about Beverly's classes and Gertrude's job. Like two adults, and Gertrude imagined that the worst part of raising her daughter was now over. She watched as the antagonism that had plagued them began to fade into memory.

Then, one morning, Beverly said she wasn't feeling well, and that she was going to stay home.

When Gertrude returned that afternoon, her daughter was gone, and there was a note on the kitchen table.

Dear Ma,

I'm sorry. I just couldn't tell you. I can't keep this up. I'm going to marry Daniel. I might as well tell you, because you'll find out anyway, but I'm pregnant. Don't get mad. It happens. But don't worry, because Daniel loves me. And he's nearly done being an apprentice, like I told you, and one day he's going to have his own garage. I'll go to school down on the Cape, after the baby grows up a bit. I don't want to be a secretary anyway. No offense. I'll call soon.

Love, Beverly

Gertrude crumpled the letter and threw it in the trash, paced the room two times before calling Estelle.

"She's pregnant." Estelle was quiet. "Did you hear me?"

"Honey, I know." Now Gertrude remained silent. She knew? She knew, but she didn't say anything? So Beverly had told Estelle first; that was even worse. Gertrude felt betrayed on both sides. "Gert? Hello?"

"Yes. I'm here."

"Gert, it's going to be fine." And, as if that were the last line in a song that Gertrude had been keeping time to, she slammed down the phone.

Leigh

I'm reckless. What am I doing at Mark's place? I have a key, but I ring the bell anyway. I didn't even go home to change. His voice comes out of the intercom, and I tell him it's me. There is a pause before the hoarse buzz allows me to push in the heavy door. I hold the handle as it rests back into the frame and walk slowly up the stairs. He's there waiting in the open doorway. I can tell he's angry, but I walk straight into him and put my arms around his middle.

Mark's a little on the heavy side. He didn't use to be when we first met. He used to play more squash and he had a wiry torso. Now he's softer, and his jaw has swelled, his chin is less distinct, the hair above his ears is greying. I lay my head sideways across his chest, like I'm trying to burrow in, and he holds me. I'm comforted until I feel his arms stiffen and he pushes me back to look at my face. I study his mouth, which is not as delicate as it used to be since his face has widened and become more toughened by years of shaving. I notice that a brown hair is sticking out of one of his nostrils.

"Where have you been? I called." I shake my head.

"Do you have coffee?" I ask him. I need to be normal, even if it's just pretend. Sometimes I feel like everything is pretend anyway. Movements we walk through trancelike.

"I need answers, that's what I need."

"I didn't ask you what you needed. I asked if you had coffee."

"No, you don't appear to care about what I need." He is still blocking the door but moves aside as I push into the apartment.

"I was on the Cape," I tell him. "I went to visit my father."

He softens when I tell him this. The product of a long and happy marriage, Mark allows for leeway in my emotional foibles when it comes to Beverly and Daniel. And now that Beverly is dead, I'm going to milk it for all it's worth. I start to cry, which is easy, though I have to admit that I do it for sympathy. Mark plugs in the coffee maker. I lean my elbows on the counter and sniffle.

"I'm sorry," I say. "You know, I think I'm fine, that none of it bothers me, but then, all of a sudden, there it is." I whiff a Kleenex out of the box he holds toward me.

"Listen Leebie, you can't just disappear." He scoops grounds and turns on the tap. He always lets the tap run for thirty seconds before using the water. Sometimes I catch him counting quietly, his fingers rubbing together under the stream of water. Today I think he only waits for twenty.

"Come on," he says, coming around to sit with me on the couch. "Don't you know I worry?" I smile weakly. I'm relieved he's over his anger, but a little disappointed as well. It was too easy. And now he's trying to be cute, to cheer me up, and it's depressing me because at least his anger was real. He reaches over and tousles my hair like I'm a child on a losing soccer team. *Buck up, you'll get 'em next time tiger.* Longingly, I watch the coffee maker as it drips.

* * *

After Beverly had recovered from her miscarriage, Gramma took a taxi to the hospital to pick her up, and they returned in the late afternoon. Beverly sat on the couch, her feet on the coffee table, and started to make up for her week of not being able to smoke. She lit a cigarette from her pack of Larks, and when that was down to the butt, she lit another one from it, etcetera.

Gramma had cleaned the house. I'd accompanied her to the laundromat, in a taxi, with trash bags full of curtains and blankets. She'd washed all the windows, cleaned the refrigerator and the oven, and had even gone to town and bought a vacuum cleaner because Beverly had only sporadically brushed the wall-to-wall carpeting with a broom. It was a different color now that it was vacuumed: dark orange, the color of a sunset, instead of the mustardy brown I was used to.

Beverly didn't say anything about the cleaning that had been done in her absence. If anything, I think it annoyed her, or maybe she took it as an insult. She flicked her ashes.

Gramma had a stew ready, in the crockpot that had previously been relegated to storing pens, jelly-jar lids, rectangles of recipes cut from the newspaper, and any other bits of junk that had ended up on the table and counters.

She ladled stew into four bowls, and we sat down to eat.

"Thanks for cooking, Ma," Beverly said, and pushed the food around her bowl before spearing a chunk of meat and eating it. "It's good. Where'd you get the recipe?"

Gramma wiped her mouth with her napkin. "It's one that your father's mother gave me. Clive loved it."

Beverly nodded and dangled her fork into her bowl from its handle. Andy and I were at opposite ends of the round table and I imagined the line of the table's diameter, connecting him to me. He looked up and caught my eye, and I'm sure he knew I needed to feel connected, so he smiled.

"The lady that was in the bed next to me, remember her?" Beverly said. "Well the most exciting thing that happened when I was there, in the hospital, was that she had a heart attack." She forked another piece of meat and chewed.

"Well? Did she live?" I was afraid for the woman with the yellow foot. I had been worried about her the day we visited.

"Oh? Now you want to know that too?" Beverly pondered the question.

"Come on and tell us," Andy said. I stared at her, and waited.

"She did. She lived," Beverly laughed. "She lived. She wasn't much fun, either, not before the heart attack and not after."

"Thank God," Gertrude said.

"Thank the doctors, Ma. Best place to be if you're going to have a heart attack."

Gramma nodded and concentrated on her stew. When we'd finished eating, she cleared the dishes. "Is that all you're going to eat, Beverly?"

"It was too much. I still don't have much of an appetite." She lit a cigarette and tapped her hand on her cup of water. "I'd love a glass of wine or something. Don't we have any wine, Ma?"

"No," Gramma said, scraping the rest of Beverly's stew into the trash. "No. There isn't."

Andy and I went to the living room and turned on the TV. Soon, Beverly pushed me over on the couch and leaned against me while we watched M*A*S*H. While the credits were rolling, Beverly stood up, kissed me on the cheek, and tousled Andy's hair. She took her car keys from on top of the speaker near the door.

"Where are you going?" Gramma said.

"The car hasn't been driven in a week, Ma. I'm going to start it to make sure it still runs."

"Can't it wait until tomorrow?"

"Why put off 'til tomorrow what you can do today?"

"I did the food shopping. And it's not as though you have a job to go to."

"Not as though you have a job to go to," Beverly mimicked her, her voice high and whiny. "God, Ma. I'm going to make sure the car starts. There's no need to get all high and mighty just 'cuz you live in a city, where it's easy to get a job. Not here on the cape, the finger stuck out in the middle of nowhere. Ready to pick the nose of Boston. Isn't it? Where're we living kids?" she turned to us.

"The snot," we both said because that's what she'd taught us: That Cape Cod was a finger poised for nose picking, and that we were the snotty finger of Massachusetts. We thought it was funny, but we were both subdued now because we knew what going out to start the car meant. We knew she'd be gone for the night.

* * *

At two in the morning, her car pulled up to the curb, the door slammed, the front door opened, and keys landed on the speaker next to the front door. I could hear Gramma whisper something and Beverly answer. I crept out of bed quietly and went to the stairs, where I could watch. Beverly was sitting on the coffee table; Gramma was on the couch, which was where she'd slept the whole time she was there with us, in between layers of blankets.

"You could ask me about my night, since you're awake," Beverly said. Gramma sat up, holding the blanket against her chest as though she'd been sleeping naked, which of course she hadn't.

"What are you going to do about Leigh?" Gramma asked, and a spear of electricity pushed into my bladder. What about me?

"What about Leigh?" Beverly asked.

"She's pulling out her hair. That's not right. Look at her, for God's sake."

"Oh she's fine," my mother said. "She's just having some anxiety about school. It'll pass."

"It's not right. She shouldn't be...."

"Alright, Ma. You can shut up about Leigh now. I was going to tell you I ran into an old friend tonight."

"Look at you," Gramma hissed. "You haven't been home one night, and you're out."

"Come on, it's no big deal...." Beverly tried to make light of what Gramma was saying, and she leaned forward as if she were going to tickle her. Gramma moved to the side. "God, Ma. You know you were always too damn strict. I'm still young. And just because you didn't ever know how to be young, to enjoy...."

"This is enjoying? You look like you're miserable."

"Well, that's why I'm trying to cheer up, meet with friends, you know. Because it's hard for me. Being alone. The baby. Too, it's hard since Estelle died."

"I know that."

"Well, she helped me."

"She also encouraged your drinking."

Beverly stood up and swayed across the living room to retrieve cigarettes from her pocketbook. "Aw, Ma. Your sister's dead. You're not gonna talk bad about her are you?"

"No. Of course not. She helped me too ... when I was alone ... with you."

"I'm without Estelle. I'm without Daniel." Beverly listed their names from behind a wagging cigarette, in a weary tone of voice, as if she were talking about things she needed to pick up at the store: I need this, I need that....

"So was I. I was alone. But I didn't go out drinking and being irresponsible."

"No," Beverly took a long drag. "You made sure you were always at home, making my life miserable. Controlling me."

Gramma lay back down and pulled the blanket around her. "I don't need to talk about this now."

"You know what, Ma? Neither do I. Neither do I. I don't *need* it either. And it's about time someone paid attention to *my* needs."

"Not a wonder she pulls her hair out," Gramma said, watching Beverly totter toward the stairs. My mother growled and stomped up as I scrambled back to my room and into bed. Often she would come into my room and wake me in the middle of the night to tell me about who she met or to make sure that Andy and I had been sleeping okay, but that night she went straight to bed, and the next morning, early, I watched from my window as Gramma got into a taxi and it pulled away from the curb.

I went back to bed and dropped hairs, one at a time, into the space next to the wall.

*　*　*

Beverly used to tell us all kinds of stuff, and she wouldn't hold anything back. She told us that her first love was Joey Cargliani, whose father owned the shop around the corner from their apartment in Lynn. He was a couple years older than Beverly; she used to go in there every single day, whether she had money or not. If she didn't have money to buy anything, she'd explain to Joey or Joey's dad that her mother had asked her to check on the price of sugar or something. One day, Joey's dad was there and Beverly says that he started to come on to her. She was only about 15, but Mr. Cargliani put his hand on hers on top of the counter, and asked her if she wanted to see the storeroom. She pulled her hand away and ran out the door. She went home and told Gramma, and, according to Beverly's version of the story, Gramma as much as told her it was her own fault for going and hanging around that shop like so much cheap trash.

So Beverly went back again the next day, and she stayed. "I learned about sex that day. It was my first time. I always wanted to prove your grandmother wrong. So I did. 'Cuz sex isn't bad, you know. Nothing to be ashamed of. Luckily it was Joey who was there that day, instead of his dad."

I remember her telling us this and us not knowing what to do with it. Like she'd handed us something hot that we couldn't let go of. I was on the sofa and Andy on the floor and we twisted our bodies, trying to put what she'd given us somewhere, but there was nowhere to put it. So we ended up with it sitting there on top of us, scorching our laps.

I think Andy changed the subject. He probably said something like this: "I know who's going to win the NBA playoffs this year, Beverly. I had a dream about it. Do you want to know? Do you, Leigh? We could make some cold, hard cash." And I probably asked him to go on, prodded him to keep talking, while Beverly moved off to the next thing—drinking vodka-sodas and making plans.

* * *

Mark takes my cup, puts it onto the table and leans into me on the sofa, trying to kiss me. Normally I like kissing, and what it leads to, but having cheated on him with Jared the surfer less than eight hours ago, I can't bring myself to respond.

"I'm sorry, Mark. I'm really tired. Can we just lie next to each other?" He moves his body up against the back of the couch and holds me from behind as we lie there, looking at the Ansel Adams print over the TV. After a couple of minutes, Mark fidgets.

"I'm uncomfortable," he says, and sits up, letting my back get cold. "Leigh, what's going on?" He has his fingers on the bridge of his nose, as if he has a sinus headache.

"Nothing's going on," I lie.

"I'm not stupid. Just because my parents are alive and married, it doesn't mean I'm stupid."

"I never said that."

"I can feel it from you. You don't think I understand you. You don't ever let me in."

I lie there silently, because what he's said is true, but I can't say it to him. Suddenly I feel incredibly stupid. How could I have given him so little credit? Of course he can sense things, probably better than I can. My intuition, which I'd always thought to be accurate and well-honed, is likely off-base, while his—having grown up in a normal household with normal parents, whose love he never questioned, was never given reason to question—might plausibly be better than mine.

"It's not that," I say evasively. He looks at me, waiting for more, but I don't have anything to follow it up with.

"If it's not that, then what is it?" he asks, predictably. That's the question I had been struggling with. I shrug, horizontal, and then sit up a bit.

"Okay, so maybe it is that a little bit. I just don't feel … like I'm the right person to be getting married."

"What are you talking about? You're not merely getting married. You're getting married to *me*." It's half-joking, this magnanimous self-confidence, but it's also real.

"I know. I know, but anyone. I don't know if I'm the marrying type."

"Marrying type? What the hell is that? There's no such thing as a marrying type or a non-marrying type. It's me you're talking to."

"I wish that made a difference. I thought it did. But it doesn't. Even with you, I'm still me." Mark, agitated, stands up and pours himself a cup of coffee. "I mean, it's all me, that's what I'm trying to say. It's not that there's anything wrong with you. In fact, there's absolutely nothing wrong with you. That's part of the problem." I feel pathetic, like I'm trying not to blame him for something that actually and against reason I think *is* his fault; but the truth that he understands, the objective truth, is that the problem is all mine. I'm playing to objectivity—because it makes more sense and inflicts less pain— and ignoring my own intuition. I continue: "The fact that there's nothing the matter with you makes the things that are wrong with me stand out in greater relief." He takes a sip of coffee before throwing the rest into the sink and filling his cup with water (after letting the tap run for only ten seconds).

"Do you want to get married or not?"

I hold my head in my hands. I don't. But I don't know if that's because it's the way I feel at this particular moment. I don't want to throw away everything I have and then realize that it was a passing phase. I decide to buy time. What I need is time.

"I do, Mark. And I'm sorry; just let me be alone for a few days to sort myself out. My mother died, and I'm not even sure how I feel about it. I'm sorry, I'm a real fuck-up."

"You are not," he says, and sits next to me on the couch. "You would be if you broke up with me, but you're not a fuck-up." He smiles and pushes a strand of hair from in front of my face.

"Very sure of yourself aren't you?" At this point, I only want to bring the argument to an end and get out, be alone.

"I am. Take a few days. You'll realize what you're missing. Just call me to let me know how you are, okay? I worry."

"Thanks," I say, and put my coffee cup on the counter before leaving.

"If you'd get a cell phone, like the rest of the people on the planet...." I smile thinly, stubborn but cute. "Hey, wait, take these," he says and retreats into the spare room. He comes back with a set of golf clubs. "I'm not going to use them. Sell them at your yard sale."

I hug him and then hoist the bag onto my shoulder before going back down the stairs to the sidewalk. When I am there, safely alone, I start to feel indignant. Why do I have to thank him for giving me time alone? Time alone is something I should be entitled to. It's as though my life is under the thumb of someone other than myself, and it feels wrong. But for the moment I am free, without any expectations, other than work, for at least a few days. I should be able to sort this stuff out, Jared the surfer and all. I get into my car and have one last cigarette on the way home.

The drive is less than ten minutes, but I flip-flop several times during it: I'm being stupid, I should let my doubts go. And guilt. I should listen to my feelings: if it's not right, it's not right. And, again, guilt. Back and forth. Back and forth, until I get home and drag Mark's golf clubs up the stairs.

I often go online and check flights. Rarely do I think I'm going to get on one—and I never follow through as far as entering my credit card number. It's just nice to know what's out there, where I might be able to go, if I wanted to. Being online like this gives the illusion of purpose, the excitement of possibility. I'm hardly surprised at myself, given the day I've had, that for once I pull out my wallet and type in the plastic numbers. Shortly an email arrives, confirming my reservation.

I ask one of the girls in the apartment downstairs to feed Buster for me— they are recent graduates, and I think there are three of them, but there could be four—all variations on extremely-fit and well-manicured.

Sure, she'd be happy to feed my cat, she tells me, and in her eyes, I think I see glee. I never complain when they play music late into the night, but if I'm gone, I'm sure they'll have a party without reservation.

May 1974

After Beverly married Daniel in the Wellfleet town hall, her pregnant belly wrapped like a gift in one of her Aunt Estelle's colorful scarves, she called Gertrude.

"So, I'm married," she said when her mother answered, as if they'd been talking about it all morning and Beverly was simply continuing the conversation.

"Oh, I see." Gertrude held the phone away from her ear. She was clutching it with all her strength and she was afraid to relax for fear she'd drop it.

"Thanks a lot for being happy for me."

Gertrude was silent for a while, listening to Beverly's young breath. "I can't...." she began, but was unable to continue saying that she couldn't be happy for her daughter. "Congratulations," she said. "I'll call your father."

"I already called him."

"Oh. You called him. First. Of course."

"Ma, stop. I had to call one of you first, didn't I? What difference does it make which one?"

"It makes a difference," Gertrude snapped. "I. I'm sorry. It's just that I raised you."

"I was going to tell you both ... so you could be here. I just, well, you didn't want to talk to me. That's the way it seemed."

"So you have a house ... somewhere to live."

"Yes. Not rented. We bought it."

"How did you?"

"Daniel's parents. They helped us out with the mortgage. It's near them, in Wellfleet. I was going to call and tell you. It was just last month. We're decorating it. You know the baby's due...."

"Yes, I know. I mean, I know about when it should be...."

"Maybe when the baby's born, you could come down. For a weekend?"

"Of course. Of course. Yes."

* * *

A few months later, Gertrude and Clive booked two rooms at a local bed and breakfast and set out on a Saturday morning to meet their new granddaughter. The air was warm and sweet with wildflowers, and the trees got scrubbier the further onto the Cape they drove.

Beverly and Daniel's house was small, but it stood alone on a plot with a tree. Beverly had grown up in an apartment, so it was a big deal to have an entire house to herself.

"It's going to be so quiet, Ma. No neighbors upstairs, clompin' around." Beverly led them up the front path—Gertrude carrying her purse and a box of Russell Stover chocolates and Clive wiping the sweat from his forehead with a handkerchief. "You like our tree? Never thought I'd own my own tree. Daddy? What do you think?"

Clive looked up through the branches. "When the leaves change, it'll be pretty." Beverly took him by the arm and led him inside while Gertrude followed. Daniel stood up from the sofa and shook both of their hands.

"The baby's asleep upstairs, but she'll wake up soon," he said, as though to deflect any attention from himself. After introductions, the four of them stood facing each other, Gertrude and Clive sizing up the situation and pretending not to.

"Let me give you a tour," Daniel said finally. The front stairs were rotting, the walls in the kitchen were still unfinished, and the downstairs bathroom wasn't insulated, but it was livable. "We've gotta get to that," Daniel kept saying, as he showed Gertrude and Clive around. "That's next on my list."

By the time the tour ended, Leigh was awake. Having Leigh there, wrapped in a pink blanket, gave them all a focus that made the time go by more easily. They passed her around and cooed and fussed and gave her a bottle until she got tired and needed another nap.

Gertrude found that she liked Daniel. He and Beverly were both so young, but otherwise, they appeared to be doing well enough. Daniel worked as an apprentice mechanic for his uncle. (Better than a starving artist thought Gertrude, like Lou, the man her sister had married, and then been left by.)

Later in the afternoon, Daniel cooked dinner. Estelle had come by, and soon her teeth and lips were slug-purple from the Chianti they were drinking. She teetered on the arm of the sofa as Daniel pulled a folding table out and arranged three chairs on the other side of it.

When Daniel approached Gertrude with the bottle to refill her glass, she waved her hand over it, saying, "No, no thank you," and looked at Estelle with poorly masked accusation that Estelle was oblivious to.

Beverly came down the stairs with Leigh in her arms and Estelle dashed over. "Oh there she is, the little angel. Oh, let me hold her, honey, I know you could use a break." Gertrude stood up but didn't approach the baby.

"Haven't you seen the baby before, Estelle? Don't you live here?"

"She's a great help," Beverly said.

"I don't see her nearly as much as I'd like to," Estelle gushed. "I wish I could do more." She turned to Beverly and lifted Leigh out of her mother's arms. Daniel was putting food onto the table: salad and spaghetti with canned mushrooms and red sauce in battered aluminum pots. Gertrude helped him arrange the chairs and lay out silverware.

"It's so nice of you to cook for us," Gertrude said. "You've both got so much to do; it really is wonderful of you."

"Oh, it's nothing. I like cooking." Daniel wiped his hands down the front of his shirt before re-fixing his ponytail.

Gertrude was famished and ate two helpings of pasta, pasty and overcooked, but with a tasty-enough sauce, and iceberg lettuce with crystalline tomatoes, probably grown in Florida and shipped north under-ripe. Estelle didn't eat, but paced back and forth with Leigh in her arms, cooing and swaying and often stopping to sip her wine.

Gertrude, who'd been holding her breath, worried that her drunken sister would drop the baby; she stood and lifted the bundle from Estelle's arms. She held Leigh, a tiny and surprisingly well-behaved baby, quiet and content. "She's so good, Beverly," she said smiling. "I don't know where she gets it; you sure weren't as quiet as this one."

"Well lo and behold, I guess I'm doing something right." Beverly finished her glass and reached for the bottle.

"Yes," Gertrude said. "You're doing just fine."

Clive stood next to Gertrude and looked into the baby's face. "She sure is a looker," he said. "Just like her mother." He put his hand absently around Gertrude's waist and winked at Beverly.

"Ho ho, now don't you two go getting all romantic on me now. Will you look at my Ma and Dad, Daniel? Pretending to be a couple."

"Hey baby, it's cool," Daniel said.

"Yeah, sure it's cool," Beverly said and went into the kitchen for her cigarettes.

"You smoke?" Gertrude said when she came back. Beverly nodded and struck a match. "You know you shouldn't around the baby."

"It won't hurt her. Probably make her stronger."

Gertrude sank onto the couch with Leigh while Clive helped Daniel to clear the dishes. Estelle sat next to her sister and prodded the baby's cheeks. "It's so nice you could come, Gertie. It really is. It's nice to have the family together, isn't it?" Gertrude looked at Estelle doubtfully. "Oh it is," Estelle said. "It's wonderful. You have a grandchild," she said to Gertrude.

"Oh Estelle, I'm sorry. I know you mean well, but you're drunk. You know you're drunk, right?"

"Oh well," she laughed and threw an arm around each woman, Beverly on her right and Gertrude on her left. "So, let's have a party, huh?"

"Here, here," Beverly said. Gertrude looked at Beverly's hand as it rested on Estelle's knee, a casual affectionate gesture that made her feel jealous.

Clive and Daniel emerged from the kitchen and Clive sat on the arm of the couch. On a stereo speaker was a plaster sculpture of a cloudbank attached to the blue sea by a pillar of rainbow. "Is that one of yours, Estelle?" Clive asked, pointing to it.

"Oh, yes. A wedding present."

It was nice of Estelle to give them a wedding present, thought Gertrude, but how childish—what those kids really needed was money.

Gertrude wasn't used to offering help, but she realized that she should do something, take Beverly shopping, for some things for the house maybe. She'd been used to having a child to take care of, and she had become used to not having one to take care of—but she wasn't sure how to navigate this new parenting terrain of living separately but helping out, being in contact. She suggested they go to the flea market the next morning.

To her dismay, Estelle, rather than offering to babysit, volunteered to go with them. Gertrude looked to Clive, hoping that he would come as well, to deflect the discomfort Gertrude knew she would feel as she watched her daughter becoming more distant from her while growing closer to Estelle (and showing it off to her mother). But Clive and Daniel were conversing in the corner. He looked so charming, Gertrude thought of her husband, there in his tweed pants and rolled-up sleeves, talking to Daniel, who rubbed his palm along his head in the direction of his ponytail.

"Okay, so ten o'clock?" Gertrude said. Both Beverly and Estelle nodded, and Beverly took the sleeping Leigh from her mother's arms and brought her upstairs.

* * *

Later that night, Gertrude and Clive crunched along the gravel to the porch of their B and B. The owner had gone to bed and most of the lights were out. They climbed the stairs, Gertrude first, and she could feel Clive behind her. Clive's room was at one end of a peach-carpeted hallway, and Gertrude's was at the other. At the top of the stairs they said *goodnight, sleep well, see you in the morning*, and each went to their room. Two doors clicked closed.

At the shared bathroom, Gertrude was brushing her teeth when Clive came up behind her.

"I'll *shust fee a linut*," she said through the muffle of toothpaste.

"No rush, no rush," Clive said, and leaned against the wall on the other side of the hallway. Gertrude spit out the toothpaste and turned.

"Sorry, I'll just be a minute," she said, and shut the door. When the toilet flushed and Gertrude came out again, Clive was gone. She went to her room and slipped her nightgown on. She could hear him, the water running, his footsteps as he got ready for bed. His door closed then and it was quiet. Gertrude lay in bed, listening to the crickets outside the window. She didn't often get a chance to hear them, so she kept the window open even though it was cool.

Down the hall she thought she heard the very quiet click of a closing door and then light footsteps making the floorboards creak. It could be anyone;

there were several other guests, and at least one was sharing their bathroom. But the footsteps stopped outside her door and a pause that seemed to last for hours was followed by a light tapping on her door.

"I didn't want to wake you if you were sleeping," Clive said. He was in his trousers and undershirt. His hair was mostly grey, on his chest and arms as well as his head, but otherwise, his body didn't look much different than it had 20 years earlier. He stepped in and enveloped her in his arms, a place more comfortable to her than anywhere, despite all they'd gone through. She breathed him in and he stayed the night.

Lying in bed the next morning, she curled up in a ball and tried to fit herself into his armpit. "I don't want to go today, God help me," she said.

"I know," he laughed. "Estelle and you aren't the best of friends anymore."

"She just inserts herself into every situation," Gertrude said, stretching out and laying her head on Clive's shoulder. "But I feel bad about it. You know what it is, though? It's the two of them together. I could take either one separately, but the two of them, the way they gang up. You could see that, couldn't you? It's not just me being crazy, is it? Clive?"

"I can see where you're coming from. Bev's happy to have an ally, I guess."

"Oh God, I know. I haven't been an ally. I've been an adversary. Judging her."

"Now now, you've done a good job, Gert. The two of you are just ... well, you're different people is all."

"It's funny, Clive. You know, I always thought you were the one who was hard to get along with."

"Me?" he laughed. "No." He kept laughing through his nose. "No, you're right. I was hard to get along with sometimes. I know that. And ... I'm sorry."

"I'm sorry too," she said. "Sorry for the times I was." Clive turned her toward him and propped himself up on his elbow.

"You do know," he said, and held his palm along the side of her face. "That I've only ever loved you?"

* * *

At ten-thirty in the morning, there was loud music playing, and Daniel was hammering something into the wall in the kitchen. Estelle opened the door when Gertrude knocked.

"Well, did we sleep in, or what?"

"Good morning. I like your outfit." Estelle was wearing a top that resembled a mass of billowy, colorful scarves from inside a magician's hat atop tight, pink pedal pushers.

"Thanks honey. I like it too. It suits me." When she turned to allow Gertrude into the house, her blouse whirled about her. Gertrude noticed that you could see her armpits inside the ample short sleeves.

"How did you all sleep?" Gertrude asked, sitting on the couch next to Beverly and smiling at Leigh, who was gurgling and kicking in her mother's lap.

"Not great," Beverly reported. "I can't complain, because she's a pretty good baby, but I think she had some gas last night."

"Do you want me to take her?"

"That's okay. We should get going if we want to get the best stuff." Beverly stood up, with Leigh on her arm.

"Did you get breakfast, Gertie?"

"Yes. Very nice. Bacon and eggs."

"Of course." They followed Beverly to the car. "The Silver Sands has a dynamite breakfast. Lou and I stayed there for a night once, when we were having the floors fixed in the house."

"It's a fine place. Good breakfast."

Estelle had tears in her eyes as she sat into the back seat with the baby in her lap. Beverly turned on the ignition.

"Are you all settled back there?" Gertrude asked, turning around in the passenger seat. "Estelle, what's the matter?"

"Nothing, nothing. Just Lou. I still have so much anger and emotion."

"Well of course you do." Gertrude said. Beverly, one hand on the steering wheel and the other arm across the back of the seat, was turned all the way around, and was looking at Estelle as the car rumbled toward the intersection of the main road.

"It's okay, she's okay," Gertrude said to her. "Better just drive."

"I'm fine, I'm fine. Just angry. Still." Estelle wiped her eyes with her thumbs, pushing her makeup into place.

Beverly turned her attention back to the road. At the stop light, she started to chant, "Ooooom. Namiyahooooh. Ringikyooooh," and Estelle joined her, their two voices gaining volume as Leigh fell asleep and Gertrude squeezed the bridge of her nose and concentrated on the sidewalk as it passed.

When they pulled into a space, Beverly got out and went around to where Estelle was struggling to stand out of the low seat with Leigh in her arms. Beverly hugged her, the two of them locked in an embrace with Leigh stuck in between. Gertrude began to worry for the baby, and whether she had enough air. Estelle stepped back and rearranged Leigh on her arm.

"You're okay?" Beverly said to her.

"Oh yes. Very powerful. And healing." She looked to Gertrude. "Couldn't you feel it, Gertie?"

Gertrude smiled thinly and nodded. "Do you want me to carry the baby?"

"Don't worry, Ma." Beverly opened the trunk. "She'd be too heavy to carry all day. Even though that's what she'd like. If she had her way."

"She loves to be held," Estelle agreed, looking into Leigh's sleeping face. Beverly and Estelle maneuvered the baby into the buggy that Beverly had taken from the trunk.

"Look at that thing," Gertrude said. "We didn't have such newfangled things when you were a baby. Imagine, it can fold down and fit in a car. What a wonderful idea."

"Things change so fast, don't they, Gertie? Since we were girls?" The three women moved off into the maze of stalls, Beverly pushing Leigh. Estelle slid her arm around Gertrude's elbow, and Gertrude was thankful for the gesture. Estelle leaned toward her sister's ear. "So, honey. How are things? You know with Clive?"

"What are you talking about? Nothing happened." Estelle stopped walking and squeezed her hand around Gertrude's elbow.

"Aha! You're being defensive. I know what that means." Gertrude pulled her along and looked straight ahead. Beverly, amongst a gaggle of old wooden furniture, was looking at a highchair. "I know you too well," Estelle went on.

"Stop that," Gertrude said, smiling. "Okay. Okay. So maybe we are close. Maybe we do … still … love each other. Don't say anything. Please. I don't want to cause anything."

"You know that's always been your problem," Estelle whispered as they neared Beverly. "Trying to keep the peace by keeping your mouth shut." Gertrude looked at her; what she was saying was absolutely right. How was it that someone so flighty most of the time could nail her so easily? Sisters. She just *knew* her. It was good to be known, actually.

"Well, I'm not going to change now. So keep your mouth shut. That looks okay," she said to Beverly as they hovered around the highchair. Beverly lifted the tray to show them where the hinge needed to be replaced.

"Daniel can fix it," Beverly declared. Leigh started to whimper. "Shit." Beverly rolled the carriage back and forth.

"He has enough to do," Gertrude said. "Don't give him any more. Let's find one that isn't broken." Leigh's whimper turned into a scream and Gertrude got to her first. "There, there," she said in a low voice as she picked the baby up and put her against her shoulder. Leigh quieted down.

"We can always come back for this one if we don't find anything else." Estelle pushed the empty carriage as they wandered ahead.

Their voices got fainter and Gertrude concentrated on feeling the baby against her shoulder. She stayed behind Beverly and Estelle, looking distractedly at used clothes, furniture, glass-covered trays of silver jewelry, toys, books.

Finally, they settled on a maple table and set of four chairs, and the wooden highchair with the broken hinge. Gertrude paid the man while Beverly and Estelle looked on.

"I'm sorry Daniel's going to have to fix the highchair," Gertrude said to Beverly as they wound their way back to the car. Estelle was pushing Leigh now, and was making wide arcing turns with the buggy, to keep her happy. Leigh sang like an owl each time Estelle whipped her in a semicircle.

"I can fix it myself." Beverly lit a cigarette.

"Yes, you probably can," Gertrude agreed. "You've always been good with things like that."

"You never know, maybe I'll be a mechanic, like Daniel."

"Is that what you want?"

"No. That's not what I want. I'm a mother now. I guess that's what I am now."

"Yes, but surely you can be other things too."

"Like you?"

"I enjoy my job."

"Yeah. But it's not your dream, is it, Ma?" Gertrude looked straight ahead.

"Where's your car? Do you remember where we parked?" Estelle turned back to them.

"I don't remember where we parked."

"I was just saying…. Weren't we here? Just next to the bathrooms there? Remember?"

Beverly did a three-sixty, the cigarette in her mouth weaving an amber circle around her. "Dunno," she said, and then, "Oh for god's sake. I always leave the keys in the ignition when it's in front of the house." She dug through her pocketbook and bits of Kleenex and foil papers from cigarette packs fell to the ground around her. "Shit. They're not here. I must've left them. Now the car's gone. Shit. Shit."

"Okay," said Gertrude, trying to stay calm. She was more worried about being stuck, about not seeing Clive for a couple of extra hours, than she was worried for Beverly because of her beat-up Rambler. "Let's just make sure. Could we be near a different bathroom? Is there more than one bathroom in the parking lot?" They looked around. There were very few cars left, and it became quickly apparent that Beverly's had been stolen. Estelle put her arms around Beverly's neck and leaned her forehead against her niece's, closed her eyes. Beverly breathed heavily, rapidly, but closed her eyes too. They began to chant "Namiyo. Ho. Ringikyo," while Gertrude bounced Leigh on her hip and held her tongue. Finally, Estelle looked up and said, "Okay. Let's find a cab."

* * *

The police station was near the Silver Sands B and B; Gertrude left Estelle and Beverly filling out forms and went to find Clive. He was on the porch, an open newspaper across his lap. Gertrude sat in the chair next to him.

"Well, the car was stolen."

"What? You're kidding."

"I wouldn't joke about something like that. Beverly left the keys in it."

Clive shook his head slowly. "Maybe they'll get it back. It'll probably break down before the thieves get very far anyway. It was probably just kids. Joking around. They'll find it."

"They were … chanting." Gertrude laughed.

"Estelle's still into her meditating and all that?"

"They both are now."

"Well, no harm."

"No harm except it distracted them and Beverly forgot the keys."

"I see your point." Clive folded the newspaper and put it next to his chair. He leaned forward to stand up, but sat back down again sharply, his hand on his abdomen.

"What's wrong?"

"Just some gas." He took a handkerchief from his pocket and wiped it across his forehead.

"Are you sure you're alright?"

"Those sausages at breakfast were so good … must've eaten too many."

"Can I get you something?"

"No, no. Sit down." He put his hand on her arm, and she sat down again slowly. "I'm fine." And then, "Too bad Daniel's parents are away this weekend."

"Yes. I'd liked to have met them. If there'd been a wedding, well, we would've…."

Clive laughed. "It was your only chance to wear a mother-of-the-bride outfit."

"It's a very good thing I don't care about such things."

"Sounds like his parents make a good living." Clive wove his fingers together on his lap.

"I'd say it's old money they're from." Gertrude marveled at how comfortable she was talking with Clive, as though they were any normal long-married couple. She was relaxed but full of energy, alive. "I'm sure they were more disappointed than we were at the rushed wedding. About being told afterward."

"Beverly says they don't like her," Clive said.

"Did she? She didn't tell me that." Gertrude touched her hair, smoothing it where it lay against her head, and lightly patted the bun at the nape of her neck.

"The uncle's just a mechanic."

"True but he married the sister…." They stopped talking as Beverly and

Estelle made their way up the path. Beverly pushed the baby carriage alongside the porch and sat down.

"Thank God we had the stroller with us, anyway. If we'd been carrying the baby...."

"She asleep?" Gertrude asked, peering into the carriage. Beverly nodded.

Estelle turned to Clive. "You heard about the car?" Clive sucked air through his teeth and shrugged.

"They'll find it, I'm sure," Gertrude said. "Beverly, honestly, you've got to remember not to leave the keys in it."

"Goddamn it, Ma. Why do you have to criticize? All the time criticize?"

"Well, it's normal, to take the keys out of the car." Gertrude looked around, as if she were talking to the trees, as if the trees would agree with her.

"Not now, though, Gert," Clive said softly. Estelle put her arm around Beverly's shoulder and looked back at her sister, her eyebrows knotted in reproach.

"Oh, heavens. I didn't mean anything. But you did leave the keys in the car."

"It's not just that, Ma. It's much more than that. I do everything wrong, don't I?"

"Oh stop feeling sorry for yourself."

Clive stood up, brushing the wrinkles out of the front of his pants. "I'm going inside."

"Wait, Daddy. You'll be going soon. I barely got a chance to see you. When are you going?" Beverly stood up and hugged Clive, her head nestled into his neck.

"Let's see." He looked at his watch over his daughter's shoulder before they separated. "I'd say if we get going by about four? How's that sound?" He looked to Gertrude.

"Fine."

"What time is it now?" Estelle asked, standing up from the porch steps, her blouse floating around her.

"Just after two."

"I've got to get going. I'm meeting someone." She paused and then went on. "A very handsome man wants to buy one of my sculptures." Her teeth jutted out in a proud smile.

Gertrude's lips were taut. "Is he married?"

"What does that matter?" Beverly said. "Didn't she say he was just buying a sculpture?"

"I hope you sell him a hundred sculptures," Clive said.

"Now, mister," Estelle said, taking Clive's shoulders, "You take care of that sister of mine."

"Okay," he said quizzically. "She can take care of herself pretty well though."

Estelle giggled. "Oh she can, she can, but she likes a little ... hanky...."

"Estelle, stop it," Gertrude snapped. "You never know when to keep your mouth shut."

"Never mind that." Clive put his arm lightly on Estelle's. "Now. Go sell sculptures, and good luck."

Gertrude and Clive, in side-by-side Adirondack chairs, watched Estelle and Beverly maneuver the carriage over the gravel driveway and down the road.

"Doesn't she ever have to work?" Gertrude said, her foot tapping on the floorboards.

"Who? Estelle? It's the weekend."

"Everyone tiptoes around Beverly. Why can't I say that she shouldn't leave the car keys in the car? Oh Clive, I worry so much about her. That's all."

"She did leave the keys in the car. Still, no one wants to be reminded...." Gertrude put her hands around the arms of the wooden chair. Clive shuffled his chair closer to hers and covered her hand with his.

"We should pack up."

"Yes." She turned her hand over and grasped his, palm to palm. "We should."

*　*　*

At ten past four, Beverly came running down the path from her front door as Gertrude and Clive pulled up.

"They found the car!" she yelled, leaning into the open window. "They found it. It must have been some kids taking it for a joyride!"

"Thank God." Gertrude's forearm rested along the bottom rim of the open window, and Beverly squeezed it before dancing around to the driver's side. Clive got out and hugged Beverly. Daniel stood at the open door of the house with Leigh in his arms, a bottle tipped into her.

He moved out of the way so they could come in, but Gertrude said they had to get going. They both had to work in the morning. Daniel stepped onto the path and reached his hand from underneath the baby to shake Clive's hand and then he kissed Gertrude on the cheek.

"Thanks so much ... for your hospitality." Gertrude moved away and opened her arms to Beverly. She sniffed while they were hugging and said, "Drinking already?" Beverly backed off.

"No, I wasn't. Jesus. It's toothpaste."

Gertrude looked at Daniel, who turned his attention to Leigh, and then at Clive, who was folding his coat and laying it on top of suitcases in the trunk of the car.

"Okay," Gertrude said. She hugged her daughter again, and as she did, she sniffed loudly, several times in a row, and then breathed out.

"You sound like you're getting a cold, Ma. You should get yourself a tissue."

"I'm fine," Gertrude said as she kissed the baby's cheek one last time and sat into the car. As they pulled away, Beverly turned and went back into the house while Daniel watched the car disappear.

Gertrude slid across the front seat, and Clive put his arm around her. As they got further away, she began to forget her worry. The smell of alcohol on her daughter's breath became less and less important. Finally, she allowed herself to feel like Katharine Hepburn leaning into Spencer Tracy as they drove slowly north.

Walnut Acres

Gertrude leans over and pushes the red button. She counts to two hundred and seventeen before Shannon comes in.

"Everything all right in here?"

"Hello, Shannon."

"Everything all right, Missus Littlefield?"

"I have a pain," Gertrude says finally.

"So do I." Shannon sighs as she approaches the bed. "So do I."

"Maybe it's in my head."

"Naw. You've gotta be full of pains. At your age. I have all kinds of pains already, and I'm only half your age." Shannon has her fingers on Gertrude's wrist and looks at the watch on her other arm. After 15 seconds she puts the old woman's arm down again and feels her forehead. "Well, you're still alive anyways. Where's the pain?"

"Here." Gertrude points to the thin valley where her shoulder meets her neck.

"Probably muscular," Shannon says, prodding the wrinkled skin like she is testing dough. "You musta slept funny."

"Does that ever happen to you?" Gertrude asks.

"Of course it does. Everybody sleeps funny sometimes. I remember this one time my neck was so stiff I couldn't brush my hair, and I had to get a haircut the next week 'cuz the brush wouldn't go through it." She is holding her elbows and looking toward the window. "You're lucky you got a window, you know."

"I know. I like to look out. But ... I...."

"You can't turn your head, huh?"

"No," Gertrude lets out a breath of ragged air as she stops trying to turn her head.

"Okay. I've got a lot of stuff to do. But if you want, I can help you get up. You want to go to the community room? Or just sit in here?"

"Thank you, Shannon."

"Which is it? The chair or the wheelchair?"

"Here. Just there in the chair is fine. By the window."

Shannon leans so her forearm is over Gertrude's chest and her other arm is behind her. "Hold on," she grunts. Gertrude grabs on, and Shannon maneuvers her up and to the edge of the bed. "Let's stop here and rest now, okay?" She straightens and puts her hands on her hips, stretches her big shoulders back.

"I don't need to rest." Gertrude is propped on the edge of the bed, her hand clamped to the rail.

"Uh huh."

"You can't possibly need to rest," Gertrude says to her. "After that."

Shannon looks at her watch. "Looky that," she says, tapping her finger on the small glass face. "I gotta go. I gotta check on the whole fourth floor still."

"But you can't leave me like this, I need help ... to get to ... there." She points her nose at the chair, a few yards away, but Shannon is still tapping her watch, and walking slowly toward the door. Gertrude can't walk on her own. She hasn't been able to walk on her own for six months or more. Before that, she had a walker, and she could get around with that. Shannon goes out the door, and Gertrude has to either try to walk on her own, or she will have to fall back onto the bed, which is too narrow. Her head will hit the rail on the other side.

"Why are you doing this to me?" she calls. "What did I do?"

After a moment, Shannon comes back, laughing through her nose. "All right. I was just kidding. Just a little joke I like to play sometimes. To keep the residents lively, you know?"

"Lively. I thought I was dead."

"Just ... remember to behave yourself," Shannon says in a raspy sing-song voice.

Gertrude can see the leaves of the maple tree and the windows across the courtyard. It's midafternoon, lull time between movement and visitors. Doctors' visits, cleaning, lunchtime, all of these things happen during the day. Then later in the evening, there'll be dinner, there'll be a few visitors.

But for now, the home is quiet. Gertrude watches the leaves move in the breeze. Blinds go down across the courtyard. She leans toward the window and lowers her head so she can make out a small square of sky up above. She sits back in the chair and closes her eyes, remembering Clara Honeywell's visit. She waits, hoping Clive will come. Being close to death should have its benefits, after all. When she opens her eyes, she is still alone. Jessie pads past her room. "Jessie!" she calls.

"How are you Missus Littlefield?" Jessie leans against the door.

"I saw Clara Honeywell."

"Ooh. Did you?"

"Yes. I did."

"And what did you want me to do?"

"I'm just telling you."

She comes in and sits on the edge of the bed across from Gertrude.

"Listen. I got some problems of my own, you know?"

"Tell me. You can tell me." Jessie looks doubtful. "I'm going to die very soon. Dead people are coming to visit me. That's how you know. There's no time for me to tell anyone your secrets."

"It's Helio."

"Yes."

"You heard us fighting."

"Oh. No. I couldn't hear."

"We really hit it off, you know. But I didn't tell him, about my boyfriend. My boyfriend's gonna come home. And what am I gonna say? Sorry you've been risking your life for our country, but by the way I met somebody else?"

"Mmm."

"I didn't tell Helio before. That's why he's mad."

"I wish I had your problems."

"Huh? What do you mean?"

"Jessie. It's all going to blow over soon. You told him, that's what's important."

"Huh. Not soon enough for him."

"Hasn't it only been a day? Two days?"

"He's really ... intense." Gertrude looks at her quizzically, waiting for more. "We've been flirting with each other since he started here."

Gertrude squints her eyes. "How long is that?"

"Gosh. He must have started. Let's see. Six months. Something like that."

"That long?" Jessie nods. "Mmmm. I didn't realize."

"You probably didn't see him. He was down in the kitchen." Jessie crosses her legs and props her chin on her fist. They sit quietly for a while before Jessie says, "So, you're seeing dead folks, huh?"

"Just one."

"My gramma said the same thing. She saw dead folks all her life."

"Is she ethnic?" Gertrude asks.

"Wha? Is she what? Ethnic? Damn, Missus Littlefield, you didn't read the book on political correctness, did you?" Jessie laughs. "Yeah, though. She was *ethnic*. She was from Haiti."

"I envy that," Gertrude says flatly.

"Envy? She was an old lady. And you're an old lady. Same thing."

"No, but I mean, ethnic people. I'm sorry I don't know how else to say it. People from warmer climates, usually. Well, they are closer to the ... spiritual world."

Jessie laughs and shakes her head. "No, no, Missus Littlefield. You've been watching too many movies. Spirituality is the same no matter how white or black you are."

"Economic insecurity would certainly lead to a greater dependence on the ... spiritual."

"Yeah, I guess maybe you have a point there." She looks at Gertrude, considering. "But look at you. You're in here. If you had some ... 'economic security,'" she mimics the words, "you'd be in a nicer place than Walnut Acres."

Gertrude waves her hand in front of her face, her wrist bent like a tree branch. "I suppose. My people. Swedes. My people were Swedes. On both sides. We're very ... thrifty, and we're good with our money."

"If you're looking for someone to leave it to, you know you can count on me." Gertrude turns away. "Well, I gotta get going." Gertrude doesn't seem to hear her. Jessie shrugs and goes out, leaving Gertrude looking at the window, where Estelle sits on the sill.

"Hey, honey."

"Well, how is it?"

"How's what?"

"You know."

"Being dead?"

"Of course. Don't be daft. What else would I be asking you about?"

"It's fine. Not so different really. You're on a sliding rule, Gertie. You're on a sliding rule."

"What's that? What do you mean?"

"I mean, it's not black and white. That's what I mean. Om. Namiyaho. Ringikyo."

"You haven't changed at all."

"No. Isn't it great?" Estelle cackles, her laugh like small pebbles raining over a tin can. Gertrude slides down in her seat, her head feels particularly heavy and she rests it forward, her chin nearly on her chest.

"It is great. I'm glad. I'm glad you came," she mumbles.

"Gramma. Who're you talking to?" Leigh stands over her. Gertrude looks up, her eyes straining to turn against the weight of her slouching head. Leigh squats in front of her.

"Leigh. What are you doing here? It's not Saturday already, is it?"

"No. It's not Saturday. You were talking when I came in. You must have been dreaming."

"Yes, just dozing."

"Gramma. I'm going to Las Vegas. I wanted to see you before I left."

"Oh."

"Beverly's dead, Gramma."

"Yes, I thought as much."

"I spoke with Simon Walsh, her friend."

"Oh."

"You knew where she was."

"I guess I did."

"Gramma, why didn't you tell me?" Gertrude tries to push herself up into a straighter sitting position. Leigh helps her. Gertrude coughs into her fist, wipes the back of her hand along the tip of her nose. Even her nose has lost substance, she notices, even her nose has become flimsy, frail.

"She asked me not to. Begged me not to. She was ashamed. I shouldn't have listened. You were more important. But I guess I felt I owed her something, as her mother, so I did as she'd asked." Gertrude is exhausted from talking.

Leigh sits on the edge of the bed. "I hate this, you know." Gertrude nods, though she's not entirely clear about what Leigh means. "This *confronting* things. People. I don't like it at all."

"So don't do it."

"I have to, Gramma."

"You don't have to go. She was sick. Very sick. It could have been from drinking. Who knows? I can tell you about it; you don't have to go." Gertrude looks at Leigh's legs as she speaks, and then, when she is done talking, looks at her granddaughter's face.

"I'm going. I bought a ticket already. Online. It was cheap. A last-minute deal. Las Vegas is a popular spot."

"I suppose it is."

"I don't like this at all. Confronting you. Okay, I'll tell you once." Leigh leans forward, drops onto her knees. "You know I love you. Here it is. I forgive you. Okay. It's okay. So."

Gertrude smiles, and there are tears in her eyes.

* * *

After Leigh has gone, Gertrude doubts herself, doubts who has been in the room with her. Was Leigh here or was it a dream? And the visits. Whether they're dreams or not, she suspects that it doesn't matter. She's getting ready to die, and either her brain is helping her to come to terms with it by recreating people from her past, or else it's real. And maybe she'll see them soon. She watches the maple tree out the window. The leaves flutter softly.

Leigh

I popped in to see Gramma, and the truth of where I was going came out of my mouth, as I had hoped it would. I'm glad. Maybe it's going to be the start of a new thing for me: telling the truth. Worrying less about what might happen. Gramma was fine. Anyway, I had to let her know I'd be out of town. I was mad at first when I found out that she'd known all along where Beverly was, but I have to admit that she's always done what's best for me.

I called Andy, and I told him too, everything. That our mother was dead (I said it loud enough for him to hear this time). And that I was going to see her friend, to see where she'd lived. "Do you want me to go with you?" he'd asked, and of course I said no, that I was fine. I knew he didn't want to go. He's happy in the house, with his friends and his job and his stability and I envy that—how easy it is for him to be happy.

"I figured she musta been. You know, dead. Or else she probably would've called."

I pitied our mother then, to think that her son felt so little of her that he didn't even cry when he found out that she'd died.

"Are you sad?" I asked him, and he said he was a little.

"But oh well. What're you gonna do?" There's something very comforting in the way Andy always has a broad cliché to cover whichever situation he finds himself in. That one was perfect. What *are* you gonna do? He wished me good luck and now here I am, on the plane, cursing myself that I forgot to request an aisle seat when I booked my ticket. I like looking out the window, but I prefer the freedom of being able to get up and go to the bathroom when I need to, without having to wake up the person next to me, or step over his crossed legs, my ass inches from his face, his drooling mouth, his snoring nose.

I am in this compromising position, straddling the business traveler to my right, when I remember suddenly that I forgot to call Mark, to tell him I was going away. The realization that I care so little for the man I have been seeing for six years, the man I am supposed to marry, that I bought a ticket, remembered to tell Gramma and Andy, got someone to feed my cat, called in sick, and boarded a plane, all without telling him, makes me jump, and my ass actually bumps the sleeping passenger in the nose, waking him up.

What a sight he wakes to.

"Oh, I'm so sorry, it's just that I remembered that I forgot to call someone, and oh my god. I'm so sorry to have woken you up. There, go back to sleep." And I'm bowing at him like a geisha and backing off down the narrow passageway toward the bathroom when I collide with a stewardess and her heavy cart of soft drinks. I should walk facing forward, instead of leading with my ass; I apologize to her too, but she is less accepting than the man whose nose I just butted, so to speak, and she scowls and asks me to please sit down until the fasten-seatbelt light goes out. I look around, desperate for a seat that is more easily accessible, but the plane is full and I have to ask the man to stand up so I can shuffle into my seat in a more dignified way. The smile on his face is made of something stiff and rubberlike. "Thanks," I say and slide the airline's magazine out of the seat pocket in front of me; I study the map of the United States.

Judging from the arc from Boston to Las Vegas, if I jump out now, I might land in one of the great lakes.

* * *

There was that one last time with Dr. Silvieri. Since I'm going to tell the truth, since I'm going to try that—telling the truth—as a way of coming clean, of letting go. What other clichés can I come up with? Starting fresh? What would Andy say? Gotta turn over a new leaf or something. There was that one last time with Dr. Silvieri.

"Hey Leigh. How's tricks little missy?" He was in his Camaro. I was half bald; I was, god, I was so *angry*. I knew very well what I was doing when I pulled my hair out. It was supposed to have been anxiety, but I could stop.

In fact I did stop, finally, after I moved in with Gramma. All she had to do was tell me to wear surgical rubber gloves when I went to bed. She used to cover my hands in cream, and put the gloves on, and tell me it was to make them soft. She did it herself: "See? Look at my hands! I'm almost seventy, and they look like the hands of a twenty-nine-year-old!" And we'd rub in the cream and slip on the gloves, and that was that. After I couldn't pull out my hair in bed at night, I forgot to do it the rest of the time too. All it took—it was so simple—*all it took* was a home that felt safe. A place and a guardian that I began to accept would still be there when I got home from school.

But around that time, with Dr. Silvieri, I was pulling day and night, vengefully. Angry and without anywhere to put the anger, or any knowledge of where the anger was coming from or why.

"What are you doing driving around and not cracking people's backs?" I asked.

"You want a ride?"

"Naw, go fix some subluxations."

"Come on, feisty. Get in the car."

"Okay." I pulled the door shut. "Drive." Slumped in the passenger seat, I watched unsurprised as he passed right by the turnoff for my house.

"Hey, where're we going?" I asked.

"Let's go to the beach."

Stan Silvieri had his own anger, and God knows where it came from and why, but for some reason he liked to spend time with me, to dance the edge of his anger and my innocence. It must have been like a drug, something you know isn't good for you but that you can't help doing.

We pulled into the parking lot. The car ticked when he turned it off.

He made me feel good. That's how lost I was, how lonely, how angry.

He put his arm around me and led me through the dunes, weaving along the sand paths through the spiky green grass that would slit your shins if you were wearing shorts and sandals. The sky was brittle blue. It would crack if you threw a rock at it. There was wind, bending the grasses and whipping sand from the tops of the dunes. We settled into a soft, sandy crevice, out of the wind, and Dr. Silvieri lay back, and I lay next to him, and we looked up at the sky, so blue it was almost purple. He breathed heavily, and I could smell the limey smell of alcohol and aftershave. I turned onto my side, away from him, and propped myself on my elbow to look at an ant that was trying to make it up the sand dune, but kept sliding backward. It didn't seem to mind that it was making no progress. It didn't give up.

"We're a lot alike, Leigh. You and I."

"Yeah? How so?" I turned my face back to the sky. "We're not alike."

"I was unhappy once."

"You're happy now, though?"

"Yes. Very happy. Right now. Like this." I stayed facing away from him but turned my head to look out the window framed by my forearm and my shoulder. He looked at me with eyes that were bluer than I remembered them, or maybe it was the sky seeping into them. He squinted at me.

"Like what?"

"This," he said and put his hand on my back, between my shoulder blades. I curled up, holding my knees with my arms and felt him push against my back. His hand was under my shirt then, on my belly and up. No one had ever touched my breasts, which were not much more than swellings under the training bra Beverly had bought me that summer. I was frozen. He moved over me, sweaty, and his chest, hairy and salty smelling, was on my face as he fumbled to take off my underwear. I was stiff and frozen, but I didn't struggle. All I could hear was my own breathing. All I could see was the sky. He wasn't violent, but the pain screamed through me anyway. And it was over quickly. He sobbed, head on his knees, after he'd pulled his pants back on. He couldn't look at me for a long time, and I pulled myself together and lay on my back, looking up at the sky and not caring what happened to me, if I died right then or not. It wouldn't have made any difference.

"I didn't put it inside you," he said when he finally turned back to me.

"No."

I ignored the hand he offered to help me up and pushed myself to my feet, and we went back to his car. He dropped me off at the end of my street and drove away slowly.

* * *

The plane touches down in a basin of terra cotta and we disembark. The stewardess smiles and wishes me a nice time in Las Vegas. The suit next to me moves off, pulling a black briefcase on wheels.

Simon Walsh has my name written on a piece of graph paper. I take it from him before bypassing his outstretched hand to kiss him on the cheek.

"Thank you so much for coming to meet me. You really didn't have to...."

"Gosh, it's not a problem at all." He reminds me of Barney Rubble, but thinner. He is wearing a T-shirt that is cut into fringes at the bottom with sporadically placed wooden beads and he has shaggy greying-yellow hair. And, to top things off, Las Vegas, when you see it from the airplane, looks a lot like Bedrock.

"I make my own hours, you see. I'm the best friend to have if you need a ride from the airport because I can take time off anytime. Except for when I have home visits, but I can schedule those myself too. Problem is of course that I end up staying up late, trying to get my work done, and then ... of course ... I have to drink so much coffee." I smile at him. He talks like a machine gun. "You want to stop for coffee? You must be tired after the flight."

"Great, yeah. I'd like that." I want to say that coffee seems like the last thing he needs, but I don't know him well enough. I can't think of what else to say, so I start to tell him about the man next to me on the plane, about how I bumped his nose with my ass. Simon laughs. His laugh is high-pitched and delicate. Jolly. Sweet and sincere.

"Your mom told me you were a mathematician."

"Yeah? Did she know that? I'm not really. I'm an accountant. For a bank." Gramma must have told Beverly that I was majoring in math. I can't believe how long it must have gone on—Gramma knowing where Beverly was and not telling us. I can't say I'm angry at her, but I'm dumbfounded.

Simon wedges my small suitcase into the trunk, amongst boxes and blankets and some toys and what else I'm not sure because he slams the trunk closed and we get into the car. "I was more a humanities guy myself. Never understood how people could want to mess around with numbers."

"You're missing the beauty."

"You're probably right." He taps his fingers on the steering wheel as we wait in line to pay the parking attendant.

"You know what I like about math?" I say, suddenly animated and refreshed by the fact that I am out of my normal surroundings. "It's that something so completely simple is at the root of the most complex matters in the universe. Everything is numbers, even people, in that they are made up of parts, percentages of each parent, grandparents. Things become easier and more ... accessible ... when you see them in their simplified form."

He turns to me, his long fingers relaxed on the top of the steering wheel. "You know, when you explain it like that, I can understand. But it's not the way my brain works, I guess. Maybe I prefer the softer edges, the fuzziness."

"Not me," I declare, leaning back and watching an ascending airplane to our right. "I like nice clean, clear edges." We pull into a gas station and Simon hops out to fill the tank. The dry heat of the desert is making me sleepy; I close my eyes and allow my body to relax.

"Have you lived here for long?" I ask as we pull back onto the road. Simon Walsh is suddenly a real person and not just the signature at the bottom of a letter, and I want to know more about him.

"Gosh. Twenty years. Can you believe that?"

"You sound ... what is it? English?"

"Nope. Australian. But I moved to the states when I was 12. First we lived in Tucson. My dad had a job there. I don't have much of an accent left. I'm surprised you noticed it."

I lean back and watch the strip malls go by. Downtown rises like Egyptian pyramids in the distance; the sky beyond the buildings is white with heat.

"I can't wait to see it at night," I say.

"It's something. Gosh. It really is a sight."

"You like it here?"

"Well, I didn't at first. But it grows on you. When you live here. It's different than coming to visit. There's some great community. Really great people. Coffee," he says. "Let's get us a coffee."

We pull into the parking lot of a Starbucks and go inside. It's cool, and the glass case with dabs of frosting stuck to the inside from the lemon scones is exactly like every other Starbucks. The only difference between this one and the one near where I work is the decor. Here are soft-toned Georgia O'Keefe prints and paintings of adobe houses. In Boston, they have darker-colored images of jazz musicians. We order coffee and go back across the sweltering parking lot to the car.

"I should have gotten iced," I say.

"Oh, it's sacrilege, as far as I'm concerned. I'm a coffee purist." He sips and holds the cup with his left hand, shifts gears with his right and steers with his forearm.

When we pull up in front of my hotel, he gets out and meets me on the sidewalk. "You know you could have stayed with me," he says. "It wouldn't be a problem."

"Thank you. It's very nice. But, the flight and hotel together were a bargain. And anyway. I didn't know you...."

We are still standing on the sidewalk, next to the car, facing each other. I feel awkward and move toward the trunk. He carries my suitcase to the door of the hotel.

"I'll pick you up at eight." He opens the glass door and puts my case in the cool, humming lobby. I wave goodbye from the reception desk as the door hushes closed and his form recedes.

* * *

It was 1985. The phone was gone. The heat was off. We had electricity, but Beverly hadn't paid that either. Then a letter came in the mail, a letter she had to sign for, and I remember the lady who delivered the mail looking past Beverly's shoulder as she scratched her signature on the clipboard. It must have looked bad: the house a mess, me with my bald spots. She caught my eye and smiled a thin, shrugging smile. I knew she felt sorry for me. At first, I wanted to go home with her, to make her my new mother. She'd come home from delivering people's mail and there I'd be, playing with an elaborate dollhouse with miniature beds and little lace blankets and tiny tea sets and I'd call her mom, and she'd bake me cookies.

But then, as Beverly was stomping across the dusty shag carpeting to the bottle of vodka in the kitchen, I realized what the letter was. "Well. We lost the house, Leigh. We lost the house." Suddenly I hated the mail lady. And her apologetic face. If she cared, why did she bring the letter?

The next week we packed up what we could fit into the trunk of the car and we left Cape Cod. "Good goddamned riddance to the snot-picking Cape!" Beverly yelled into the air as we rolled over the Sagamore Bridge and onto the more solid ground of mainland Massachusetts.

Andy and I laughed tensely. I was glad that we would finally get to see where Beverly grew up: the playground she'd described, the corner store, the shoe factory, and the train that takes you into Boston. And I was glad that I wasn't going to see Dr. Silvieri anymore.

She stopped at a pay phone at the Sagamore rotary to tell Gramma we were coming while Andy and I waited in the car. It was summer, and my legs felt like strings of taffy inside my Wranglers.

August 1976

Daniel drove. Estelle sat with Leigh on her lap in the back, and Beverly, who was pregnant for the second time, sat in the passenger seat, chain-smoking out the window. Daniel had never been to Lynn, and Beverly hadn't been back since she left.

"Your poor mother," Estelle said. "So many years alone, and just when she and Clive were happy again...."

"She spent enough years alone; she should be used to it." Beverly had slouched down the seat and she had to stretch her arm to reach the top of the window to flick her ashes.

"We're all used to it, honey. Doesn't make it any nicer."

"He's lucky," Daniel repeated what they'd been saying for the past two days since they'd learned of Clive's death, "that it didn't last long. I mean, it's better he didn't have to suffer too much."

"I wanted to get a chance...." Beverly said, but couldn't go on.

"Honey, you thought he had months," Estelle's voice dropped to a whisper. "Don't blame yourself. Nobody could've known it would go ... so ... fast."

"Jesus, Beverly, don't light another one," Daniel said. Beverly went ahead and lit a new cigarette before pushing the old one out the slit at the top of the window. Daniel waved a hand in front of his face and lowered his window all the way, even though they were on the highway.

Finally, Beverly threw her cigarette out the window and leaned her head on her arm against the car door. She cried, humming high whines through her closed mouth, like a wounded dog. In the back seat, Estelle massaged Leigh's feet and sang to her as they drove north.

* * *

In the church, Gertrude stood erect while Beverly sniffed loudly. "I half-expected some of his ex-girlfriends," Gertrude whispered to Estelle.

"There's still time."

Gertrude elbowed her. "I was only kidding."

A tissue bloomed from Beverly's face, and her belly was a basketball. Gertrude squeezed her daughter's knee, and Beverly pushed her mother's hand away.

Gertrude managed to swallow the words that made their way to her lips. *You've got too much makeup on*, she wanted to say, but didn't. For a moment, she let herself forget about Clive and instead wondered why the only thing she could think to say to her obviously distraught daughter was that she was wearing too much makeup. *But it's because I care*, she thought. She cared that Beverly was going to look ridiculous at the reception, shaking people's hands and blubbering with greasy black stains of eye makeup sliding down her cheeks. It was cheap and absurd-looking, and Gertrude wanted to wet a washcloth and wipe it all away, the way she had her daughter's snotty face when she was a little girl.

Gertrude held herself, her arms crossed across her abdomen, and focused on the gaudy flowers arranged on top of the shiny brown box. Inside was Clive's body. Beverly blew her nose loudly.

Later, people came through the apartment and Gertrude sat with Estelle at the kitchen table, drinking coffee. One at a time they came to the table, put a hand on her shoulder: Clive's coworkers, her coworkers, what little family either of them had, Clive's cousins from New Jersey, friends from their old neighborhood, friends from their apartment building, even some friends from high school, where Clive and Gertrude had fallen in love.

Most of them knew that she and Clive had been separated, and she wanted to make sure they could see that they had, in the end, reunited—that Clive had been her one true love, and she'd been his. She'd nursed him through his short-lived illness, taken an unpaid leave of absence so she could be by his side as he withered away, his body like wood that's been on the forest floor for years.

She'd left his coat on the hook by the door, his pipe in the holder, the ashtray clean but the pipe's burnt tobacco still caked inside the bowl. Their wedding picture was propped on the mantel.

Beverly chatted loudly in the living room, her voice rising in decibel level with each drink. Leigh toddled from furniture leg to human leg, and cried for Daniel to pick her up. Gertrude was talking with Clive's boss from the insurance company when she heard a crash in the living room, and she ran in to find Beverly being helped up by Mr. and Mrs. Taft. On the floor was an upturned plate of deviled eggs. Mrs. Taft tried to pick up the eggs. Mustardy paste was smeared into the carpet. Mr. Taft still held onto Beverly's arm, as though he were afraid she'd fall again.

"She's upset," Mr. Taft said conspiratorially to Gertrude.

"We're all upset. Thank you." She crouched down to help Mrs. Taft clean up the mess. Mrs. Taft put her hand on Gertrude's arm and squeezed. "She's pregnant, Gertrude. She shouldn't be drinking like that."

"I'm quite aware of that," Gertrude said, standing abruptly and going to the kitchen for a wet rag.

"Mr. Taft," Beverly was saying, her voice too high, "I remember one time when I was just a kid and we used to jump rope down in front of the building. Your son, Buck, well he was older than us, just a couple years, but you know the way at that age, a couple of years. It's like a lifetime." Mr. Taft nodded sympathetically, but he turned his face away, perhaps because Beverly was spitting when she talked.

"Beverly," Gertrude interrupted her. "I think you should go lie down."

"What are you talking about?"

Gertrude continued to scrub the rug with a wet rag, even when all the egg had already come out. "I think you should lie down. You're upset."

"Yeah. I am."

"Please, go lie down." Gertrude's hand tightened on the rag at her side and egg came off on her skirt.

"I miss him." Beverly slumped onto the sofa. "I really miss him." She put her head in her hands.

"We should go," Mrs. Taft said to Mr. Taft. "You know where we are if you need us." She took Gertrude's hands in hers. Gertrude turned her face away but left her hands in her neighbor's. "We're only up one floor."

"I know where you live," Gertrude said, trying not to be unkind. "You've lived there as long as I have."

Mr. and Mrs. Taft left, and soon the living room was empty. The people who remained were in the kitchen.

"Get up," Gertrude hissed at her daughter. Beverly looked up at her through glazed eyes.

"Where's Daniel?"

"He went out, to the park, with Leigh."

"He's never here when I need him, Ma."

"He's taking care of your daughter."

"I mean what I say."

"You're drunk. You're pregnant." Beverly nodded in agreement.

"I know. You're right, Ma. I'm upset. I miss Daddy."

"No reason to neglect your child. Your children."

"I don't mean to."

"I know you don't. Just go to bed. You'll feel better later." Beverly went quietly down the hall to her old room.

Simon is in the lobby, sitting on a small sofa. On the floor is a cardboard box. He pushes it aside with his foot as he stands to greet me. We wave to each other, even though we are only standing a few feet apart, because we kissed on the cheek once and now we're not sure what the protocol should be.

The box, he tells me, has some of my mother's things. The hotel lobby is the last place I want to look through it, so I take it to my room while Simon waits for me. We go for dinner and eat steak and potatoes in a restaurant that is Western-themed and has black-and-white pictures from Las Vegas's heydays: train station, casinos, nuclear explosions.

"So she'd been sober?" I ask.

"Yes. She was sober." Simon puts his knife and fork down. "She got sober, and she was doing really well. She did way better than I did when I got sober first, or was that the second time? Well, once she made the break, and after the hard times, the beginning is always hard. Actually, it's always hard, but anyway, it was too late." He slows down to locate some succinct phrases: "She found out she had cancer. That's why she didn't get in touch with you."

I'm struck for a moment by the bizarre fact that over steak a stranger is telling me how my mother died. And then I'm appalled that my second thought is for myself, the genetic significance. Here I am, finally finding out how my mother died and what's my reaction? To worry that I'll get it too. My grandfather, my mother, the chances seem stacked against me.

"So you were in AA?" I glance at his club soda with cranberry juice.

"AA, NA, you name it. All the As. Gambling, drugs, alcohol. The only addiction I let myself keep going is coffee. I love coffee."

"You don't smoke?"

"Never did. Thank God, because I'm sure I'd have done my best to give myself lung cancer. Never did get cancer. Never got the chance." He is forking food into his mouth speedily. "I'm HIV positive, that's bad enough."

I stop chewing and swallow. I wait for him to elaborate.

"What?" he says, laughing at my surprise. "It's okay. I don't have Aids yet."

"Yes, but."

"I used to shoot heroin. Used to. Used to do a lot of things." He wipes his mouth, and I notice that he has very small and delicate hands.

"So, did my mother...?"

"No, she drank. She, she was an alcoholic, that was her problem."

"You're lucky to be alive."

He stops eating; his fork hovers midway between plate and mouth. "You got that right. Here's to being alive." And he raises his glass. I pick up mine, and we clink them together.

* * *

Andy and I were settled in Gramma's house, but Beverly only lasted a week. She met someone at a bar (of course), and said that he'd told her about a job at a ski resort. The plan was that she'd go out there, and then send us the money to come as soon as she could.

Within a day or two, she had all of her stuff packed into a beige vinyl suitcase with bumper stickers on it, the Grateful Dead's rainbow-hued dancing bears and Peace and Love. When Andy and I got up in the morning, she was at the kitchen table, which was laid with four plates and there was a platter of French toast in the middle. Gramma had gone for a walk, Beverly told us, and the three of us ate breakfast together.

She promised she'd send for us. We believed we'd see her soon. We believed she'd send for us. Or, if she didn't send for us, that she'd be back. But she didn't send for us. And she didn't come back.

That was the last Andy and I ever saw of our mother.

A month later, when it became clear that she wasn't coming back, Gramma called Daniel in Delaware, and he drove to Lynn. He slept on the couch for a couple of nights and had hush-toned conversations with Gramma in the kitchen while Andy and I sat looking at the TV.

It was August and Daniel said he would take us back-to-school shopping at the mall. We didn't know where we'd be going to school and nobody offered any information. There was no more house in Wellfleet, and Beverly hadn't sent for us, so that meant we'd either be staying here in Lynn with Gramma or going to Delaware with Daniel and Delilah. I figured that wherever it was, it wouldn't be for long, because we'd be moving to Colorado soon enough.

It was one of those New England late-summer days that make you long for the winter. So hot it was hard to move and our armpits and upper thighs stuck together under our clothes. Andy had gotten a terrible rash, and parts of it were so raw that they bled, so I was constantly blotting the blood from the back of his neck with a wad of toilet paper that I kept crumpled in the pocket of my shorts. Andy was surly from the heat and sat in the back whacking his knuckles on the door handle while Daniel drove us to the mall with all the windows open.

"Did Gramma tell you that Beverly hasn't called?" I asked him.

"I know." He glanced over at me, then concentrated on the road ahead.

"We miss her."

Andy, I'm sure, couldn't hear us because of the choking hot wind blowing in the open windows.

"I know. I understand that you would." He was a narrow person, all the narrower in the big Mercedes that he'd bought for cheap and rebuilt. "What size are you now? You're both getting so big."

"Where are we going to school?"

"I don't know. Your gramma and I have been discussing it."

"Are we going with you?"

"I don't know. We'll see. Our place is pretty small."

Ever since Daniel had moved away, we'd started getting birthday and Christmas cards with Delilah's cheerful signature underneath his; she used to dot the I with a bubble heart. I assumed it was Delilah who didn't want us. I still hope that's the case, but I've never had the nerve to ask.

We pulled into the parking lot and walked into the rushing, cool air conditioning. At JC Penney, Daniel sat outside the dressing room in first the girls' and then the boys' sections, and waited for us to come out. I tried on everything inside and then carried out an armload of things I wanted and an armload of things I didn't. Andy tried on each thing and then came out to show us, one item at a time. A couple of shirts didn't fit him very well, but we had to buy them anyway because the rash on his neck had left blood stains on the collars.

Daniel and I didn't speak very much while we waited for Andy to try things on, but once, while we watched Andy's feet fall through the rumpled corduroy of another pair of wranglers, Daniel turned to me and said, "I really miss you guys."

Then take us with you and kick that bitch Delilah out! I wanted to scream. Instead, I smiled a small smile.

"Leigh?"

"Yeah."

"Your gramma told me not to say anything, but you have to stop pulling out your hair."

"I know," I said. But heat pushed at the backs of my eyes as I struggled not to cry.

"Okay. That's good," and he put his hand for a moment on top of my headband, as if he wanted to ruffle my hair, but of course he couldn't because there was hardly anything but fuzz. I forgave him for everything at that moment, that easily. I wanted him back. I wanted him to take care of me.

At the checkout, Daniel pulled out his wallet and paid for our new clothes. I could see in the place where he kept his license, the top of a picture of Delilah, her lemon-sherbet hair and a slim rectangle of surprised forehead.

I was too timid to ask if he had pictures of us in there.

After dinner on the night before Daniel was to leave, we had a special cake that Gramma had made, and we were polite with each other because none of us really knew one another, except for Andy and I, and nobody spoke about Beverly.

When we were done eating, Gramma got up to make coffee. Daniel cleared his throat and said, "Your gramma and I were talking and, uh, we decided that it's best if you two stay here with her, for a little while, and see how you like it."

Gramma came back to the table and smiled at us. "There's a school down the block, and I've been asked to cut back my hours at the museum anyway, so I'll be here when you get home in the afternoons. We'll see how it goes."

"Until Beverly sends us the bus ticket?" Andy asked.

"Yes, that's right," Gramma said.

"Or maybe in a few months, you'll come to Delaware," Daniel offered.

"That's okay," Andy said, and it was unclear whether he meant *No thanks* or *Sure*.

"Can we watch TV?" I asked.

*   *   *

I find myself avoiding talking about Beverly. Simon Walsh has turned out to be someone whose company I am enjoying, and I guess I'm not ready to talk about her. Or maybe I want to feel like I know him better.

We go bowling after dinner, to a place in the old part of Las Vegas. Simon tells me that most of Las Vegas's famous strip is actually located outside of the city of Las Vegas.

"When I gambled it was here. Now when I go out, I go out around here. Not that I go out much, but still you can see it's got a lot more character. Speaking of character, you'll find much better characters around here too." I put my hand on his arm, and he stops talking.

"Has anyone ever told you that you talk a million miles a minute?"

He laughs his high-pitched delighted laugh and goes on. "They have told me that, as a matter of fact. A few people have told me. Others probably just leave me alone. The people who care, now they tell me...."

I laugh and point to the lane. It's his turn. He takes a ball and teeters to the line, heaves it right down the middle. The ball is probably bigger than his waist and I tell him after he knocks down all but one pin that it seems physically unfeasible that he should be able to hold a ball without it pulling him over.

"I eat. You saw me eat." He sits down, sips soda from a waxy cup. "I've always been thin. Even before the drugs."

It's my turn, but I don't get up.

"When I was a girl," I pause, and he looks at me, waiting. "I was raped. By my mother's boss. I never told her. But I never forgave her either. Not for that, and not for abandoning us." I get up and take a ball, hurl it down the lane, and it slides straight into the right-hand gutter. So does the next ball and the next. I turn and look at Simon.

"Go on. Take one more," he says. "Take one more. I won't tell a soul." I turn and try again. And it goes straight down the middle, cleaning out all the pins but one on each edge.

"Not bad," he says as I sit down. I lean forward, put my hands between my knees.

"She did some terrible things, your mother. You know." He taps his fingers on the bench between his legs. "She ... well...."

"I've never seen you stuck for words."

He laughs and puts an arm around me, and hugs me to him, and puts his free hand on my head, and pats my hair. We stay that way for what seems like a very long time.

"You should look in the box," he says. "That I gave to you. Beverly made me promise I'd get it to you. I don't know exactly what's in it. But I know she thought it was important."

"I will, I'll look at it," I tell him, motioning toward where the balls tap each other into place. "But not until I win this game."

* * *

Gramma took me for the first haircut I'd had in four years. It is thinner than it should be—even to this day—but the stylist did a Dorothy Hamill cut, and that afternoon Gramma took the headband out of my hand, before I could put it on, and stuffed it into her purse. She could've thrown it in the garbage, but I guess she was hedging her bets. Or maybe she wanted us both to remember it, to keep it from happening again.

Andy was at the occupational therapist and we had half an hour to kill.

"Where should we go?" Gramma asked. "You feel like ice cream?"

"We should bring Andy," I said.

"I guess you're right. So, what then?"

"I wish I could show Beverly my haircut," I said, looking away from what I knew would be a worried expression.

"I've tried to find her, Leigh. I've done everything I could do." We walked down the sidewalk, me with my hands shoved into my pants pockets, Gramma with her purse clutched in front of her. The wind blew in our faces, and we both looked at the ground.

"Like what?" I asked, trying to sound curious rather than accusatory.

"I notified the authorities in Boulder. That she's missing. I did that a week after she left. And I call them at least once a month, to make sure they're still looking. She got off the bus in Boulder. But no one's seen her since."

"So she did go there."

"Yes."

"Well, that's where she must be." We'd had this or similar conversations before. I knew everything Gramma had just told me. But she told me again and again, never getting annoyed that I was asking as if I didn't know, never shutting me down. She must have been as worried as I was, if not more worried. "Do you think she's okay?" I asked.

"I hope so, sweetie. I hope so."

I used to think that Boulder was a dark and scary place and that somehow it was holding Beverly captive against her will.

"Can we go there?"

"Maybe one of these days, if you want, but I don't think it's going to do any good."

"But maybe we can find her."

"Well, we can't go while you're in school, so let's stop talking about it and go get Andy."

Gramma had converted a laundry room–storage closet at the end of the hallway into a tiny room for Andy, and that night I snuck out of my room, which had been Beverly's when she was growing up, and down the hall to Andy's, and I got into bed beside him. We could hear the distant enthusiasm of a talk show from the living-room TV.

"Andy," I said, pushing him. "Andy, wake up."

"What?" he said, moving over, his back still toward me. He had gone through puberty already and was as big and hairy as a man. We'd both changed a lot. I wondered if Beverly would recognize us.

"Beverly's in Boulder, and I don't think she has the money to get home."

"Boulder?"

"Boulder, Colorado. I think we should go find her."

"Why?"

"Don't be stupid. I just told you. Because maybe she doesn't have the money to get home."

"She could call."

"But maybe she's scared we'll be mad."

"Well, what can we do about it?" He turned over to face me.

"We should find her." Our knees were touching. He clutched his hands together, pulled at his fingers, one after another, and then started to wiggle the fingers of his right like they were the tentacles of a sea anemone.

"Stop that," I said, and slammed my hand on his to keep it still.

"Ow," he whispered.

"Well?" I asked, my hand still resting on his.

"Well what?"

"Will we find her?"

"How?"

"Go there."

"Aw, Leigh," he said shaking his head.

"Oh never mind." I got up. He watched me go and turned to face the other way as I eased the door shut.

Back in my own room, I pulled the atlas off the shelf and looked for the millionth time at Boulder. I still don't know what made me suddenly think I could actually go and find her. Maybe it was the haircut; I wanted to show her my Dorothy Hamill cut, to show her that I was okay. Maybe if she saw that I was okay, she'd be able to get better too.

I didn't want to live with her again. I didn't actually miss her that much. Maybe I wanted to show her that I wasn't unhappy—not to make her feel bad that I'd been unhappy before, but because I thought I could help her now. Or maybe I was just curious, to see her. To see if we could be friends. To see if I could forgive her.

Life with Gramma was uneventful. I had school to keep me occupied, I went twice a week to the swim classes that Gramma had signed me up for, and I played interminable games of checkers with Andy in the afternoons. Three years passed that way, and I was nearly sixteen, and I was doing well in school, getting good grades because I couldn't manage to fit in, either with the jocks or the druggies or the preppies, or even with the arty crowd. Nobody was mean to me, but I didn't talk much. I did my work, slipped through each day making as little noise as possible. I did well in math, and teachers said I'd probably be able to get a scholarship to go to college.

Gramma had started savings accounts for Andy and me, and I knew where she kept the passbooks, between two cookbooks in the kitchen. I took mine the next morning, and on the way home from school I took out a hundred dollars. The teller probably shouldn't have given it to me, but she was elderly and may not have been able to see very well how young I was. The next day, instead of going to school, I went to Central Square and caught the bus to Boston.

"Where're you going?" Andy called as I turned down Market Street instead of going toward school.

"To find Beverly."

He resumed walking, one hand shielding the side of his head, as if I were something hot that might set his hair on fire.

The bus left at ten o'clock and I thought it would arrive at eight the next morning.

Well, it arrived at eight in the morning, but two days later. We pulled in to Terre Haute, Indiana, and I got off the bus thinking it was Boulder. Luckily the bus driver saw me sitting inside the terminal, eating a McDonald's hamburger on one of the benches, and called to me. "Hey, aren't you going all the way to Boulder?" He wore a Greyhound uniform, but he had tattoos all over his forearms and a silver hoop in his ear. I stood up, clutching my school bag in front of me.

"You mean ... this isn't Boulder?"

"Naw. This is Indiana, girl. You got twenty-four hours to go." He laughed and walked me back to the bus. "Good thing I noticed you, you'da been stuck here."

I slid back into my seat and sipped until my soda was gone; I made slurping noises, crumpled the wrappers from my lunch, shoved it all into my backpack, and started twisting my hair into knots.

When I think about Gramma, finding out what I'd done and having to leave Andy with Mrs. Taft upstairs, then trailing me on the bus that left the next day, it must have been terrible for her. If it felt like a long trip to me, it must have felt doubly long to her.

What did I think I'd find when I arrived in Boulder? Did I think I'd just hang around downtown until I saw Beverly come trotting down the steps of an apartment building? And if that were the case, if Beverly were fine and happy, then wouldn't that mean that Andy and I were, in fact, the root of her troubles? And if she weren't okay? What might she be? In a doorway, dirty, decrepit, her hand sticking out onto the sidewalk from where she slept under newspapers? What would that mean? What was I going to do? Pick her up? Wash her off? Save her life? So she'd be forever indebted? So Gramma and Andy would be overwhelmed with gratitude and respect?

And what if I couldn't find her? She could've gone to California, to San Francisco, where she used to say she wanted to go. I should have taken more money from the bank. I couldn't afford to go all the way to California. I twisted hairs around my fingers while I rode the bus, my eyes sliding over and over the same sentence in the book I was supposed to be reading for English, the Oxford Book of English Literature. My fingers would twist the hair, but luckily I couldn't pull without being conscious of what I was doing. I must've twisted my hair up into so many knots that my head resembled an over-loved teddy bear when the bus finally eased into the station. I was sleepy and disoriented, and I thought the two stocky police officers were waiting for me to step down so they could board the bus. It took me a long moment to realize that they were there for me.

After I spent a day in the police station, eating pizza, playing solitaire, Gramma showed up, grabbed me into her arms with all her strength and held me desperately to her.

We did spend the day ostensibly looking for Beverly. We went for lunch, we did some shopping, and then we caught the bus that left that evening. Gramma never reprimanded me once. I'm still thankful to her for that.

We went home. Gramma tenderly, patiently, combed the knots out of my hair. I leaned against her and watched the telephone poles fly past.

Walnut Acres

Gertrude opens her eyes to the ceiling. Even without glasses, she can see yellow water stains. One is the shape of South America—another place she'll never travel to. Her eyes scan the periphery of the room, but they are sluggish—cartoon Mexicans at siesta time. She can hear voices.

"You change her."

"Come on, Shannon. I'm nearly outta here. I have a date."

"Oh, good for you."

"God she smells."

"You can't leave her that way and then leave your shift. You have to make sure everything's done."

"Fine. Go read a magazine, that's what you're good at. I'll do it."

Jessie appears in Gertrude's field of vision. She leans toward her and whispers, "She's a fat cow."

Gertrude tries to laugh, but can manage only a smile. Jessie hoists her blankets down to the end of the bed, leaving her exposed to the cold air before she closes the door. When she comes back, she pulls off Gertrude's pants and slides on a new pair. "Wheeew," she says, wrapping them into the waste bag. Gertrude squeezes her eyes shut; tears push out and roll down the sides of her face. "I'm going out with Helio tonight." Jessie covers her back up—clean and dry. Gertrude opens her eyes.

"Good," she whispers. "He's … a … nice … man."

"You're not doing too good today, are you?" Jessie sits on the edge of the bed and takes Gertrude's hand in hers.

"No."

"I'll get the doctor."

"No."

Jessie leans her face towards Gertrude's, their eyes level. "You don't want a doctor?"

"No."

Jessie squeezes her hand. "Okay. No doctor. You comfortable?"

"Yes."

"Okay. I am going to see you here when I come in tomorrow, right?"

"Right."

"You gotta stick around, Missus Littlefield, and I'll tell you how my date goes." Jessie begins to clean the room, humming, wiping the sink, dusting the windowsill. She looks at the watch on her arm and comes to the bed. "I do have to get going. You sure you're okay?"

"Of course I am," Gertrude says, with more force than she knew she had. She startles Jessie.

"Well, all right then. I guess you are. I'll see you tomorrow." Jessie leaves the door open. Gertrude is thankful that she's not closed in, that she can sense the people walking past. She sees Jessie's pink parka at the door and looks over the bridge of her nose at her, and smiles, lifts her hand a few inches from the mattress and waves, and then Jessie is gone. Gertrude closes her eyes and rests, comforted by the hallway sounds of people passing, walkers clicking, the shuffling footsteps of residents whose mobility isn't yet lost, wheelchairs rolling past in harmony with the efficient clip of attendants' white clogs.

* * *

"Daddy's waiting for you, Ma." Gertrude looks up to see her daughter.

"Long time," she manages.

"Not so long. It was nice of you to come, you know."

"Nice? It wasn't nice. It was my ... responsibility. You were my responsibility. I made mistakes."

Beverly stands and approaches the bed, lies down, puts her arm around her mother's waist.

"Naw. Don't blame yourself. I was okay, in the end. Turns out that's what matters. Isn't that a blessing?"

"Yes, it really is," is all Gertrude can think to respond.

"Estelle and I chant together sometimes, you know."

"Yes."

"I won't chant for you though, Ma. You never liked it."

"No, Beverly. I never did."

"Daddy said to say hi."

Gertrude lifts her chin and tries to see her daughter's face, but she is gone and Gertrude is left alone again. The visits are always so short. She wishes people would stay longer.

* * *

"Time for your pills. It's a good thing you have me here to remind you. All of you. You'd all as likely forget to take them, huh? Missus Littlefield?" Gertrude is looking at Shannon with eyes struck by terror. She cannot move. She cannot speak. "You okay? You in there?" Gertrude blinks at her, the only movement she seems to have any control over. Shannon lifts the old woman's arm and drops it back onto the bed. She leans forward, her ear an inch from Gertrude's face. "If you wasn't breathing, I'd say you were dead. Well, I'll get a doctor. Don't worry, Missus Littlefield." And with that, she whooshes out the door; the movement of her heavy body makes the air in the room swirl about, diffusing the fake-floral smell of her perfume.

November 2000

"I'm sick, Ma."

"Yes. Are you in pain?"

"No. Not right now. Sometimes. For the most part, I do okay. I go to work."

"You have a job?" Gertrude was sitting on the edge of the sofa, her hands on her knees.

"I used to deal cards. I was good at it. Then I was a bartender." Beverly laughed, a wheezing smoker's laugh. "That was a mistake. Now I work in an office. They treat me good." Gertrude chewed her bottom lip.

"Why don't you come home? I could...."

"No," Beverly got up and twisted the rod on the blinds so the stripes of orange sunlight got smaller on the opposite wall of the living room. "No way. I'm not going back there. I couldn't."

"But you have children."

"You didn't say anything to them? About coming here? About me?"

"They think I'm in New Hampshire playing bridge."

"Good." Beverly sat back on the foldout chair opposite her mother and twined her bony fingers together. "That's good."

"They should know."

"You can't tell them. You promised." Beverly's hands shook as she pulled a cigarette from a pack on the coffee table. "Anyway, they're not kids anymore."

"You should take better care of yourself."

"See that? That's why I can't go home. I'm gonna die, Ma. But not from smoking. I don't drink anymore. Leave me alone to have a cigarette."

Gertrude leaned back into the sofa and covered her face with both hands. "Maybe," she said from behind her hands. "Maybe it will go into remission."

"It might. That's true. But not from me not smoking. You want something? Something to drink? Tea? You like tea."

"No no. I'm fine. Fine." Beverly, who'd been half-standing, ready to get something from the kitchen, sat back down again, took a long inhale. She flicked her ashes, and Gertrude noticed that she had a blue-green tattoo on her hand. She almost asked about it, then decided not to.

"So tell me. Andy, he's still at the CVS?"

"He graduated." Gertrude stood up. "Actually I will make tea. Don't get up, I can find everything." She went into the kitchen and filled the sticky kettle from the tap.

"You look good, Ma."

Gertrude lit the stove. "Thank you."

"No really. I mean, how old are you? You're eighty, nearly, aren't you?"

"Older."

"Happy birthday." She took another drag and let it out slowly. "To you. No, you really do. You're strong."

Gertrude sat back down while she waited for the kettle. Beverly's apartment was small, but relatively clean. Disorderly, but habitable.

"Andy is loving his job. Developing photos. And he has a new living situation. It's nice. It's in Everett, and it's near his job, and he's very happy there, and independent. He's friends with everybody."

Beverly's hand shook as she smoked. "That's great, Ma. He was always such a nice kid. So nice. And Leigh?"

"She's well too."

"She still working at that job you said she had?"

"Yes."

"She's happy?"

Gertrude nodded her head. "Mmm hmm." Beverly chose to believe her, even though the affirmation wasn't very convincing.

"Good. I'm glad. She was a little ... troubled. As a kid."

"She's fine. Just fine."

The kettle began to whine. Gertrude got up. "You want a cup?"

"Yeah. Sure. Why not."

As Gertrude put their two cups on the table, Beverly said, "You sure you only want to stay the one night, Ma? You could go to the casinos. Ya never know, they're full of retired people. Nice old men...."

Gertrude shook her head. "It's been so difficult not to tell them. Now that they're older. Why hide?"

"You can't tell them. If you do, I'll never forgive you." Beverly tapped her fingers on her knee, in the same way that Gertrude always did. Gertrude noticed the gesture and recognized it. Tap tap tap, lightly. Gentle worry. "I bet she's smart. Leigh." She became more animated, and her fingers stopped tapping. "Leigh. I bet she's real smart."

"Yes, she is. She's done well. You know she looked for you once." Beverly wiped at her eyes with the back of her hand.

"Oh yeah?"

"She took the bus from Boston to Boulder, without telling me." Beverly didn't respond, but hung her head. Ash fell onto her lap, and she brushed at it absently. "Two days it took. She thought it was only going to be overnight. She didn't read the dates on the arrival times."

"Not as smart as we thought." Beverly laughed, put out her cigarette, and covered her face with her hands, her shoulders rounding up next to her ears, while Gertrude scanned the room for tissues.

"Here," Gertrude pushed a roll of toilet paper under her daughter's crumpled face. Beverly took it and blew her nose.

"That's the kind of sadness used to make me drink," she said finally, a thin painful smile across her gaunt face. She pushed her hair into a ponytail and stood up. "Come on. Let's go get something to eat. You must be starved."

"You have the energy."

"I'm okay. I finished chemo a week ago. You shoulda seen me then."

"Your hair. Doesn't it affect hair?"

"Didn't fall out. Go figure. Guess I'm lucky."

Gertrude almost mentioned Leigh's hair, and how she wasn't so lucky, but stopped herself.

* * *

On the flight home, Gertrude fell asleep. She hadn't slept well on Beverly's sofa and she was still tired from the flight out just two days earlier. She dreamed that Clive was with her on the airplane, and that he had his arm around her.

She was leaning very comfortably on the arm of the young man next to her. He wore a business suit, jacket and all, and he was sweating.

"I'm sorry," she said when she woke up and realized she'd been resting against him. He smiled at her stiffly and mumbled that it was okay as he slid his jacket off.

"I was dreaming. Of my husband."

"It's okay," the man said, turning away, and she wondered why he'd let her sleep against him if it made him so uncomfortable.

"Don't worry," she reassured him. "You're nothing like him."

He unbuckled his seatbelt and folded his jacket into the overhead compartment.

*   *   *

Back in Lynn, Gertrude unpacked slowly. She'd only been gone a couple of days, so there wasn't much in her case: an extra blouse, undergarments, a scarf for her hair because she'd had it done the morning before she left.

She hadn't expected to go. She'd received other letters from Beverly, and she usually threw them away after writing a response. This one she'd saved, and she'd booked a ticket. It wasn't so much that Beverly was sick, or that they hadn't seen each other in almost two decades, as it was the fact that Gertrude herself was getting old. She realized as she was unpacking that it was irrelevant whether their seeing each other again, their reconciliation, had helped Beverly or not. Even though she'd gone under the assumption that she was going to help Beverly, it turned out that she'd needed the visit, needed to feel at peace, as much as or more than Beverly did.

She wandered the living room with a yellow dust rag, touching the surfaces of things. Then she put on her coat and went out the door.

Leigh was at her desk when Gertrude stepped off the elevator and asked the receptionist to point her in the direction of her granddaughter.

"Gramma, what are you doing here?"

"I was in the area."

"What the hell were you doing in this area?"

"Okay. I was bored. Can't a person be bored?" Gertrude sat down just inside the cubicle's entrance. There wasn't room for much more than a desk, two chairs, and some bookshelves; and Gertrude felt claustrophobic. In contrast, she knew that the smallness of the room made Leigh feel safe.

"Of course." Leigh looked at her quizzically. "Are you sure...."

"I'm fine." Gertrude lowered the top half of a book's spine from the shelf near her seat. "Okay, most of my friends are dead. What am I supposed to do? Find new old people to hang around with?"

"No, of course you shouldn't."

"Just because I'm old, doesn't mean I'm automatically going to be friends with other old people. Handbook of Financial Accounting. Hmm. Looks thrilling."

"Yeah. You'd really like that one."

"I'm sure."

"So it wasn't a great bridge weekend I take it?"

"What? Oh that. No. Well, yes. It was fine. You know, I like bridge." Leigh looked at her skeptically. Leigh's boss passed by.

"I, ah, I need that report. The meeting's at five."

"Of course."

He nodded his head at Gertrude, a gesture that could have been mistaken for checking her out, if she'd been younger, and left.

"Well, you're obviously busy."

"He's got a meeting," Leigh whispered. "He needs me to do the legwork so he can present the information."

"I gathered something like that."

"I can meet for lunch though. A quick lunch."

"No, no. I'll let you be."

"Gramma." Leigh put her hand on Gertrude's forearm. "It's a great surprise. You've never dropped in like this." She leaned back, her ear to the air as if listening for sounds. "You're sure everything's alright?"

"Everything is fine. Couldn't be better. I'll leave you now." She unfolded herself from the chair, shook free the wrinkles in her blouse. "By the way. I notice you're a lot better at keeping things organized here than you are in your apartment."

Leigh laughed. "Yes. I am. I know. But I'm going to clean my place this weekend. You can come help me organize."

"Well, if you'd like. Though I'm sure at my age, I'd just be a nuisance."

"I'll pick you up." Gertrude smiled at her, leaned over to kiss her on the forehead, and left. Leigh watched her round the corner and pad down the carpeted hallway before turning back to her figures.

Leigh

Back in my hotel room, I pick up the phone and call Mark.

"Jesus, Leigh. Las Vegas? Why didn't you tell me you were going?"

"I know, I'm sorry. I thought maybe you could just be there, here, on the phone with me. My mother left me a box of things."

"It's late."

"I know it's late."

"It's later here," he says, as if I didn't know that.

"Mark, I'm sorry I didn't tell you I was coming out here."

"When did you make these plans?" He sounds so cold.

"Last minute. I just kind of decided and then went." His breathing sounds bullish.

"Leigh, we have to talk."

"Okay. Yes. We do have to talk." I wonder if I've been selfish, thinking that he should be there for me, on the phone, when I open the box. I hadn't thought too much about whether he'd be mad or not. I was Taking Some Space. I wonder if there's any way he could have found out about Jared, the surfer, and I marvel again at my recklessness, my sudden propensity for *doing*, as opposed to thinking. But I am not so different from before. After all, I was the girl who took off on a bus all alone at sixteen to find my mother. The doing somehow makes the thinking less suffocating.

Mark and I hang up, without saying I love you. I open the box.

* * *

Andy walked in sideways, one hand in a fist at his forehead and a grin on his face. "Guess what Mr. Taft has?"

Gramma and I had just returned from our afternoon in Boulder and two-day bus journey home, and Andy came downstairs from where he'd been staying with Mr. and Mrs. Taft. I'd taken a shower and was on the sofa in my pajamas. He sat next to me, and I grabbed him and hugged him around the neck. The place where his scalp met his neck smelled almost like the black coffee with sugar that Gramma drank every morning. He waited patiently until I'd let him go. "A *ham* radio!"

I leaned into the sofa and listened to him recount his days with the Tafts. Mr. Taft had introduced Andy to the monstrous device that took up a whole corner of the living room, and Andy had spoken to a man in Shanghai. "In China!" Andy yelled. "All the way in China. And then there was this guy in guess where? You'll never guess. It's an island. Guess."

"I dunno. Nantucket."

"Nope. Haw-a-ii! And it's like he's right there, talking to you even though, you know how far away he is in Hawaii? When it's day here, it's night there. That's how far."

Gramma sat down next to Andy. She had on her pink-flowered nightgown and bathrobe. She'd brought us three cups of tea and put them on the coffee table. I remember sitting there with the two of them, mug in my hands, and feeling warm. It seemed so simple that we could sit together in the evening, drinking tea, and I couldn't understand why Beverly was unable to give us this. Safety. Comfort. I remembered Beverly's stories about her mother, about how critical she'd been, how cold, and I had a hard time reconciling my gramma with the person my mother had told me about.

"So you didn't find Beverly anyhow," Andy said, after he'd finished telling us about Mr. Taft's ham radio. I shook my head.

"Oh well, that's life," he said. "I'm sure she's okay."

Gramma collected our empty mugs, and we went to bed. We had school the next morning.

* * *

Inside the box is a pair of shoes and I put them on the floor. They're Peter Pan boots, purple suede. I wonder—not for the first time—about her sanity. What would make her think I wanted her old shoes? There are photographs: some of me and Andy and Daniel, a baby picture of me on a pink blanket with white celestial fuzz around the oval border, and, more interestingly, there are some of her after she'd left, in bell bottoms, in a prairie skirt, her hair no longer bleached but her natural brown, and without makeup. In one she is standing in front of a cactus with a man I don't recognize.

I put the photos back in their envelope—developed at CVS, by the way, by someone working the same job that Andy does in Everett. It feels like there is some cosmic game going on here.

She also left me her wedding ring (what am I going to do with that? I'll jinx myself if I wear it), a couple of Barbie dolls (they must be for Andy), and a headband like the one I used to wear. At the bottom of the box is a letter, written on paper pulled from a spiral notebook. I unfold it. There is one letter addressed to Andy and one addressed to me.

Dear Leigh,

Hi honey. God I miss you. I know, I know, why don't I call then? Why don't I send for you? You have every right to ask me those questions. I just don't know exactly how to answer them.

I used to think I was so brave. But look at me. I'm so scared.

I've written you this letter, in my head, so many times. And now, here I am, with paper and a pen, and I can't seem to make the things I want to say come out.

Basically, you're not going to believe this, but I've stayed away because I thought you'd be better off without me. No, I don't want pity, and I'm not trying to make you feel bad for me or to make myself seem like a martyr.

Leigh, something happened to you, when you were young. And it's my fault. I know you're older now, and I know you're doing okay, and you're happy. And you even have a boyfriend. Your gramma has been keeping me up to date. I couldn't have lived without that, without knowing that you were okay.

You came home one day, Leigh, and something in you had changed. Maybe it wasn't the day. Maybe you'd been that way all along, but on that day, I knew, I don't know what was different or why, but I knew when I looked at you that I had failed.

I've been sober for five years. I got sober and it was like I'd been sleeping and having dreams but then when I got sober, it was like I realized that the dreams were real. They weren't dreams, really. They were nightmares. They were reality. And they were my own fault. I wanted to get back in touch with you, to salvage whatever we could salvage, but I couldn't bring myself to do it, and now I'm sick. I regret a lot of things, but leaving you and Andy with Ma was something that I'm glad I did. Not selfishly. At the time, it was selfish. I left you, and I just drank myself silly, honey. It was real stupid. But if I was going to be an alcoholic, then I'm glad I didn't drag you around with me.

Your gramma did a much better job than I could've done, considering my addiction. I'm grateful to her for that.

Anyway, my sweet girl, in the box, you found my shoes. I don't know why I want you to have them. They're not very used, and I guess I thought if you wanted to have something of me, then well, you might like to wear them sometimes. I think they're cool. There's my wedding ring. I just didn't know what else to do with it. Melt it down and make yourself something. And for Andy, I'm returning his Barbie dolls, the ones I took with me because I wanted to have something and also because they were always getting him into trouble. Ha. Remember that?

The headband I bought for you a long, long time ago, not long enough ago as I should've. But I've held onto it all this time. I hope you don't ever need it, but I was thinking of you, anyway….

Well, how do you like that? My hand hurts I've been writing so fast. I guess I got it all down. Mostly all I want to say is that I love you. And I'm sorry.

Love, Beverly (Mom) p.s. There's a picture of me with my second husband. He turned out to be an asshole, even more of an asshole than your father, but I was happy with him for a little while.

Tears slide down my cheeks and I pull off the brown flats I'd been wearing and slide my feet into Beverly's purple boots. They fit. I walk around the room a few times before taking them off and getting into bed.

* * *

It's a long trip from Boston to Las Vegas, especially if you're only going to stay a day and a half. I'm tired. Simon drops me at the airport, chattering the whole while, pointing out landmarks as we pass them. I promise I'll come visit him another time. He feels like a friend. A close friend. But I know that with time, our connection will flag. Our connection is Beverly, after all. And Beverly is dead. Besides, he lives so far away.

I push Beverly's box into the overhead compartment and slide across, into the window seat again, hopeful in that guilty sort of selfish way, when you pray that nobody sits down next to you. Thankful when nobody does, I put my coat on the seat next to me, stretch out, and fall asleep.

Mark picks me up. We are face to face, and I'm not sure if I should kiss him or not.

"Thanks for coming."

"It's late," he says, turning away. "What else would I have done?" I follow him to the car in silence.

He seems strange, like someone I've never met before. He breathes heavily through his nose as he puts the car into reverse. His car still smells like upholstery, even though he's had it for five years. On the floor is a three-sectioned holder with tissues, armor-all, and a yellow chamois rag. I pull out my wallet and try to give him two dollars for the tunnel, but he flicks open a compartment in between the seats and takes the money from there.

"I really don't know why you're so mad at me," I say finally.

"I'm not mad."

"You sure seem mad."

"I'm just defending myself." The yellow lights inside the tunnel make him look old. We emerge into the streetlights and headlights of Haymarket, and they flash across his face, reflect in his darting eyes as he hunts for the best lane.

"What are you defending yourself against? What's that mean?" I'm more curious than defensive, and I'm starting to feel guilty.

"You. I don't know what you're going to do next."

"That's ridiculous," I say, because he'd be right if he knew the truth, but since he doesn't, what he's saying doesn't make sense. "All I did was get a letter, saying my mother had died, and I took a couple of trips. You know, I guess, figuring stuff out. Thinking."

"And none of it, Leigh. None of it includes me."

"Yes, that's true," I say meekly. "And I'm sorry." He swerves into the passing lane. His eyes are wet. He's not crying, really, but there are definitely some tears there, and suddenly I'm overcome with the heaviness of what I've been doing to him, how I've been treating him, and overwhelmed by the fact that he loves me this much. I hadn't realized it.

"I've taken you for granted," I tell him and look out the window at barrels and pylons, their orange dulled by the dark of nighttime. He nods and keeps driving. When he parks the car in front of my place, I ask him if he'd like to come up for a little while. He points his nose at the digital clock in the dashboard and shakes his head.

"Okay. Fine. I'll call you tomorrow."

He turns on me then, a werewolf who's just woken up from a slumber to find the moon is full. "Don't call me, Leigh." He says my name with emphasis on the L, the ee trailing after like a tail. "Unless you are sure you want to be with me."

"But...."

"No. No more. Okay, listen. I'm not getting any younger, and to be honest, there are other people who'd be more than happy to be with me."

Jealousy, bolt of lightning that it is, fires this out of my mouth: "Oh, so you have someone lined up?"

Jealousy is supposed to work like hypochondria. You become afraid that you're mortally ill as a way of preventing yourself from becoming mortally ill. Jump to the worst-case scenario as a way of preventing it from happening. It doesn't happen that way for me tonight.

"I'm just saying that there are other options for me."

"Are you seeing ... someone ... already?"

"No." He's softer now. "No, I'm not seeing anybody. Look. I'm just telling you that there's no more time. I'm not waiting anymore. If you're going to be normal." Normal. I hate when he plants his flag on Terra Normal. "To get married, like what the plan was. That *was* the plan. Then fine. Call me tomorrow. But no more trips, no more not returning phone calls. No more doubt."

"So who is she?"

He shakes his head, smiling tensely. "It doesn't matter. There isn't anything happening. I'm just telling you that I'm not going to wait. So?"

I stare out the windshield. The park at the edge of the University campus is under construction, boarded off by plywood planks. Seems these days like everything in the greater Boston area is under construction. When I look at him, it is with sadness. He returns my look with contempt.

"I'll call you. We can finish this tomorrow. Thanks for the lift." And I take my bag from the back seat and slide out. He drives away slowly as I turn the key in the front door.

Upstairs Buster greets me by rubbing against my shins and purring madly. I pour Friskies into his bowl. Thankfully my brain takes a break for the rest of the night and I am able to fall into a deep sleep.

Walnut Acres

The light eclipses the doctor's face as it moves from one of Gertrude's eyes to the other. She sees Shannon looking over the doctor's shoulder and hears them speaking about her, as if she can't hear them. As if she were already dead. But she's not dead. Not yet. She can feel the sheets, the prod of the doctor's fingers and tools. "We can run some more tests, but. It's best to keep her comfortable."

When the doctor leaves, Shannon makes light of things. "Missus Littlefield. You're just being stubborn. Just like usual." And she arranges the pillows around Gertrude's head, tucks the blankets under her legs. Gertrude falls asleep. Again.

When she wakes, she feels numb. Leigh is looking into her drawn face, holding her soft white hand, running her finger along the pearl blue veins that rise from the surface.

The ridges in Gertrude's fingernails are like a tree's trunk, the way it wears its age, the years countable. Gertrude can feel Leigh's hand on hers, the coarse sheet lying over her legs, the rising and falling of her chest as she breathes, the rims of the plastic-framed glasses that Leigh has perched on her face, mimicking who she used to be. From behind thick lenses, she follows the figures moving around the room.

Leigh rests her head on her grandmother's hand. "I miss you Gramma. I miss talking to you." Gertrude's eyes are filmy, the lids pink. They blink a few times and close gently.

"Well, how is she?" Jessie enters the room and begins bustling about the periphery, wiping surfaces after spraying them with orange fluid and emptying the trash: medical detritus, gauze, sterile wrappers; wadded up tissues like mangled and drunken origami birds because Leigh cries, her back to her grandmother, quietly, if there's no one around.

"I guess she's okay," Leigh says. "It's hard to tell."

Jessie moves in to take Gertrude's pulse. She slides her arm down behind the old woman's back and shifts her over. The movement sends a streak of pain down Gertrude's right arm; her eyes go wide for a moment, but no one notices. Leigh leans back in the vinyl armchair, crosses and then re-crosses her legs.

"Still no movement or speech?" Jessie asks, looking at Gertrude but speaking to Leigh.

"No," Leigh says. "Nothing."

"You're gonna be just fine," she says to Gertrude, and puts the heel of her hand on her forehead. "I don't think there's a fever, but I'll take your temperature anyway. That okay?" Gertrude's eyes follow her. She knows Jessie is just looking for ways to make herself useful.

Outside in the hallway, Helio sweeps dirt into a dustpan attached to the end of a long handle. He pokes his head in the doorway.

"Hey there, Missus Littlefield. How we feeling today?"

"She's okay," says Jessie. "Just doesn't want to talk right now. That right?"

"How're you doin'?" he asks Jessie.

"I'm fine." She slides a plastic cover over the end of the thermometer and opens Gertrude's mouth by pushing down on her chin.

Helio comes into the room. Gertrude's eyes watch him approach. He puts his face near hers and smiles. Leigh is behind him as he lowers his face to the level of her grandmother's. He whispers, "How are you, my friend?" He takes her hand and kisses it, and then leaves.

Jessie shakes down the thermometer, writes something on a clipboard. "That's Helio," Jessie says to Leigh, as if it explains anything. "He's a big flirt, that's what he is, isn't he Missus Littlefield?" She puts the clipboard back into its holder on the wall.

Andy arrives, and Jessie squeezes past him in the doorway.

"How's Gramma?"

"Well, like I said, she's been immobile like this, no speech, no movement." Leigh sits on the wide windowsill. Cool air comes out of the vent.

"Yeah, but why? Do they know why?"

"They still don't know."

Andy is wearing his look of concentration, his brow muddled into the center of his forehead. Now that he's getting older, his frowning has left a deep crease that dips down to the bridge of his nose. He stands in the middle of the room, his fingers tapping against his thighs. "She can hear you," Leigh tells him. "Go talk to her." Andy approaches the bed slowly. He is still furrowed, looking at Gertrude's face, her tiny shriveled body, her uncombed white hair, dry and wispy; she looks nothing like the grandmother who used to hoist him onto her lap, even though he weighed well over a hundred and thirty pounds at nine years old.

"Hi Gramma." He sits in the chair; the metal legs whine under his weight. He pulls the fingers of one hand back with the other hand until the palms at the knuckles are stretched white and glossy, and then pulls the other, and then the other, back and forth, again and again. Leigh picks up a magazine from Gertrude's bedside table.

"How are you?" Andy says to his grandmother. "Oh yeah, you can't talk. I guess you're fine. I hope you're fine." They sit in silence, Andy pulling his fingers. Gertrude closes her eyes.

"How's work?" Leigh says to Andy, filling silence.

"Good. We're getting a new manager."

"You wouldn't think about applying to be a manager yourself, would you?"

"No way," he says. "No way. You couldn't pay me to do that."

"Well, they would pay you. Anyway, I know you could do it." She turns to Gertrude. "He could be the manager, couldn't he, Gramma? See, Gramma thinks you can do it, too. You're an underachiever."

"I like doing the photos. I get to see them all you know, all the pictures that everybody takes. And it's a big responsibility. You know I had to go to that conference."

"You told me."

"Yeah, well if I see anything bad ... you know ... then I have to report it."

"Okay, okay. Do the photos. As long as you like it."

"I like it." Andy stares past Gertrude's head and jiggles his leg. Leigh looks at the magazine on her lap.

"So you never told me about your trip," Andy says to Leigh, as if she hasn't just gotten back the night before. As if she'd gone to Las Vegas months ago.

"I met a friend of Beverly's," Leigh tells him. "A nice man. I have a letter for you. From her." She rustles through her purse and takes out the folded paper.

"What's it say?" He says, reaching for it.

"I don't know, I didn't read it."

"No?"

"Of course not. She wrote one to me. I read that one." Andy partially unfolds the paper and then re-creases it, flicks it with his fingernail and finally hoists the bottom of his windbreaker up and slides it into the pocket of his jeans. Leigh plunges her hand back into the depths of her handbag.

"Here. This is for you too." She offers him one of the Barbie dolls and roots around for other.

"Aw, Leigh. I don't want that."

"Okay. Okay. I'll keep it." She puts the doll and her sister back into the darkness of her bag.

"You wanna watch TV? You think Gramma wants to watch TV?"

"I doubt it."

"You wanna watch some?"

"I don't care. Go ahead and turn it on."

Andy turns on the TV. It is a documentary: a tiger gaining on an antelope. "Look, Leigh, she likes it," he says, pointing to Gertrude. "National Geographic channel." Gertrude is looking at the TV. Her eyes roll slowly in Andy's direction. His eyes are the exact same color as Clive's; brownish green; like the seaweed that washes up on the beach in Lynn, the kind with the bubbles of air in each strand, bubbles that look like they should make a popping noise when you burst them, but instead just collapse quietly. Andy bites the cuticle of his middle finger, and they both turn back to the TV. The antelope succumbs. Leigh's fingers dance distractedly on the pages of her magazine.

* * *

Helio is clinking around under the sink when Gertrude wakes up next. Leigh and Andy are gone.

"Hey there," Jessie pokes her head in the doorway.

"Hey."

"Well?"

"Well what?"

"Well. Well, how are you?"

"Fine." Helio talks to Jessie over his shoulder.

"Oh. Good. You're supposed to ask me now. How are you, Jessie? I'm fine. Oh, that's good. I'm glad to hear that."

"Sorry," he says, sitting back cross-legged and swiveling to face her. "Sorry. How are you?"

"I'm fine too," she says tersely and leaves. Helio sighs and looks at Gertrude, whose eyes are open.

"I didn't know you were awake." She blinks several times.

Gertrude looks at her hand where it lies at the edge of the mattress. Finally, two of her fingers raise themselves like animals looking up from a trough. She breathes slowly, her chest rattles.

"What is it?" Helio puts his ear close to her face.

Her eyes flick around. Tears pool in their bottom lids.

Gertrude knows that if your life is short, like a short section of wallpaper, then it doesn't matter so much if it's a tiny bit crooked. When your life stretches on, however, like a tall room, and you start at the tiniest angle, the imbalance—initially unnoticeable—becomes more pronounced. And you stray further and further, making the wrong decisions, time after time. And then your crookedness becomes more apparent and you overlap some strips of wallpaper and pull too far from others. Things begin to show, in your posture, in your face.

She wants to ask Helio how he sees her but she knows. She knows, whatever mistakes she made, she did her best. He sits on the chair and takes her hand in his. Her hand is soft and fragile, and his are like two rowboats, cupped around it. Then he is Clive, and he puts her hand back down on the mattress and climbs onto the bed and lies down next to her. His breathing calms her the way a washing machine can calm an infant. "I've missed you, Gertie." He envelops her. "How I've missed you."

April 1974

With a flourish, Clive placed his pipe-holder ashtray on the table between the two chairs in the living room. Gertrude commented on the state of the chairs: that he'd have to do a lot of sitting in his in order to catch up. Hers was worn from reading and television watching, while his had been empty for twenty years. They held hands, and in the evening Gertrude cooked a meal, and the next morning Clive whistled contentedly as he worked on the dripping tap in the bathtub.

It wasn't, of course, always rosy. They had gotten used to having things a certain way, each of them alone over the past two decades becoming comfortable that way, and suddenly now they were meant to share themselves again. Gertrude got grumpy when Clive stippled the sink with tiny shaved hairs, left the toilet seat up. Clive got annoyed when Gertrude asked him questions while he was trying to read. He left wet towels on the bed and wiped his face with the dish-drying cloth. She forgot to shut off lights and ran the water while she brushed her teeth. "You know, you just wasted about a gallon of water," Clive would say. She'd nod but forget the next morning, and he would lie in bed listening to the water rush out of the faucet and straight down the drain while Gertrude examined her face in the mirror, her mouth filled with toothpaste foam.

But they could see out. That was the difference. Twenty years earlier a mood would overtake Clive, Gertrude would become insecure, which would make him even more annoyed, worsening his mood and so on until it seemed impossible that they would ever inhabit the easy relationship that they had had when they first got married. Now, after all the years that had passed, when one of his moods struck, she'd leave the house and go window shopping or visit with a friend. And he'd get beyond it more quickly, remembering with his wife gone for the afternoon that he missed her and wanted her back, and seeing himself much more clearly than he ever could when they were younger. She'd arrange bridge games with Mr. and Mrs. Taft, set up the card table in the living room. They'd leave the news on while they played. The house felt full.

*　*　*

But while Gertrude and Clive were playing house, their daughter's life was disintegrating. Daniel was tired of his wife's unpredictable fits of rage. She was drinking way too much, openly much of time, but hiding it as well. Daniel, who'd been good-natured about his sudden wife and child, the unexpected marriage, was happy to have shocked and disappointed his overbearing parents and glad again when they handed him the money to buy a rundown house. But the baby came to mean little more to him than an extension of the wife whose constant demands and eventual utter disappointment made him feel at first small and inadequate and later exasperated, indifferent. Crying in the bassinet, adding to the chaos of misunderstood fury and heartfelt antagonism.

There were plenty of other women, rich women, Mercedes owners who would come from various distances to his uncle's garage, and he started to entertain the idea that perhaps there would be a way out. Though he didn't act on any of his flirtations at first, he enjoyed knowing he was sexy. Young with grease on his hands and vital in some way he was not at home—these women (there were a number of them) would gaze and smile and one even took his hand and said *Meet me later why don't you?* Beverly could feel him growing distant, and her jealousy drove him yet further away, and in turn she started to drink even more.

She wandered into town one day, aiming Leigh in her baby carriage toward the garage, and Daniel, when he saw her coming, wiped the grease from his hands with a dirty pink rag and shook his dismal head. She'd bleached her naturally chestnut hair, and it was a bad match for her skin tone, which took on a greenish hue under the streaky yellow and he found her increasingly ugly to look at. Though she wasn't ugly, not really. But Daniel was becoming incapable of generosity in his assessment of her.

"Thought we could go for lunch," Beverly said in a tone that implied some underlying sarcasm and Daniel picked up that he was being accused of saying no even before he'd said no.

"Fine. Sure," he replied, and her face registered surprise and something close to happiness. "Let me wash up." He went to the sink in the back of the garage after cracking the door and saying something to his uncle in the office. He scrubbed his hands and dried them on a blue industrial paper towel.

"She wouldn't take a nap."

"It's a nice day."

"Yeah, so I thought, well. Why not, and come down. See if you could get off for a bit."

"She's asleep now."

"Like a baby," and they both laughed grudgingly, not hearty or comfortable.

"Well. We go to Dill's?" And Beverly said sure, and this was before Delilah came on the scene; before Delilah had even graduated high school in fact, and they parked Leigh in the corner by the bar and slid into a booth. Beverly ordered a bloody Mary and Daniel had a beer, and after the first half a drink they were both a little more relaxed. Beverly ordered a second. The food had just been placed in front of them and she finished the second drink halfway through the meal and ordered a third, and Daniel didn't understand alcoholism, the personality change that was a chemical reaction between her body and alcohol, but blamed it entirely on her, and the demon that lived inside her. Which was a reasonable assumption, but if she'd controlled the drinking, the demon would've followed. How could he know that? And when it was him that she attacked, calling him a momma's boy and a rich kid and saying how he wouldn't have anything if it weren't for his parents? He got up, threw some crumpled bills onto the table, and walked out.

He left Beverly to her misery, but he walked right past his daughter as well.

Leigh soon woke up and Beverly fed her a bottle and pushed her home angrily.

Things weren't always that bad between them, but their fights were unpredictable. Any random thing could light the fuse under Beverly, and she'd suddenly be filled with resentment. Other times, she seemed content, taking care of Leigh, making dinner for Daniel. And he'd come home and almost be happy as well.

It should be said that not all of their problems were the result of Beverly's alcoholism. Daniel could also be cruel, in the way of a boy from a well-off family who rejects the path suggested (strongly) by his parents, but still harbors the suspicion that he could have done better for himself. The meanness manifested when he was going to be late but wouldn't call. Or when he'd sit on the armchair with his paper and not speak a word for the entire evening—until Beverly would become enraged and snatch the paper away, and then he'd go to bed, wishing there were a spare room, and instead perform a gravitational miracle by sleeping on the precipice of their mattress with half of his body not even touching it. He didn't generally say nasty things, and he wouldn't get violent, but he could clam up and shut down better than a turtle. And that was how he managed to win most of their fights, with Beverly in a heap on the floor, begging him to please speak to her and apologizing for everything she'd done and then some. And they'd make up—which was what they were doing when Andy was conceived—and they'd be okay for maybe a week or two or three until something, as likely boredom as anything else, would cause Beverly to make some demand, some comment, and Daniel would become silently derisive, and so forth, until all hell would break loose and Daniel would shut down and work late.

* * *

Gertrude and Clive had a good year and a half. Even before Clive got sick, Gertrude would occasionally be struck by the horrible fact that they were growing older, that this couldn't last forever. When his stomach pains became more frequent, Gertrude urged him to go to the doctor. He put it off. "It's gas," he'd say, pushing his fingers sideways into his solar plexus. By the time he finally went to the doctor, and the diagnosis made its way home through a network of specialists, it was too advanced, and there was nothing they could do. It wasn't long before they moved a bed into the living room and kept the TV going all day long, to give Clive a sense of movement and color and the illusion that he was still a part of the world.

Estelle spent some time with them, and Gertrude was grateful for it, even though her sister's belief in spirits and amorphous vision of an afterlife was pure silliness to Gertrude's ears.

Clive, for a lifetime of skepticism, was willing to entertain Estelle's crackpot spirituality. Gertrude came in one afternoon, pulling her rolling shopping tote, to find Estelle and Clive chanting together. Her sister had a scarf wrapped around her head and sat cross-legged by Clive's feet. They both had their eyes closed and their voices together, chanting *om shanti shanti om*, was both moving and ridiculous. Estelle's voice nasal and crackly from her years as a smoker and Clive's face sunken like someone had wrapped it in Saran wrap and pulled. His mouth moved. His lips had become thin from the illness, and Gertrude wondered as she watched them open and close, propelled by the bones in his jaw, what lips were made of—that they could lose their substance as Clive's had. She pulled the tote through the living room and into the kitchen and as their voices died down and the groceries were put away she came in to find Estelle holding both of Clive's hands and staring into his eyes. Gertrude cleared her throat, and Estelle loosened her grip and leaned back, beatific.

* * *

"What does it do for you?" Gertrude asked her husband later that night. She was lying alongside him on the narrow bed, and the television was flickering, the only light in the house.

Clive chuckled weakly to the ceiling. "It makes her happy. I don't know." His paleness was startling, especially in the television glow, but Gertrude forced herself not to look away.

"But you don't believe it."

His voice clattered in his throat. "Does it matter?"

"Are you scared?" Gertrude whispered.

"Not really. It hurts, Gertie."

"I know. I'm sorry." She stayed as still as possible, and Clive's eyelids fell up and down slowly before settling over his eyes. She watched the TV over his feet where they stuck up under the blanket. The sound was low, but she could make out the voices. They stayed that way until the program ended and the screen was shrouded in static. She turned it off before going to her bed.

* * *

A year after Clive died, Estelle collapsed at the pier and was dead before the ambulance had arrived at the hospital. It turned out she had a heart anomaly that was asymptomatic, that could have caused her to die suddenly at any moment.

While alcohol propelled Beverly further and further into the delusion that it was saving her by easing the pain, Gertrude was mourning her husband and then her sister. Weeks after they buried Estelle, Gertrude called Beverly.

"I thought you and Daniel and the kids might like to come up and visit. Christmas maybe."

"I dunno, Ma. I'm not feeling in the mood for being social."

"Well, it's good for you to get out."

"I guess. I'm in a slump. You know. I just. I'm all alone."

"Fine. You're alone. I'm alone, why not spend some time together?"

"Yeah. The kids. They're not so easy."

"Beverly, you have your children."

"Dammit, don't lecture me. It's not easy. You only had one. Two's different. And the baby. They say he's not right. He should be walking. He's not walking. I can't handle it. And my husband, he's not there for me. You don't know what it's like." Gertrude could hear her daughter lighting a cigarette. "You had a good husband that you dumped. Me, I got a bad husband. Doesn't care."

"I didn't call to compare husbands," Gertrude said. "Do you want to come up or don't you?"

"Naw. You got your life, Ma. You never cared so much anyway did you?"

"Of course I did," she said quietly, wounded. "Call me if you change your mind."

Beverly didn't change her mind.

The Funeral

Walnut Acres Municipal Nursing Home handles many of the details, which Leigh is thankful for. Gertrude had already paid for her own funeral, and all Leigh had to do was contact friends and family. The room isn't full, but it's far from empty. Daniel sits several rows from the back with Delilah, who looks uncomfortable, her mouth stiff and her jaw tense, though she produces a forced smile and shrugs her shoulders slightly whenever she catches anyone's eye. Daniel wears a blazer and khaki pants. The blazer has a small duck embroidered on the pocket. He pulls a pair of glasses from his pocket to read the folio he'd been handed by the funeral-home director. Delilah stares at the casket.

The priest is young; Gertrude had known him only slightly, as she hadn't been a regular churchgoer. Leigh sits with Andy, and when Mark sits on her other side, she squeezes his knee and offers him a thankful smile.

Joshua Cleggan is here with his daughter, a heavy woman in a lavender skirt and matching jacket, and next to her is Helio. (Jessie told him that she can't take time off every time an old person passes, but Helio has the day off anyway.) Most of the old people are friends she'd made later in life, but some of her old friends' children are here. Leigh is surprised at the number of people she doesn't recognize and is reminded that her gramma had been more than just her gramma; she'd been an entire life.

When the time comes, Leigh unfolds her notes and stands up. There is rustling and murmuring. The room is like a dandelion gone to seed that the wind has jiggled. Low coughs break away and float toward the ceiling. The front of the room gives Leigh a sense of entitlement that almost makes her unafraid and the faces are kind, looking up at her expectantly. *Poor girl*, some of them must be thinking, those who have known her since she arrived at her gramma's house an obviously troubled waif.

In middle school, even in Lynn, where there were plenty of dysfunctional kids from broken families (families were breaking all over America, but in the cities, you didn't have to hide it quite so vigorously), her bald patches set her apart from the other kids. Some of the people who had known her then—shy and awkward and sad—are here now, and Leigh knows they are marveling at her pearl earrings, her tailored black suit, and at the hair that hangs down her back like a horse's tail, tied at the nape of her neck with a black ribbon.

She smiles, triumphant, proud of herself and her gramma.

But there is always the heart of her younger self, cowering there in the machete grass of the sand dune, with Dr. Silvieri. She can see herself, with him, walking the beach, his velour tracksuit top unzipped to the level of his sternum and her in an Indian skirt and one of the flannel shirts that Daniel had left behind and the black men's combat boots that she'd found at the flea, but she banishes the memory—something at which she has years of practice—and begins to speak.

"My gramma saved my life." She looks at Daniel. Delilah is made of cardboard, but Leigh thinks she sees remorse in Daniel's face, or perhaps just sympathy. "I remember," she says, forcing herself to go on, though her body is shaky and tense and she feels as though she might faint. "This one time. When my gramma was teaching me to drive. She had only learned a few years earlier herself. I remember I was in the driver's seat and she was next to me, and ... she ... well. She was an old woman already, even then." Leigh's mind focuses on the memory she is relating, and suddenly speaking becomes much easier. "But she wasn't old, in so many ways... I drove down the wrong way. Just crossed the double yellow lines and went on the wrong side. Now there wasn't anyone coming, but on the right was a big puddle, and I wanted to miss it. And I remember her so clearly. Saying, 'Honey, if it suits you to drive on the other side, so long as nobody's in danger, then just do it. Always use your own instinct, your own brain, and don't be afraid that someone knows better than you do just because they wrote the rules.'"

When Leigh looks up, she sees Simon Walsh sitting in the back. He winks and gives her a thumbs-up.

"Daring advice. But it was good advice." She goes on to describe Gertrude as someone who was courageous and who strove to do what was right; she was someone who could admit when she was wrong, a quality that is not as common as you might think. Leigh's voice trembles, and she feels light as she finishes talking, as though she's just emerged from an illness and can finally do the things that healthy people take for granted.

When she returns to her seat, she leans into Andy, and he puts a hand on her shoulder and taps it like it is an old dog's head.

* * *

After the service, there are coffee and pastries and rolls stuffed with deli meats. Leigh finds Simon.

"What are you doing here? You didn't say you were going to come. You didn't have to come."

"I didn't want to say anything until I knew I could swing it. Last minute deal." He is wearing a corduroy blazer and is freshly-shaven. He's gotten a haircut too, which makes Leigh feel uncertain of his identity. She's not sure why she still, childishly, feels thrown off when people change their appearances. Like when Daniel cut off his long hair. She is ashamed at how uncomfortable she feels after they'd been so close in Las Vegas. Perhaps it's because he knows too much about her.

"I could've picked you up at the airport...."

"Not at all. I wouldn't have you do that. You have enough to do. How are you? Okay?"

Leigh nods. "Fine. I'm fine. I really am. Surprisingly."

"Could hit you later."

"Yes, it could. But I'll worry about that when it happens." Leigh can see her brother speaking with Mark. She can't hear their conversation, but she can tell that it is superficial from their expressions and the distance between them. "Do you want to meet my brother?" she asks. "How long are you staying?"

"Oh, I have a friend I'd like to visit," he says quickly as they make their way to where Andy and Mark are eating sandwiches.

"Well, there's room on my couch, if you want.... This is Andy. Andy, this is Simon, a friend of Beverly's, you know, that I told you about."

"It's nice to meet you," Andy says, pumping Simon's hand. Simon laughs and shakes his hand out after Andy has released his grip.

"Your mother told me about your superhuman strengths."

"Sorry," Andy laughs. "Sorry."

"You know, it's nice you came," Leigh says to Simon. "Because you're the only person who was at both of their funerals." For a moment she feels envious, as though he's taken something from her, played a role that she should have played, but then she is also grateful for his presence. "It pulls them back together somehow." Simon is nodding in the way of someone with an exceptional instinct for letting others speak. But Leigh is done.

"I've been wanting to come out to the East Coast anyway."

"Do you have some other plans?"

"Several people to visit. You were at the top of the list though." Leigh relaxes as he tells her and Andy about a family friend from Australia whom he hasn't seen in years but has kept in touch with, a former boss who now works for the Boston Housing Authority, and a woman he's known since they were teenagers following the Grateful Dead.

"You sure have a lot of friends."

"The world's a big place. Lotta people in it," he says. "There are a few I should call, but I won't. If you can't spend quality time with a person, what's the point? Don't you think?" Leigh and Andy both nod.

Mark has moved away, ostensibly to get a pastry, and Leigh can feel him watching her. She excuses herself, leaving Andy and Simon, and makes her way over to him.

"Did I do okay?" she asks. "You know. Speaking. Public speaking isn't my strongest suit."

"I thought it would be longer," he says.

"Well, it was going to be longer. I had a lot to say. In fact, I had more written down, but it was enough. You know the way my voice always used to do that scratchy shaky thing whenever I had to talk at a meeting."

"It was fine. Just fine," he says.

They stand together in silence until Mark blurts out, "Listen. I'm um, I'm sorry. I haven't been you know, supportive."

"You're here," she says.

He leans over and kisses her on the cheek. "You know you should have asked me, to help you prepare, the eulogy. I could help you."

"That's okay."

"You're going to be fine, Leeby." He puts his palm on the side of her head.

"Of course I'm going to be fine," she snaps and moves her head away from his hand. "I'm sorry. I'm ... sorry."

"What is it?" he says. "What is it that you're so mad at? You're projecting, you know." His voice lowers to a whisper, and he points his nose in Daniel's direction. "It's him you're really mad at. You need to learn to recognize that."

And it's one of those moments of startling clarity because he's right. Leigh is beginning to feel faint.

"My grandmother just died."

"I know. I'm sorry. First your mother,"

"I guess you're right about my father...."

Mark smiles, part sympathetic, part I-told-you-so.

"Anyway, who's that guy?" Leigh is a little disappointed that their conversation is turning away from something real, as uncomfortable as it was. They spend so much time on bland details.

"That's a friend of Beverly's." Leigh turns to look at Simon and Andy deep in conversation. "He's HIV positive," she says and immediately regrets having said it.

"It was nice that he came."

Leigh is thrown off by how uncritical he is. She had expected judgment and she realizes she must have been hoping for judgment, or she wouldn't have said it. She had been hoping to shock, for whatever reason.

"Come meet him," she says and leads him across the room.

* * *

She remembers the first time Mark met her brother. The three of them had gone for a meal at a nice restaurant, Mark's idea. He'd wanted to make a good impression of course, and it had charmed Leigh. But Andy isn't great company when he's uncomfortable. When they arrived at the restaurant, they had to wait in the bar. Leigh and Mark ordered cocktails, and Andy ordered a coke. Mark called for a Bailey's Irish Cream and handed the short, heavy glass to Andy, saying, "Try this, Andy man. You gotta loosen up and have a drink." At first, Andy enjoyed the attention, and sipped at the drink and laughed. But his humor had worn thin quickly as the bar became more and more crowded and Andy kept getting bumped into by people who weren't always friendly. He began weaving his fingers and dropped his drink on the floor. Leigh told him it was okay, but he was getting more and more nervous; the hostess looked angry as she mopped up the sticky liquid. Finally, they were led to a table in the center of the room. Andy didn't know what to order, and the waitress seemed impatient, even though, Leigh thought, with entrees upwards of 25 dollars, she ought to have been a bit more gracious. A minimum-wage earner, Andy got even more uncomfortable about the prices and tried to order just an appetizer. Mark ordered him lobster. Leigh, who had started out the evening proud of Mark and his largesse, had begun to feel sorry about the whole ordeal and to wish they'd gotten Chinese take-out and rented a movie.

* * *

"So what do you do in Las Vegas?" Mark is asking Simon, and Leigh is embarrassed by the triteness of the question, though she understands that conversation needs to be made. Simon, who has mayonnaise on his chin, tells Mark—in the rapid-fire way he has of speaking—about his job, about his former addiction, about his friendship with Beverly. Mark seems shallow, commonplace next to Simon's survivor-humor. Simon is talking about his job; he works with kids who are at-risk, helps to get them into schools and away from dangerous neighborhoods, negotiates for their parents, and occasionally has to recommend that they be removed from their homes, which is hard, but he only does it if it's terribly clear that it needs to be done....

He wipes the mayonnaise from his chin, and even though it is still lodged between the knuckles of his hand, she feels relieved. But Simon wouldn't have been embarrassed if she'd pointed it out to him, she realizes, and suddenly the mayonnaise on Simon's knuckle encapsulates everything that is wrong with Mark. Leigh is for a moment painfully aware that if she is going to spend her life with anyone, she wants that person to be someone who doesn't mind being in public with mayonnaise on his chin.

"Did you ever meet Gertrude?" Mark brings the conversation back to the reason they're here. Simon nods.

"Once. She came to visit Beverly, and I met her then. Great woman. Spirited. It's funny to meet your friend's parent, don't you think? Especially a mother of a woman or a father of a son? Isn't it? You know, you can see the factory where the product was produced. Right?"

To Leigh's surprise, Andy answers him first. "Yeah," he says. "I know what you mean. It's like seeing where someone comes from."

"Yeah man," Simon nods, encouraging Andy to go on.

"Well, I have this friend, Kevin, he used to love Leigh, but anyway she already had a boyfriend. Well, Kevin's my best friend, and I met his dad, and they were just alike."

Leigh is watching her brother affectionately.

"I disagree," Mark says suddenly, in the tone he uses for meetings at work. "I never met Leigh's mother, but I have met her father, and I don't see much of him in either Leigh or Mark." Leigh's smile has tightened.

"I can see her mother in her," Simon says. "Just the good parts ... of which there were many."

"Not from what I've heard," Mark says, and Leigh cringes at his callousness.

"But I haven't met her father." Simon goes on.

"You haven't introduced them?" Mark says to Leigh. He scans the room and sees Daniel and Delilah standing together, sipping coffee from paper cups. "He's over there."

Daniel sees Mark pointing at him and comes over, Delilah in his wake. Mark is too comfortable, magnanimous, which annoys Leigh.

"This is a friend of Beverly's," Leigh says. "Daniel, Delilah, this is Simon Walsh, who came all the way from Las Vegas."

Delilah seems somewhat more at ease than earlier. She shakes Simon's hand and smiles warmly, then turns to Mark, and gushes about how she hasn't seen him in such a long time, and how they must all get together soon. "Family," she says, "is so important, isn't it?" Leigh catches Andy's eye for a split second, and a tiny smirk passes between them.

"It is," Mark says without the slightest irony, "It's fundamental." He turns to Daniel. "How's business? Keeping busy?"

"I don't go in much anymore," Daniel says, "but the garage is still busy. Cars will always break, and even if they don't, they need to be tuned up. Especially the newer ones, with all the automatic features. I'm not worried about it slowing down anytime soon."

"Leigh tells me you've been doing more metalwork?"

Daniel nods and Leigh can see that his enthusiasm, even though he doesn't say much, is similar to Simon's when he talks about his work.

Sometimes she can forgive Daniel and sometimes she can't. Even though it may be true that a lot of her anger is because of him, her disappointment and sadness are sporadic, usually according to when it serves her interest to feel like a victim. She's proud of him at this moment, listening to him talk about something he loves to do. He's become an artist, Leigh realizes, and she's happy for him.

While Daniel and Mark are talking, Delilah leans toward Leigh and asks about Helio, who is eating sandwiches and talking to Joshua Cleggan's daughter.

"He's from the nursing home."

"Well isn't that nice of him to come," Delilah says. "You're sure he's not just here for the free food?"

"No, I saw him with my gramma. And he really liked her."

"I was only kidding, of course."

Delilah melts into Daniel's arm, looks at her watch, draws his attention to it until he says, "Yes, we'd better get going."

Leigh is suddenly dying for a drink, and wishes she'd insisted on there being wine and beer served at the reception, even though it's still only noon.

People clear out quickly then, and Leigh, Andy, Simon, and Mark go to a bar. It is Leigh's suggestion, and the three men bring her to a nearby café, where Leigh orders whiskey, Mark has a beer, Andy has a coke, and Simon drinks coffee.

"I'm channeling my mother," Leigh jokes as she orders a second and then a third whiskey. Simon continues to regale them with stories of Las Vegas and Mark laughs too loudly and throws back beer, his Adam's apple bobbing. Soon Andy has had enough and wants to be back home, in his house, with his friends. Leigh hugs him sloppily and becomes slightly morose after he's gone because he'd seemed distant—something she's not used to, but of course, being drunk, she doesn't put it together and he doesn't realize either that her drunkenness is what's disturbing him, poking at all kinds of emotional substrata he'd rather leave dormant, and to comfort herself, she orders another drink.

* * *

"God I'm an idiot. Oh god. Sorry. I really am." Leigh sits back onto the floor. "Stupid, get this drunk." Simon is crouched next to her. He hands her a glass of water, and she wipes her mouth with a wad of toilet paper. She's not sure how she got home. "I'm no different. From her."

"You're very different."

"Why don't I know it?" She leans against the tub, toilet paper pressed to her nose.

"Well you never saw her after she cleaned herself up." Simon slides over next to her, takes the glass of water she hands him and holds it on top of his crossed thighs.

"I need to clean myself up."

"You're different. It's a one-off. You'll feel so terrible you won't do it again for a long, long time. That's the difference."

"I had sex with a stranger, you know," she says, turning her splotchy face toward him behind the clump of toilet paper, like a geisha being coy behind her fan. "Just a couple of weeks ago. I was in a sand dune. Fucking a stranger. Like some animal." She purses her lips together, cries.

"That was stupid," Simon offers matter-of-factly.

"I know," she laughs.

"I've seen a lot worse than you, you know. Just so you know."

"I don't know how that's supposed to make me feel." She wipes at her face, leaving a streak of makeup and teary mucus. "God I'm disgusting."

Simon has stood up and is soaking a washcloth under the tap. Leigh takes it and lays it over her face. Her nose and lips and chin push little hills in the wet fabric, and she sucks some water from it into her mouth. Simon lays his hand on her face and wipes the cloth back from her cheeks to her hair. Leigh enjoys the clean, tight feel of the dampness drying on her skin.

"Where's Mark?" she says finally, nearly sober now after having thrown up. Simon nods his head toward the living room.

"He didn't hear," Leigh begins in a panic.

"No, no," he says quickly, and then, more thoughtfully, "I don't think so."

She raises an eyebrow at him. He shakes his head. "No. He didn't. He was watching TV when I came in to make sure you weren't drowning."

"Good. I guess," she says, and then, "Andy went home early."

"He's a nice man, your brother." Simon tosses the wet washcloth into the sink. "You've done a good job with him, you know."

Leigh pulls her knees into her chest and hugs them. "I didn't do anything. He's always been good."

"You've taken care of him," Simon says. "Your mother told me that too." He scratches beneath his eye with the back of his finger. "It seems to me that you've been taking care of people for a long time—your brother, your grandmother."

"No. Family's not like that. We've taken care of each other." She puts her head onto her knees for a long while, and when she lifts it again, says, "I'm afraid. I don't know what I might be capable of." Simon seems to make himself physically smaller as he leaves room for Leigh to say what she needs to say.

"Hey," comes Mark's voice from the other side of the door, interrupting. "You okay?" He opens it wide enough to put his head through. "She okay?" he says to Simon, who nods. "I'm gonna head off, Leeby. Okay?"

"Sorry," she says. "Sorry I'm such a mess."

"Don't worry about it." He is holding the remote control, and he swings it into the bathroom to show it to her. "I'm going to leave this on top of the TV, where you can find it." It's a lame attempt at a joke, and nobody laughs, except Mark. "She's such a slob, Simon. You can never even find the remote."

Simon stands up, takes the remote control and offers Mark a handshake. "It was nice to meet you."

"Yeah, you too." Mark leans over and kisses the top of Leigh's head. "You should get yourself cleaned up," he says quietly. She nods tightly and waves goodbye with a tense palm. She sighs loudly after the door of the apartment closes and as Mark's feet are scuffing down the stairs to the street. They sit in silence for a while, Simon against the base of the sink and Leigh against the tub. She begins to laugh then.

"Whatever I'm capable of," she says with a wry smile, "he's not going to save me from it. That's clear. At least I know that."

Simon reaches over his head and pulls the washcloth from the sink. She takes it, wipes her face, then hands it back to him to refresh.

"Maybe once you stop worrying about what you're capable of, you'll realize that you don't need to be clinging so tightly. Maybe it's the clinging that makes it seem like if you let go you might fall into some pit of snakes. Maybe if you let go," Simon lays the washcloth over his knee, not caring that it's making a wet spot on his pants, or that it's got Leigh's tears and mucus mixed with the tap water. "You'll realize that your feet are actually on the ground and that there's nowhere to fall to."

"You think I'll be able to just walk around then? On the ground?"

"I think you'll be able to just walk around then. On the ground."

"No snakes?"

"No snakes."

Leigh

The doorbell rings and Buster and I are in bed. Well I'm in it, he's on it. I'm awake, but it's early. Too early for someone to be ringing the bell. I look at the clock on the nightstand: not quite seven. The bell rings again, and I shuffle to the door of my apartment and go down the two flights to street level. I can see through the oval glass two people going back down the steps. I open the door, and they turn around. They are an older couple, in their early seventies maybe. She's wearing a woven shawl clipped together in front with a pewter dragon pin, and he's wearing an Irish knit sweater. They make their way back up the seven wooden stairs. They look like people who care how their clothes are made. There's nothing made in China on this pair, but you can tell it's not because they're rich.

"The yard sale?" The woman says. She holds a page from a newspaper spotted with red circles. "Isn't it today?"

"The yard sale!" I gasp. I'd advertised it and then forgotten all about it. "Gosh. You see I was getting married," I explain, "and then it turned out that I'm not. Not now anyway. I'm not giving up my apartment. And so, oh gosh, I should put up a sign or something, in case other people come by." The man raises his hand to me, as if I'd just offered him something and he doesn't want it.

"It's okay. Come on Maddie. Let's hit the next one."

"We're not going anywhere without stopping for coffee first," she says as she follows him. Suddenly, as though she'd just remembered something, she turns, puts her hand on my arm. On her fingers are several sterling rings with large gemstones. "I'm sorry for your trouble. I really am." She makes a face that looks like she's going to make a kissy noise, but instead she whistles. "Unless I should be happy for you. One never knows these days."

"I was just about to make coffee," I offer, my voice going up a notch.

"Really, come on up."

"Oh, no, we couldn't." The woman begins, but her husband turns and climbs back up the stairs and waits for me to move out of the way.

"Of course we can. She advertised a yard sale. We oughtta let her give us coffee." I smile. "She'd feel bad if we didn't, wouldn't you? Didn't catch your name."

"Leigh," I tell him, and they follow me up the stairs to my train wreck of an apartment.

"Herbert," he points to himself, and then, "my wife, Madeleine. Looks like you could use to have a yard sale." Buster darts past their legs and into the kitchen.

"Well, yes, I was sort of ... rearranging." I clear piles of papers from the kitchen table.

It turns out that Herbert and Madeleine have recently retired, and are filling their hours and making a little extra cash by buying and selling antiques. "Little treasures," Madeleine says, "I've always loved finding treasures." She admires a vase that I have in the middle of the table.

"It was my grandmother's," I tell her. "She recently passed away." I caress the side of the vase with my forefinger.

"I'm sorry," Madeleine says, for the second time since I've met her. I'm starting to wonder how apparent it is that I'm someone to be pitied. "I'm so sorry."

I pour three mugs of coffee, and give Madeleine and Herbert the two mugs that still have handles. "Oh god, I'm sorry. I'm out of milk," I say, putting the cups down.

"We both take it black," Herbert says.

"I'm really sorry about the confusion," I say again. "I can't believe I forgot...."

"It's no trouble at all," Madeleine says.

"It is," Herbert interrupts her. "It's a pain in the ass."

I look at him, and I can't help laughing because his language sounds so out of place. He looks like he should be timid, an absent-minded professor of philosophy or a twittering leprechaun in his Aran sweater. He smiles at me. "But it's okay. We haven't really gotten this whole ... antiques buying ... business started." He says the words *antiques buying* as though he's talking about something mysterious and wonderful that he is about to embark on, but about which he feels the need to be humble. Antiques buying ... Lear jet flying ... spying on the Iranians with my own homemade satellite system ... business.

"It sounds like a nice way to make some extra money," I offer benignly. "You can spend time together."

They look at each other affectionately, and I am simultaneously envious of their relationship and heartened by the fact that it exists. Suddenly Herbert gasps. He is looking at the countertop, and I assume that Buster is up there eating butter, but when I turn in my chair, I see only the regular piles of magazines, cereal boxes, coffee cans.

"Is that a Malibu Barbie?" He asks, standing up and nearing Andy's Barbie dolls.

"Malibu? I have no idea. It's my brother's." They both look at me for an awkward moment. "Well, from when he was a kid." We approach the counter and look down at the two Barbies.

"That's Francine!" Herbert exclaims, pointing to the other doll. Francine's hair is redder than Barbie's, but she has the same improbable blue eyes, tiny waist and long legs.

"You like them?"

"You have any idea what these are worth?" I shake my head and pick up my broken-handled mug of black coffee.

"'Bout a hundred wouldn't you say, Herbert?" Madeleine asks, touching Francine's smooth shin.

"Take them," I say. They both look at me. "Really. Take them."

"No, no we couldn't." Madeleine looks to her husband for confirmation.

"No, of course not. If you'd like to sell them, well, we would buy them if the price is right."

"Make me an offer," I say. Herbert pulls the wallet from his pants pocket and holds it at an angle as though he were using it to reflect sunlight on the opposite wall.

"Fifty," he says.

"Too much."

"Each."

"Oh come on."

"Fair's fair," Madeleine chimes in. "We're only going to sell them, it wouldn't be right to take them for less than they're worth."

"Well," I say, remembering that they are Andy's, and that he could use the money. "I guess if you're sure you'll make a profit on them. Would you like a cookie?" I hand them the Barbies and put a tin of cookies on the table. "They're homemade," I say. They each take one and nibble. I had come across the recipe in my gramma's things. When she made them, they were delicious, crispy and spicy, but I haven't managed to reproduce those qualities. Mine are too hard and they taste like aluminum. Herbert and Madeleine finish theirs and then politely refuse a second.

On the way to the door, Madeleine stops and elbows Herbert, who has the two Barbie dolls wrapped like genies in a newspaper carpet. She points her nose in the direction of Mark's golf clubs, which are leaning against the wall next to the television.

"Right," Herbert says. "Right." He turns to me. "You wanna sell those clubs?"

"Herbert tried golfing for the first time last summer, and he loved it, didn't you, Herb?"

He nods. "Love a set of clubs." I grab the clubs and carry them downstairs. Herbert opens the trunk of his car, a beat-up Toyota hatchback, the color of tarnished copper, and takes out his wallet while I put them in.

"Nope. They're yours, seriously," I say, and push his hand with the wallet back toward him. It's a struggle, but I refuse to back down, and after several minutes of both Herbert and Madeleine pushing money at me, I win out. I watch them drive away, with Andy's Barbies and Mark's golf clubs in the back.

The summer has begun in earnest, and there are tulips in the small patch of lawn, the product of a previous tenant's effort. It's still early enough that very few cars pass. The college kids have gone home for the summer, and many people will be away from the city for the long weekend. It occurs to me that more people might come by for the yard sale I've advertised, so I go back upstairs and start lugging down records and books I've already read and don't want to read twice. Costume jewelry, clothes, dishes, an electric percolator, a wire fruit bowl. I make trip after trip, pour myself a second cup of coffee, and wait for people to come.

Acknowledgments

Carobeth Laird's memoir, *Limbo*, was a helpful resource as I imagined what life might be like in a nursing home.

I wouldn't have had the confidence to try to publish anything if it weren't for my sage and super-supportive writer's group: Past and present members include Lisa Heiserman Perkins, Peter Brown, Laurie Covens, Cathy Armer, Bob Dall, Bill Ellet, Kari Bodnarchuk, the amazing Tehila Lieberman, and salt-of-the-Earth Lucy McCauley.

A few other writer and reader friends read drafts of *Long Division* and offered advice and/or encouragement. Elizabeth Christopher, Phil Hamell, Kathy Rushe, JoEllen Paine, and Stephen Russell: Thanks to you.

Thanks to Deb Jarnes for the title and the homework assignment.

And finally, thanks to Colin, Aidan, and Emmet Hamell, for everything else.

About the Author

Sara B. Fraser's fiction has appeared in various literary magazines, such as carve, salamander, whimperbang, wilderness house literary review, and stonecrop. She lives in massachusetts and works as a high-school teacher. This is her first novel.

Thank you so much for reading one of our **Literary Fiction** novels.
If you enjoyed our book, please check out our recommended title for your
next great read!

The Five Wishes by Mr. Murray McBride by Joe Siple

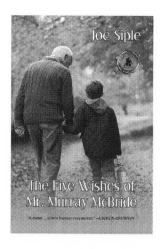

2018 Maxy Award "Book of the Year"

"A sweet...tale of human connection...will feel familiar to fans of Hallmark

movies." *–KIRKUS REVIEWS*

"An emotional story that will leave readers meditating on the life-saving

magic of kindness." *–Indie Reader*

View other Black Rose Writing titles at www.blackrosewriting.com/books

and use promo code **PRINT** to receive a **20% discount** when purchasing.

Made in the
USA
Middletown, DE